Statue of
Limitations

Statue of Limitations

Kate Collins

KENSINGTON BOOKS
www.KensingtonBooks.com

KENSINGTON BOOKS are published by

Kensington Publishing Corp.
119 West 40th Street
New York, NY 10018

All Kensington titles, imprints, and distributed lines are available at special quantity discounts for bulk purchases for sales promotion, premiums, fund-raising, and educational or institutional use.

Special book excerpts or customized printings can also be created to fit specific needs. For details, write or phone the office of the Kensington Sales Manager: Kensington Publishing Corp., 119 West 40th Street, New York, NY 10018. Attn. Sales Department. Phone: 1-800-221-2647.

First Kensington Books mass-market printing: February 2020
ISBN-13: 978-1-4967-2433-5
ISBN-10: 1-4967-2433-X

ISBN-13: 978-1-4967-2434-2 (ebook)
ISBN-10: 1-4967-2434-8 (ebook)

10 9 8 7 6 5 4 3 2 1

Printed in the United States of America

This book is dedicated to all those crazy Greeks I've come to know and love and try my best to understand. It's also dedicated to all of us Athenas who are true warrior goddesses, standing up for what is right and just and never, ever forgetting that a bully is just a coward in disguise. If you carry nothing else away from this book it should be this: Speak your truth. Your body, mind, and spirit will thank you.

Acknowledgments

I'd like to thank my agent, Jessica Faust, for her wisdom and encouragement; Martin Biro and Kensington for believing in me; and my editor, Tara Gavin, for carrying on bravely under tremendous mountains of work.

I'd like to thank my assistant (and son), Jason Eberhardt, who has incredible vision and editorial skills, not to mention is a great storyteller in his own right.

I'd like to thank my daughter Julia, for her inner guiding light and creativity in her own endeavors. It takes a lot of talent to turn a hobby into a career, and she did it in spades.

I would also like to thank those ancient Greeks for coming up with such a wonderful cast of gods and goddesses, if only I could find one.

What you leave behind is not what is engraved in stone monuments, but what is woven into the lives of others.

—Pericles

PREFACE

IT'S ALL GREEK TO ME
blog by Goddess Anon

Chaos Reigns

I've read your comments and I'm truly flattered. I know many of you want me to reveal my true identity, but trust me, it's better this way. My life has been nothing but chaos lately, and I can't give you any more details than that. But I can give you a little backstory.

First of all, I come from a big, noisy, and nosy Greek family consisting of several annoying siblings, a meddling mother firmly committed to the idea that I should marry a nice Greek boy, a father who, although not fully Greek, has totally embraced the culture, and my grandparents, Pappoús (or Pappu, as we pronounce it) and Yiayiá (actually it's spelled Oiaoiá, but I'll keep it simple).

Secondly, when I was young, I prayed for a handsome white knight to come along to rescue me, and guess what? Nothing. Ever. Happened. I finally figured out I'd have to do it myself. So, at the ripe old age of twenty-four, I packed a suitcase, moved to the closest big city, got a studio apart-

ment and a low-paying job at a big company, and worked my way up until I reached a level of success that made me happier than I'd ever dreamed possible.

I also met and married a very successful, non-Greek businessman, which caused all kinds of uproar back home. So along with a wedding gift, my mother gave me her prediction of my future with this man: he'll break your heart; after your divorce you'll never be able to support yourself in the city; then you'll come back home where you belong.

Oh, how I prayed that she would be wrong, but once again my prayers went unanswered, because, much to my consternation, it turned out that she was right.

Ten years later, my corporate job was eliminated and my husband divorced me, leaving me in debt up to my ears but unchaining me from a bitter marriage that made me feel invisible and wary of ever getting close to a man again. So, with a young child to support, I packed up our belongings, along with my pride, and returned home into the welcoming—or should I say gloating—arms of my family.

Now my child and I not only live in the big family house, but I also work for the family business, which at least enables me to earn my own money so I can move into my own place one day. In the meantime, my child, who'd been left so distraught by the divorce, does seem to be blossoming here in the midst of our eccentric but strong fam—

CHAPTER ONE

Monday, 8:10 p.m.

My computer monitor flickered briefly, and the screen went black. The lights in the ceiling high above my desk made a buzzing sound and then they, too, went dark. The window beside my desk offered little help. The bright May sun had set fifteen minutes ago.

Muttering under my breath, I reached for my cell phone only to remember that I'd set it on the oak console table on the opposite side of the office. A bolt of lightning momentarily illuminated the room, enabling me to make my way around the old oak desk and across the wood floor to the table. At a sudden heavy thud from somewhere outside the room, I paused. Standing in the dark beside the table, I waited, listening.

Hearing nothing more, I did a quick mental inventory. My father, John Spencer, who owned Spencer's Garden Center, and my youngest sister, Delphi, had left when the shop closed at eight. I'd turned on the CLOSED sign and bolted the door myself. Then, with no one around, I'd retreated to the office to write my blog—my way of releasing my pent-up frustrations. The store was completely empty, so what had caused the noise?

I located my phone, switched on the flashlight, and shined it at the open doorway. Thunder rumbled in the distance as I quietly peered out into the huge garden center.

The office where I worked was on the right side of the shop behind the L-shaped checkout counter. I could see that the cash register hadn't been touched, the bolt on the big red doors was still thrown, nothing on any of the shelves had been disturbed, none of the outdoor wall decor was askew, and no windows had been broken. That was a relief. But I still had to track down the source of the noise.

Over a century ago the garden center had been a barn on the very northern edge of Sequoia, Michigan, the last building on Greene Street. Now, with a brand-new arched roof, big picture windows, a high-beamed ceiling, cream-colored shiplap walls, and a shiny oak floor, Spencer's was one of the most attractive buildings along the mile stretch of tourist shops. I'd always loved being there—I had a natural green thumb—but I'd never expected to make it my life's work.

Another thud turned me in the direction of the out-door garden area, located on an acre lot behind the barn, and then I had my answer. It was Oscar, our friendly neighborhood raccoon, who liked to steal shiny objects. He'd pilfered any number of items from the area where we kept garden décor. I wasn't about to let him take another one.

Using my cell phone's flashlight as my guide, I headed toward the back exit, walking down the left side past rows of indoor plants, garden supplies, tools, and small decorative pots. Circling the long, oak plank conference table at the rear of the barn, I pushed the glass door open and stepped outside just as the electricity came back on. Hanging lanterns around the perimeter of a ballroom-sized area right outside the building illuminated a cement floor and a wide aisle down the middle that divided the area into two sections. The left side was filled with shelves overflowing with flowering annuals, perennials, and vegetables, while the right side contained stone, clay, glass, and cement garden sculptures, water fountains, large decorative planters, wrought-iron benches, and patio furniture.

I caught movement from the corner of my eye and backed against the door with a sharp gasp.

A man was crouched at the base of a life-sized marble statue of the Goddess Athena, now lying on her back in the grass. He had an open pocketknife in his hand and his cell phone was propped nearby, its flashlight aimed at the statue's base. He jumped to his feet, obviously as shocked to see me as I was to see him.

"Drop that knife and don't move a muscle." I thrust my phone forward, the beam pointed at his face and my trembling finger on the home button. "I've got the police on the line."

If only that were true.

The hanging lights flickered, threatening to go out again.

"Okay," he said in a calm voice. "No problem." Moving slowly, he placed the knife on the ground and raised his hands above his head. "I'm sorry. I didn't mean to alarm you."

"You broke into our shop. What did you *think* that would do to me?"

"Hold on a minute," he said in a rising voice. "I did

not break into the shop. I was *told* to stay here until someone could help me, and that was"—he tipped his wrist to see his watch—"over twenty minutes ago."

I gave him a skeptical glance. "You've been out here for twenty minutes?"

"*Over* twenty minutes. Again, I'm sorry for alarming you, but I was just doing what I was told."

Undeniably good-looking, the man had dark hair that was parted on the side and combed away from his face, big golden-brown eyes, a firm mouth, and a strong jawline. My gaze was drawn down to his expensive tan suede bomber jacket that showed off his muscular shoulders, dark blue jeans that revealed an athletic build, and noticeably pricey navy leather loafers.

His expression seemed sincere, but the truth was that I was alone with a stranger behind a big barn on Greene Street, the main thoroughfare of our small lakeside town, with only my phone and my wits to protect me. The other shops had already closed and any tourists who'd stuck around would no doubt be comfortably seated inside a restaurant or one of the local sports bars. With the storm quickly approaching, who would hear my cry for help?

I jumped at a sudden clap of thunder. With all the bravery I could muster, still holding my phone, I pointed toward the lane that ran behind the shops on Greene. "You need to leave right now."

"Will you at least give me a chance to prove I'm telling the truth? If you don't believe me, I'll go."

A strong eastern wind blew through the garden area, shifting the hanging lanterns, and causing my long blue sweater to billow out around my white jeans. I could smell the rain coming.

Brushing long strands of light brown hair away from my face, I said, "Make it fast."

"The young woman who waited on me—I didn't get her name—is probably in her late twenties, with lots of curly black hair tied with some kind of fuzzy purple thing. She had on a purple sweater, jeans, and bright green flip-flops. She was shorter than you but had more . . ." He gave me a sweeping glance, his eyes moving from my long brown hair all the way down to my white flats. He saw the narrowing of my gaze, and finished with "color in her cheeks."

That wasn't what he'd meant to say and we both knew it. He had just described Delphi, my airhead of a sister who, like my other two sisters, Maia and Selene, had the curvaceous bodies, shorter stature, and olive complexions of my Greek-American mother, Hera Karras Spencer. I, on the other hand, was the only one who had inherited the pale skin, slender form and straight light brown hair of my English-blooded father.

It was quite likely that Delphi had gotten busy with something and had forgotten to tell me. Her absent-mindedness was common enough to convince me the man could be telling the truth; but still, what did he intend to do with that knife?

I gestured toward the statue. "What were you doing?"

"Can I put my hands down? My arms are tired."

At my curt nod he said, "Thank you. I'm Case Donnelly by the way."

As he walked closer, holding out his hand to shake mine, I realized I was still clutching my cell phone.

"You might want to put that away." His mouth quirked as though trying to hide a grin. "I'm guessing the police hung up a long time ago or they'd have been here by now."

I stood my ground, my gaze locked with his.

"And your flashlight app is on, by the way."

He wasn't missing a trick. Feeling a blush starting, I

turned off the app, slid the phone in my back pocket, and took his hand. "Athena Spencer," I said in a crisp, businesslike voice. I'd gone back to my maiden name when my divorce had become final.

"Athena." He looked impressed. "Like your *Treasure of Athena.*"

That he knew the statue's name surprised me since it wasn't written on any tag.

"It's a pleasure to meet you, Athena. Are you the owner here?"

His charming smile and warm, firm grip left me a little breathless. I dropped his hand and stepped back, feeling awkward and at the same time angry with him for causing it. "I'm the business manager. My father owns the garden center. Now would you answer my question, please?"

"I'd be glad to." He gestured toward the overturned figure. "I was trying to find out if the statue is authentic."

"She's authentic."

"Do you have the legal paperwork to prove it?"

Feeling my temper on the rise I said, "Yes. It's called a sales receipt."

"And does it say on this sales receipt that the statue is by the Greek sculptor Antonius?"

I paused to think. Had I seen the name Antonius anywhere on the receipt in the file marked *Statue*? I'd only noticed that it *was* a receipt because it had been sticking up out of the file when I was putting something else away. Who was Antonius anyway?

As though reading my thoughts Case said, "Antonius is a Roman artist from the early twelfth century who became famous posthumously for his sculptures of Greek gods and goddesses."

I lifted my chin. "As a matter of fact, I do know that."

Not. "And anyway, it doesn't matter. The statue isn't for sale."

"That's okay. I wasn't interested in buying it. But just out of curiosity, may I see the receipt?"

His impertinence irritated me. "No, you may not. It's late, I'm hungry, and I was supposed to meet someone for dinner ten minutes ago."

Case studied me with a shrewdness that made me uneasy. "It's just after eight o'clock. Why isn't the garden center open?"

"All of the shops in town close at eight. You're not from around here, are you?"

Completely ignoring my question, he glanced back at the statue. "I'm betting you paid a lot of money for her."

His sudden switch of topics threw me off guard. Plus, I was growing hungrier—and angrier—by the second. I hadn't wanted to dine so late anyway, especially not with Kevin Coreopsis, the "good Greek boy" my mother was encouraging me to see, but of course, when did my wishes ever count? I would've much rather had dinner with my son at The Parthenon with the rest of the family.

"First of all, I didn't buy the statue. My grandfather did. He was going to use it at his diner, but it was too large. Secondly, how much he paid isn't your concern. Now, would you please keep your promise and leave?"

"I'll take that as a yes, she did cost a lot of money. I hope your grandfather at least bought her from a reputable art dealer."

"Not that it's any of your business, but he bought her at an estate sale." Why had I told Case that?

My stomach rumbled, reminding me why.

"So, an auctioneer sold it to him? Is the auction house reliable?"

I balled my hands into fists, not about to admit that neither the auctioneer nor the auction house was one I knew anything about. I hadn't even been aware that Pappoús had purchased it until it was delivered.

"Okay," Case said, "I'll mark that down as a *you don't know*. Whose estate was up for auction?"

I pulled my cell phone out of my pocket. "Get out now or I really will call the police."

"One more question. Did the auctioneer inform your grandfather that someone had applied a thin layer of cement over the bottom of the statue where the sculptor's name should be?"

I glanced in surprise at the sandal-clad feet of the marble Athena and saw that Case had indeed scraped off a bit of what appeared to be a cement coating.

"I'll take that as no," he said. "Therefore, my question for you is, why would someone put cement over the sculptor's name unless it wasn't a genuine Antonius?"

I absorbed the information with a sinking feeling in the pit of my stomach. Had my *pappoús* been ripped off?

Case straightened his jacket cuffs, clearly satisfied that he'd made his point.

And indeed, he had. With one eye on the black clouds overhead I asked, "How long will it take you to find out if she's authentic?"

"Five minutes, and I won't even charge you for my services."

I stared at him in surprise.

Case smiled, revealing a charming dimple in his cheek. "I'm joking."

His teasing helped break the tension between us, and I couldn't help but smile back. I glanced at my watch. "All right, Case Donnelly, you've got five minutes."

As he crouched down to work, my nerves kicked in.

What if this outrageously expensive statue was a fake, not even worth what we'd paid to move it from the Talbots' estate to the diner and then to Spencer's? I felt sick to my stomach thinking about it.

I'd protested mightily that it was too big for the diner and too far out of my grandparents' budget anyway, but as always, my voice went unheard. The family had gathered behind my stubborn *pappoús* because he was the head of the family and his decisions were final, regardless of what his college-educated granddaughter had to say.

The problem was twofold: it was too large for The Parthenon's front entryway, and Spencer's was stuck with it until we could convince Pappoús we needed to sell it, which didn't seem likely. He loved his *Treasure of Athena* and would often bring his lunch down and sit at one of the outdoor tables gazing at her as though waiting for her to come to life.

As Case worked, I had to admit that the statue was beautiful. I hadn't seen such exquisite detail in a sculpture since I'd toured Greek museums with my family years ago.

Standing at over six feet tall, Athena wore a traditional flowing toga gathered over one shoulder with a clasp so that the material draped down over her small, firm breasts. Another layer of material swirled down from her waist to the sandals on her feet. Her hair was swept up beneath a helmet that covered the top of her head. Her arms were bare and slender, but her strength was evident. One hand rested on her right hip, the other hand was outstretched in greeting. She was the goddess of war and wisdom, strong, courageous, and independent, none of which I felt.

Case blew away the dust he'd scraped off, uncovering a small brass plate attached to the bottom of one of

Athena's soles. I knelt down for a closer look as he wiped off the brass with his palm. "There's your marking."

I squinted at the etching but couldn't make sense of it. "Is that in Greek?"

"You don't read Greek?"

"I usually skipped Greek school. Does that mean the statue's an authentic Antonius?"

"She's authentic, all right, and worth a small fortune."

As he hoisted the sculpture back to its standing position, I stared at it in awe, my heart racing as the words *small fortune* echoed in my head. We owned an authentic Greek Antonius? Surely Pappoús wouldn't mind selling now. And just think what they could do with that money to spruce up the interior of their outdated diner.

Case held out a hand to help me up. "There's one more thing you should know about her, Athena."

"And that is?"

He brushed dirt off the statue's exquisite marble face. "She's mine."

CHAPTER TWO

A bolt of lightning lit up the night sky, and the clouds opened up, the sudden downpour sending me dashing for the door. I pushed it open, gritting my teeth in anger as Case followed me inside.

"That statue is *not* yours," I called over my shoulder, "and I knew I shouldn't have trusted you. I should've called the police when I had the chance."

"Call them right now if you want, but remember, you told me you wanted to know whether she was authentic."

I whirled on him. "I'm supposed to believe that some ancient Greek letters—which I can't read by the way—prove you own her?"

In a calm voice he said, "No, the proof of ownership is hidden inside a compartment beneath that brass plate."

"You really expect me to believe that?"

"As soon as the rain stops, I'll go back outside and show you."

"Not happening for two reasons." I tapped my watch.

"I have to leave right now, and my grandfather bought her fair and square. The end."

Case pulled out a chair at the long oak table and sat down. "Show me the sales receipt and I'll go."

"What?" I spluttered. "You promised you'd go if I let you prove you didn't break in."

"I will go—as soon as I see the sales receipt."

"Look, I'm hungry and late as it is. If you want to see the receipt, you'll have to come back in the morning. The garden center opens at nine a.m."

"Be reasonable, Athena. How long will it take you to pull out a piece of paper? Another two minutes? As you said, you're already late."

My cell phone beeped to signal an incoming text. I glanced at the screen and saw Kevin's name: *Maître d' will hold our table only ten more minutes. Better hurry. Xoxo K.*

Muttering under my breath, I texted back: *Be there shortly.*

Case cleared his throat. "Boyfriend getting impatient?"

I scowled at him, but he merely smiled and tapped his fingers on the tabletop.

"Fine. I'll show you but then you *have* to leave."

"You have my word on it."

I marched through the big converted barn and into the office, my leather flats pounding the wooden floor. Still muttering, I yanked open the old green filing cabinet and rustled through the files. I found the one marked *Statue* and thumbed through the papers until I found the receipt. I was ready to pull it out when a thought occurred to me. The only way this stranger could've tracked the statue to our business was to know we'd purchased it at the estate sale. Then why was he playing dumb?

I felt a cold shudder ripple down my spine. What if

my instincts were wrong? My mother had often told me that I was too trusting, especially with strangers. And it *was* strange that I'd just let a man I didn't know inside the building with me. I straightened at the thought, feeling the sudden need to escape.

I turned to find Case casually leaning against the doorway, looking around with interest. I had to admit that he was quite attractive and really did seem like he was telling the truth, but something about him still bothered me. Trying not to betray my nerves, I pretended to search further, then shut the filing cabinet with a bang. "I don't have it."

He studied me for a few seconds. "I see. Then who does?"

"I'm assuming you know where my grandfather acquired the statue, so I suggest you take it up with them."

"You're talking about the Talbots?"

I nodded and pulled out my phone. "Now, I'm going to ask you one last time to leave or I will call the—"

"Not necessary. That's all I needed to know. Have a nice dinner."

With that, he turned and walked out.

"What were you thinking, Athena?" Kevin scolded, making me feel as though I were five years old. "You could've been killed. You should've run back inside, locked the door, and called for help."

What I was *thinking* was that I should've eaten supper with my son instead of sitting here listening to Kevin's annoying lecture. I'd had enough of those during my marriage to last a lifetime. The only reason I'd accepted his late date was to keep my mother off my back. As long as she believed I was seeing a "good Greek boy" she wouldn't try to fix me up with anyone else. As the quote went, "Better the devil you know than the devil you don't." At least I was dining at an upscale Italian restaurant, a nice change of pace from Greek food.

Kevin paused as the waiter refilled our water glasses. "Next time phone the police before you go exploring a noise in the dark. Or better yet, call me. I would've come right over and thrown that *bástardos* out on his ear."

I reached for my water glass, thought better of it, and picked up my wine instead, trying to control the urge to fire back at him that I wasn't some helpless female who needed a big, strong male to protect her—even though I felt that way sometimes.

But all I said was, "I'll take that under advisement, counselor."

"You don't have to be snippy." He reached for his glass and finished his merlot in one big gulp.

My guilt kicked in instantly. "I'm sorry, Kev. It's been a long day. Let's change the subject."

"Good thinking." He snapped his fingers to get our waiter's attention and held up his empty wineglass. I ducked my head, afraid to see the expressions on the other diners' faces. What kind of person snapped his fingers at a server?

"By the way," Kevin said, as the waiter filled his glass hastily, "I was asked to do a presentation for a political science class at Sequoia Community College. The professor asked me to speak on *Roe v. Wade*. So I've been mulling over a few ideas. . . ."

I sipped my wine as he talked, thinking back to when I'd first met Kevin Coreopsis thirteen years ago, when our mothers had arranged for us to attend the annual high school spring dance together. The nice-looking, curly haired senior class president and I had dated casually until he'd gone east to attend college and law school. We'd lost touch completely after he'd taken a position as a bankruptcy attorney at a high-powered New York law firm, and I'd moved to Chicago, and that had been fine with me.

Last winter Kevin had moved back to our small town of Sequoia to "reconnect with" his "roots," as he'd called it. But I'd learned through the Greek grapevine that he'd actually returned because he'd been let go by his firm. Now he worked at a local law firm as a legal aide. It was quite a step down from his previous position, but he kept saying something big was in the works, he just couldn't talk about it yet. I had a feeling it was something he made up to save face.

Kevin was still handsome and fit, although his face had rounded out and his dark hair had thinned, but there were so many things that annoyed me about him. The main one was his possessiveness. As soon as I'd come back home, my mom had invited him over for dinner, and ever since, he'd acted as though it was a given that we were a couple and therefore he should know everything about my life. For that reason alone, I chose not to tell him about the *Treasure of Athena*'s history and potential worth.

I caught sight of a very large bald man in an ill-fitting brown suit heading toward us. I immediately grabbed my menu and opened it up, whispering to Kevin from behind it, "Don't look now but here comes Donald Fatsis."

A wet, folded newspaper landed with a plop next to my water glass, an article on it circled in red. "Do you believe this?"

Fatsis, owner of the Acropolis Art Gallery, a pricey shop on the block of Greene Street known as Little Greece, yanked out the chair between Kevin and me and dropped his portly body onto it. He slapped one beefy hand on top of the newspaper. "That greedy son of a—" He caught himself as diners around us began turning their heads, but then began talking again just as loudly. "Talbot Junior is going ahead with his father's plans."

"What?" I was so stunned I had to set my wine down before I spilled it. "I thought Grayson Talbot Senior canceled the project, and even signed a document to that effect."

"He did, but we don't have the document," Fatsis grumbled. "The GMA let him walk right out of the meeting with it and his promise to file it with the court. And then, what do you know, he up and dies before filing the damn thing."

"Then someone has to have it," I said. "What about his assistant, Harry Pepper?"

"I'd bet good money that Talbot's son had that document destroyed," Fatsis said, "so *he* could go ahead with the project. Remember, Junior's even more dangerous now that Senior's kicked the bucket. He's younger, greedier, and has much more influence on the town council now that he has control of the entire Talbot fortune."

I reached for my glass to take a steadying sip. That meant The Parthenon, as well as my grandparents' apartment above it, was once again in jeopardy, as was all of Little Greece. I felt a knot forming in the pit of my stomach.

It wasn't until after I'd moved back home that I'd learned about the plan to raze the block of Greek-owned shops and build a huge condominium complex in its place. My family had been in a state of panic but hadn't told me because of what I had been going through at the time. The condominium project had been the brainchild of real estate mogul Grayson Talbot Sr., and his son Grayson Talbot Jr., the most ruthless, politically connected, and extremely disliked men in town.

The Greek Merchants' Association, or the GMA, had met with the town council and the Talbots many times, begging them to reconsider how their project would hurt not only the families who owned the shops but also the town itself, whose main flow of income came from tourism. But the Talbots had refused to budge, and the councilmen, as usual, had sided with them, their position being that Little Greece was old and outdated, a hindrance to drawing in more tourists, which was far from the truth.

But then, at the last Greek Merchants' Association meeting, Talbot Sr., in an apparent change of heart, had canceled the project, shocking not only the GMA but Talbot's son as well, who had immediately walked out. However, shortly before Talbot Sr. could file the necessary papers to officially stop the project, he'd died in what the coroner had ruled an accidental drowning in his bathtub, something no one in the Greek community believed. As my mother said, it was simply too coincidental.

And to make things even more suspicious, none of the town officials had demanded an inquiry, and Talbot Jr., or Sonny, as he was called by my family, hadn't even ordered an autopsy. When I heard that, a red flag was raised instantly in my mind. My first instinct had been to tell my father to have the GMA fight the council's ruling, question the coroner, and demand answers, but Kevin had talked me out of it, reminding me that the Talbots owned this town and there wasn't anything the GMA could do.

"Remind me again, Donald," Kevin asked, "when is the next GMA meeting?"

"Tomorrow at eight p.m. at Spencer's," Fatsis answered.

"Which is when you should've brought this up," Kevin said, giving the man a withering glance. "We were in the middle of a conversation."

Actually, it was more like a monologue.

"Well, excuse *me*," Fatsis said snidely. "The evening newspaper just came out and I thought you'd want to know."

"I already knew," Kevin fired back.

I stared at him in surprise. "You knew and didn't tell me?"

His face flushed a deep red. "I didn't want to spoil our dinner."

I narrowed my eyes at Kevin, then turned back to Don. "Thanks for the information."

"You're welcome." Fatsis pushed himself to his feet and pulled out a handkerchief to mop his perspiring face, pausing to say, "I hope to see you at the meeting this time, Athena." And then he ambled toward the door.

"Didn't I say you should have come?" Kevin asked in his superior tone of voice.

I hated arguments, so I held my tongue.

As soon as Fatsis was gone, I picked up the newspaper to read the article and then wished I hadn't. As Fatsis had said, the plan to level the entire block of Little Greece was still going forward despite the now deceased landowner's last-minute promise to halt it. "Demolition Phase One is scheduled to begin in thirteen days," I said to Kevin, "and you didn't think to tell me? You know The Parthenon is on that block!"

"I found out just this morning." Kevin shook out his napkin and placed it on his lap, as though it was no big deal. "The GMA is going to need a court injunction to halt the project until they can get a hearing on the matter."

"Seriously, Kevin, do you really think a judge will rule against the Talbot Corporation in favor of a handful of Greek shop owners? I still say the best approach—"

"Don't worry about it, honey." He reached across the table to pat my hand. "I'll be there to guide them through the filing process."

"I can predict right now the GMA won't go along with taking the matter to court."

"That's why you should attend tomorrow's meeting with me. Our two voices combined could be very persuasive. Because of your newspaper experience and knowledge of big city politics, they trust you. With your encouragement, I'll bet they'll even let me speak for them before the town council." He gave my hand a squeeze. "Admit it, Athena, we'd make quite a team."

I eased my hand away from his. Kevin might have thought he had good intentions, but sometimes—make that most of the time—he came across as way too self-important.

"Hey," he said, lifting my chin, "why so down in the mouth? I'm here for you. Now wipe off that scowl and give me a *big* smile."

I hated it when he treated me like a child. But because his feelings were so easily hurt, I merely took a deep breath and gave him that big, fake smile he wanted.

"Good. Just remember, no matter what happens, I will be there for you. Now I want you to put your hand in mine and promise me you won't let this new development get you down."

Truthfully, *he* was getting me down.

"Come on," he said again. "Give me your hand."

At that moment the waiter set a basket of Italian bread between us.

"Thank God," I said on a sigh, and reached for the basket.

Kevin gave me a puzzled look. "Thank God?"

Thinking quickly, I said, "*Thank God* the bread's here." I picked out a slice and reached for the butter. "I'm starving."

IT'S ALL GREEK TO ME
blog by Goddess Anon

Someone Please Bore a Hole Through My Brain

This evening I had to suffer through a dinner with the biggest bore on the face of the planet. He actually snapped his fingers to get the waiter's attention. Who does that? And then when I thought my day couldn't get any worse . . .

CHAPTER THREE

Tuesday

After seeing Nicholas off to school, I headed to The Parthenon for a cup of Greek coffee before the diner opened to the public. I couldn't wait to share the news about the *Treasure of Athena* and what it could mean for my grandparents. To my surprise I found my sisters Maia and Selene and my mother gathered at the counter, laughing and poking one another. I peered between their shoulders, saw them reading my blog on Selene's laptop, and my palms immediately began to sweat.

"Reading tea leaves!" Maia said, she and the others chortling. "That sounds exactly like something Delphi would do."

"Except Delphi reads coffee grounds," I said, wiping my palms on my slacks.

"Coffee grounds, tea leaves, what's the difference?" Selene asked. "It's still funny."

I honestly hadn't thought my online journal would take off so quickly—or that my sisters would find it. I had been very careful to keep any personal references out of the blog. Now I had even more reason to do so. If my family were to find out I was talking about them, they wouldn't find it so amusing, and I'd be in the doghouse. But who knew? Maybe they'd learn something from it.

Maia pointed to Selene's hairdo-of-the-day, her long black curls puffed out at least three inches on one side of her head, a huge silver comb holding back the other side. "Remember the blog where Goddess Anon wrote about her sister's big hairdo? Look at yours today."

"I like my hair this way," Selene said with a pout. She worked as a hair stylist at Over the Top Hair Salon and liked to style her hair differently every day. Today she was wearing a soft green knit top with the shoulders cut out, white jeans, and white T-strap sandals, while Maia, an instructor at the Zen Garden Yoga Center, had on a bright pink yoga tank top with matching bra and black-and-pink-print yoga pants with black sandals.

My mother, The Parthenon's manager, wore her usual Grecian blue blouse, black skirt, a heavy, gold bangle bracelet, matching necklace, and a pair of chunky gold earrings she and my dad had bought in Santorini on their honeymoon. Her thick, short black curls framed her plump face and her dark eyes shone with her vitality and verve for life.

With plates balanced along her arms, Yiayiá backed through one of the kitchen doors and set the toast and egg breakfasts in front of my sisters. I looked up from the laptop when I heard Pappoús clink his trusty metal spatula against the order wheel to get my attention.

"Athena, breakfast for you?"

"I ate with Nicholas," I called. He gave me a nod and a wink and went back to work.

My mother clicked her tongue in disgust as she pointed to the last entry. "This poor young woman has an *anóitos* boyfriend who snaps his fingers at the waiters. Who does he think he is?"

"You're right about him being a fool, Mama," Maia said, showing off her knowledge of the language. "I'd dump him if I were her. There are plenty of other fish in the sea."

"Too bad I don't know this girl," Mama said. "I could match her up with the man of her dreams"—she snapped her fingers—"just like that. I *am* Hera, you know."

I couldn't hold back a shudder.

My mother was named Hera after the goddess of goddesses, women, and marriage, and firmly believed that her true calling in life was to be a matchmaker. She'd named all four of her daughters after women of Greek mythology: Selene, at thirty-six the oldest of us, after the goddess of the moon; me, Athena, her second child, after the goddess of war, wisdom, poetry, and art; and Maia, twenty-eight, after the goddess of the fields, which fit her because she was a vegetarian, something none of the family was able to wrap their Mediterranean minds around.

Delphi, however, had been named after the famed Oracle of Delphi, a high priestess who gave people predictions and guidance. At first offended that she hadn't been given a goddess name, my baby sister had finally pounced upon the oracle myth, deciding that she, too, like her namesake, could help people with her gift of foresight. The scary thing was that every once in a while, she actually got it right.

My mother nudged me. "Everything going well between you and Kevin?"

"Couldn't be better," I said, scooting onto a stool at

the counter as Yiayiá served up my coffee. "Shouldn't all of you be finishing up? It's almost time to open the diner."

"We still have a few minutes," Selene said, still hunched over the computer. "This is a hoot, Thenie. You should read it."

"That's okay," I said, "I have better things to do with my time."

"Like having a good breakfast," Mama said. "You're too skinny, Athena. You should've had Pappoús make you warm toast and a nice ham and feta omelet."

"Thanks, but you know I eat with Nicholas."

"Bring that boy here then," she said. "We'll fatten him up. He's too skinny."

"He has to catch the bus, Mama."

"The bus goes right by the diner every morning," Mama said in her no-nonsense voice. "I'll talk to Janice. She'll stop right out front. Problem solved. Now, eat Maia's eggs before you leave. She never eats them."

"Vegetarian," Maia reminded her with a mouth full of toast and jelly.

"I'd better get moving," Selene said as she shut the computer. "You don't know what you're missing, Thenie. Everyone at the hair salon reads the blog. It's a riot."

I wanted to give myself a high five. My boss at the paper had said I didn't have a strong enough voice to be an author, but I couldn't express my excitement in front of my family. "Good for them" was all I said.

Maia turned on her stool and tugged my long hair. "Try reading it sometime. Maybe it'd put a smile on your face instead of that frown you're wearing."

"Where's Delphi?" Mama asked. "Has anyone seen her?"

"She's running late as usual," Maia said. "She said

she had to take something to the garden center she found at a flea market yesterday."

"Speaking of Spencer's"—I finished my coffee and slid off the stool—"I've got to get to work. See you all at dinner."

Mama crooked her finger at me. "Thenie, come here a minute."

I followed her into the kitchen. "What's up?"

She stroked a strand of hair away from my forehead. "I know why you look so down today, my *moró*. Your dad and I heard the news about the condominium project and feel the same way. We're at our wits' ends trying to figure out how to stop it."

Actually, she was right about me feeling down. I hadn't been able to shake the dreadful thought of Little Greece being demolished, along with the diner my grandparents had run since they were a young married couple, and the apartment they'd lived in just as long. I was surprised that this hadn't been the topic of this morning's conversation. But perhaps they'd discussed it before I'd arrived.

Obviously, something needed to be done to stop the demolition, but the only solution I'd come up with was that everyone in Little Greece needed to modernize their shops, which wasn't going to happen overnight. For The Parthenon, that meant repairing and painting the stucco front, putting in a new floor, painting over the old, faded murals of Greece on the walls, and—the biggest change of all—adding modern items to the menu similar to those I'd seen in Greek restaurants in Chicago.

Before that could happen, however, Pappoús had to be convinced to sell the *Treasure of Athena* so he'd have the money he needed. That also meant convincing Case Donnelly that Pappoús was, in fact, the owner of the statue. If he wanted it for his family's museum, he'd have to buy it. But I needed to find that proof of ownership first.

Perhaps Kevin was right. The Greek Merchants' Association would have to file an injunction against the Talbots to stall for time. That would give the shop owners the opportunity to start modernizing. I made a mental note to bring it up at the meeting.

"We can start by making sure everyone is at the GMA meeting tonight to listen to what Kevin and I have to say," I told my mom. "Maybe our ideas will help."

Oops. There I was, making plans for speaking at their meeting. I wanted to smack myself on the forehead for allowing myself to be sucked back into the Greek drama again.

Mama put her arm around my shoulders and gave me a squeeze. "Kevin is a smart boy, isn't he? I knew you and he would get back together."

I had to suppress that shudder again.

I arrived at the garden center to find Delphi lugging a tall, wrought-iron whirligig through the store heading for the outdoor garden area. She was wearing a Southwestern poncho in purples, creams, and greens, a bright purple scarf around her neck, blue jeans, and purple flats. She waved an elbow at me and proceeded to back straight out the door into the yard.

Because my dad didn't have a strict dress code and I worked mainly in the office as bookkeeper, I wore whatever I wanted. Today I'd chosen cream pants with a mint green and cream top and a mint green cardigan.

My dad had created the job for me when I came back home, which provided me with income and didn't require too much of my time. The relaxed schedule also allowed me to have breakfast and dinner with my son and take time off for school events. During our busy season, I also helped customers in the garden center with selection and design. I didn't have any formal training, but I did have a passion for it. Plus, I'd practically grown up at the garden center, learning all about horticulture from my father.

Right now, however, I often had hours to fill. So, besides filling in as salesperson and cashier when Delphi or Dad were busy, I'd also given the big indoor center and outdoor garden area a more modern feeling, as my dad tended not to notice those things and Delphi's head was usually in the clouds. Sometimes I even had time to work on my blog, but usually I saved that for after closing time, when I had the office to myself.

Dad had inherited Spencer's Garden Center from his father, who had purchased the abandoned building and its acreage for a pittance and started a business doing what he loved best—growing plants. Spencer's sat at the northern end of Greene Street, at the very edge of the tourist area, across from Lake Michigan and four blocks up from Little Greece, where The Parthenon was located.

"Thenie," my dad said, stepping out of the office, "there's a news bulletin on TV you should hear."

I started to follow him when Delphi stuck her head into the shop and called, "Thenie! Hurry! It's the statue!" Then she gestured for me to come to the garden area.

"I'll be back in a minute, Pops," I called, and hurried toward the back door, fearing what I'd find. As soon as I stepped outside, Delphi pointed to the statue, which was now back down on the ground. "Someone must have broken in last night and knocked it over. I hope it's not damaged."

My heart raced in dread as I knelt at the statue's base. And there I saw the little brass plate with the etching on it hanging open at its hinge, exposing a hidden cavity, just as Case Donnelly had described. I used my flashlight app to look inside, but the compartment was empty.

I muttered a curse under my breath. Case must have returned to get his proof of ownership, because he was the only one I knew who was aware of the secret compartment. *Damn it!* Why had I trusted him? I pressed the brass plate back in place, heard it snap shut, and rose in a fury. "Help me get her up."

"Should we call the police?" Delphi asked.

I wanted to but I had no proof Case had taken the document, and without proof, what was the point of calling them? I fumed under my breath at Case. Perhaps I *should* say something was taken and give them his name and description. That would teach him not to mess with me. The only thing was, my conscience wouldn't let me.

To avoid alarming my sister any further I said, "I'll bet it was Oscar. I heard him rooting around out here last night before I left to go to dinner. He must have jumped on top of the statue to get over the fence and knocked her off balance."

A small raccoon who we guessed was not even one year old tipping over a marble statue seemed like a hard sell, but Delphi bought it wholeheartedly. Working together, we hefted the statue to her feet and brushed her off. Heading inside, we met Dad coming out, a shocked look on his face.

"Harry Pepper's dead."

"Mr. Talbot's assistant?" I asked.

"They're already calling it a homicide," he said, starting back toward the office. He shook his head in disbelief. "Poor Harry. I just can't believe it."

Mama knocked on the front picture window, so Delphi hurried to let her in the door. "John, girls," she said breathlessly, "did you hear about Harry?"

As the four of us stood in front of the TV mounted up in a corner of the office, Mama said, "Didn't I tell you something fishy was going on? First Grayson Talbot dies in a freak accident, and now his assistant is murdered. That can't be a coincidence."

The text scrolling across the bottom of the screen read: *Harry Pepper, longtime assistant to the late Grayson Talbot Sr., was found dead inside the Talbot mansion early this morning. Anyone with information is urged to call the Sequoia Police Department's Detective Bureau. Stay tuned for further updates.*

A frightening thought raced through my mind. The *Treasure of Athena* had been owned by Grayson Talbot Sr. The Talbots' estate sale was where my *pappoús* had acquired it. Had Case come back to Spencer's looking for his proof of ownership, found the statue's compartment empty, and gone to the Talbot mansion seeking it?

I was shaking as I sat down behind the desk.

Three things were apparent: Case had been determined to prove he owned the statue; he had conned me into showing him where I kept the paperwork; and Harry Pepper, who was in the process of tying up the deceased mogul's business affairs, had access to all of Talbot's documents, which might have included the missing proof of ownership.

Could the man I met yesterday be a cold-blooded murderer?

CHAPTER FOUR

"**I** don't believe it," I muttered, then realized I'd said it aloud and quickly went to the coffee machine on the console table and put in a pod to make myself a cup of decaf.

"I know exactly how you feel," Mama said, putting her arm around me for a squeeze.

I stirred sugar into my coffee and tried to pull my thoughts together. I wanted to tell *someone* about my scare from the night before, but the last thing I needed was another lecture like Kevin's. I also didn't want to admit to anyone that I might have made a huge mistake trusting a stranger, yet the truth was that Case Donnelly could be a murderer. He had gone to great lengths to find the statue and was now on the hunt for his proof of ownership. Would he have killed someone to reclaim them both?

Delphi was standing in front of the desk reading something on her cell phone.

"Here's what I found online," she said. "Police believe someone entered Grayson Talbot's office through a pair of open French doors on the home's main level and forced Harry Pepper to open the safe. According to Grayson Talbot Junior, who found the body, Pepper was slumped over a desk, apparently having been murdered by suffocation."

With a heavy sigh, my dad took off his glasses and polished them with a tissue. Tall, slender, and fair-haired like me, he had on his standard blue work shirt with navy jeans and black sneakers. "I can't believe anyone would've wanted to kill Harry. How is your father doing, Hera?"

"Poor papa," Mama said. "He was so distraught at the news he cried. He actually cried." Turning to us she said, "I don't know if you girls remember this, but Harry and your *pappoús* started The Parthenon together as young men. For a time, they were as close as brothers, until the economy took a nosedive and the tourists stopped coming. It was so bad The Parthenon nearly closed."

"But Yiayiá saved the day," Delphi said. "Right?"

"Yes, she did," Mama replied. "She changed the menu, spruced up the décor, and took over the front of the restaurant. But that caused a falling-out between your *pappoús* and Harry, who wanted to keep everything the way it was. Then Harry got a job offer from Grayson Talbot and reluctantly accepted."

Dad sighed heavily. "Poor Harry. He was such a gentle man. I can't believe anyone could've done this to him."

"Bad things happen when you get involved with the Talbots," Mama continued. "When Harry accepted the job, it upset my father greatly, and the two men went their separate ways. They didn't talk much after that, but I would see Harry around sometimes. He was always kind to me."

Delphi went over to her and gave her a hug, laying her head on Mom's shoulder. "I'm sorry, Mama."

"Thank you, my little *moró*," she said, patting her back, using the Greek word for "baby." No matter how old we were, we would always be her babies.

She went over to give my dad a hug and kiss. "I have to get back to the diner, John. I just wanted to make sure you'd heard."

Dad tilted up her chin and smiled. "Thank you, Hera, my dear. I'll see you at home this evening."

"Girls, I'll see you at the diner later," Mama said as she swept out the door.

"I'm going to have a cup of coffee," I said. "Dad, would you like one?"

"No, thanks, Thenie." After another deep sigh, Dad put his glasses back on and checked his watch. "Time to open the shop. Life moves on."

"I'll take a cup." Delphi dropped into one of the wicker chairs facing the desk and propped her feet on top. "My usual—half-cream, one packet of sugar."

I took an empty cup off the shelf above the coffee maker and handed it to her. "Here. You have legs." As I turned to go, I gasped inwardly. I'd sounded just like my mother.

Carrying my steaming cup of coffee back to the desk, I sat down to work, trying without success to stop thinking about Harry's murder. I couldn't help but feel somewhat responsible even though my gut was telling me Case was not a killer. Still, the facts added up and the guilt weighed heavily on my conscience.

By ten thirty, I had finished half of my daily accounting work, made myself another cup of coffee, and gone out into the shop to take a break. Dad was restocking a shelf of fertilizer and Delphi was seated across from an elderly lady at the long table at the back of the shop having a cup of coffee with her.

I recognized Mrs. Bird right away. I'd helped her choose perennials for her garden just a week ago, after Delphi had called in sick. I saw her swirl the coffee in Mrs. Bird's cup and immediately headed toward them. My sister was about to give the poor woman one of her predictions.

Reading coffee grounds was Delphi's favorite diversion. She'd make a customer a cup of Greek coffee, a thick, sweet brew with a layer of fine coffee grounds at the bottom, then chatter away until the coffee was gone and only the grounds were left. At that point she would give the cup a few swirls, creating a pattern in the grounds, then interpret them.

Some customers enjoyed her so-called predictions, while others played along with her, not wanting to hurt her feelings. Then there were those like Mrs. Bird, elderly and highly nervous, who might take one of Delphi's foresights too seriously.

When I got there Mrs. Bird was listening to Delphi with wide, alarmed eyes, while my harebrained sister talked a mile a minute.

"Delphi?"

She gave me an innocent gaze. "What?"

"Phone call for you in the office."

Delphi gave me a scowl. "Take a message, please."

"Mrs. Bird," I asked, "are you feeling okay?"

The elderly woman gave me a beseeching look, her pale blue eyes wide with concern. "Not really."

"Whatever my sister said to upset you, I apologize. Delphi, a word with you, please?"

"I was only giving Mrs. Bird good news," Delphi said. "I told her that her husband is coming back home, and all is forgiven."

"That's just it," Mrs. Bird said, wringing her thin hands in trepidation. "I don't want my husband to come back home. He's dead."

After seeing Mrs. Bird safely to the door, I stepped outside to stretch my legs and take in some fresh air. The day was mild and sunny with a cooling breeze coming off the lake, so I crossed the street and began to stroll along the boardwalk, gazing out at the blue water. Across from me were the boutiques, art shops, antique shops, pubs, restaurants, and gift shops that made Sequoia such a popular tourist attraction.

Four blocks down I came to the section of Greene Street that made up Little Greece, where a Greek Fest was held every June. Sequoia also had a big arts and crafts festival in July along with monthly concerts all summer and fall in the band shell at Sequoia Park along the lake. But as I passed the first shop on the block, an art gallery called the Acropolis, owned by Don Fatsis, I was reminded once again of Talbot's project.

How deplorable to think that an entire block of shops would be history in less than two weeks, and a big, modern condominium stuck in the middle of our charming downtown, where the tallest buildings were a mere three stories high. How wrong that the diner started by my *yiayiá* and *pappoús* would be gone. It made me furious.

I turned around and headed back, stopping to study the diner. I could picture a beautiful blue door with white columns on both sides, a coat of fresh white stucco, and large windows across the front that took advantage of the beautiful lake view. And while I wanted to encourage my grandparents to remodel, I'd promised myself I wouldn't get involved.

Then why had I told Kevin I'd attend the meeting? I had to remind myself that what I truly needed to focus on was my own life, working toward independence for Nicholas and me, and holding onto the *Treasure of Athena* for Pappoús.

At noon, Delphi and I headed to The Parthenon for lunch while Dad handled the garden center for the hour we were gone. It was a dead time anyway, as most tourists and even the locals were eating then.

Inside the family diner, deep red booths lined the dark golden-yellow walls decorated with gigantic murals—the Acropolis on one side and the Parthenon on the other. The long, faded yellow lunch counter with its red leather–cushioned stools separated the diner into two halves, each side with booths and tables that were almost all full. Behind the yellow counter was a wide pass-through window that showed Yiayiá and Pappoús hard at work in the galley kitchen at the back. Ancient black-and-white linoleum covered the floor, and the smell of oregano, basil, garlic, and lamb filled the air.

We said hello to Gayla, the hostess, seated on a stool at the small checkout counter to the left of the door, and headed for the last booth on the left side that Mama always reserved for family. As usual, she had a large bowl of feta cheese, kalamata olives, and cherry tomatoes waiting, along with glasses of water, hunks of homemade bread, and tzatziki, a cucumber yogurt dip.

"Were there any updates on the murder?" Mama asked, as she scooted in next to Delphi, seated across from me. My sisters Maia and Selene hadn't arrived yet.

"Just the same news they had on this morning," I said.

"That's all the customers are talking about," Mama said. "There hasn't been so much chatter since Mr. Talbot drowned in his bathtub."

A sudden hush fell over the diner. I swiveled to look at the TV over the counter where everyone was staring.

"What's happening?" Mama asked, rising.

A customer said, "Another report about the murder. They just showed footage of a man caught on security cameras leaving the Talbot mansion."

"Wait a minute." Delphi placed her fingertips at her temples. "I'm getting a vision."

I got up to move closer to the TV as the surveillance video played again. The images were somewhat grainy, but I could still make out the home's white bricks, a row of huge viburnums along the front in full bloom, and a pair of open black French doors. A moment later I saw a dark-haired man dressed in a tan bomber jacket, navy jeans, and dark shoes run out of the doors and begin jogging out of frame.

"Hey!" Delphi said, pointing toward the TV, "I've seen that guy before."

A cold knot formed in my stomach. I'd seen him, too. It was Case Donnelly.

CHAPTER FIVE

My mother stared at Delphi in alarm. "You saw that man? Here in town?"

"Yes!" Delphi answered. "That's what my vision was about. And Thenie—"

Before she could say more, I burst in with "—had a vision, too!"

Mama stared at me openmouthedly. "*You* had a vision?"

"Yes!" I pointed toward the TV. "Right now, in that news report, just like Delphi did." I gave my baby sister a light kick under the table. "Right?"

"Ouch." Scowling at me, she reached for her ankle.

"For a moment I thought you were serious, Athena." Mama rolled her eyes and fixed her apron, bracelets jangling. "I'll be right back. Behave, you two."

Delphi waited until Mama was out of earshot before whispering, "That was mean. I really did get a vision."

"It wasn't a vision," I hissed, glancing around to be sure no one could hear us. "You *remembered* seeing a man at the shop who resembled the guy in the video."

"I'm telling you it wasn't a memory. I know the difference." She reached across the table and took my hands. "You've got to believe me. The man who came to see the statue"—she dropped her voice to a whisper—"*is Harry Pepper's murderer.*" She sat back as though vindicated. "There. I've said it. Now you've got to call the police."

"Call the police for what?" Maia dropped her purse onto the bench next to Delphi, sat down, and began rolling her shoulders, her hair still in a ponytail from yoga class. Mama plopped down beside her.

"Something knocked over Pappoús's statue and I think it's that impish little Oscar." I narrowed my eyes at my youngest sister. "If you wouldn't feed him, Delph, he wouldn't come around."

"Dad feeds him, too," Delphi argued, completely oblivious to the subject change. "Besides, how can we stop feeding him? He was abandoned by his mother and depends on us to live."

"And you know this how?" Maia asked.

"I saw it in a vision, just like the vision I had about . . . ow!" Delphi gave me another scowl but wisely let it go rather than being kicked a third time.

I breathed a sigh of relief. Yet as I reached for an olive, I was struck by the fact that I was protecting Case. And why? What was keeping me from turning him in? Was it the fear that the police might be pursuing an innocent man—or was there a deeper reason?

"Are you talking about Oscar again?" my sister Selene asked, as Mama got up to let her in the booth.

"How did you get here so early?" Mama asked. "I thought you had a client."

"She canceled."

"I like your hair better that way, Selene," Maia said.

"Thanks." Selene patted her hair—long black curls

pulled to the back of her head, fastened with a tortoise-shell clip, and then fanned out like a peacock's tail. "I redid it. I didn't want to look like that woman described in the blog."

Delphi pressed her fingers to her temples. "I'm getting a message about the blog."

"Delphi," I said, trying to get her off the subject, "pass the bread basket this way."

"What's the latest on Pappoús's statue?" Maia asked, as Delphi shoved the basket down my way with a frown. "Are we going to have an unveiling for it?"

"The pedestal base is coming tomorrow," I answered. "We should take advantage of the opportunity to do some kind of promotion. How about this coming Friday? Delphi and I can organize it."

"Oh, joy," Delphi said in a bored tone. She slid out of the booth. "I'm going to the kitchen to ask Yiayiá to make some *keftedákia*. Anyone want some?"

"I do," Selene said through a mouthful of feta.

"Meatballs again?" Maia rolled her eyes. Eye rolls were a given in my family.

"That's better than what *you* eat," Selene said. "I'll bet there's a protein bar that tastes like cardboard in your purse right now."

"It doesn't taste like cardboard. It's nutty and delicious and packed with nutrition. Besides, you know Mama's rule. Always carry food for emergencies."

"Yes, *real* food." Selene rolled her eyes and Maia stuck out her tongue at her.

I said nothing because I had a protein bar in my purse, too, but I made a mental note of their argument for a future blog article.

While Delphi was in the kitchen, another news bulletin came on, interrupting our conversation. Once again, with a sick feeling in the pit of my stomach, I watched the blurry image of a man closely resembling Case jogging away from the Talbot mansion. The bulletin was followed by a phone number of the Sequoia Police Department and a request for anyone with information on the man's identity to come forward. And once again I felt torn, still hoping the man I'd met in the garden was not the image I saw on the TV video.

"Something strange is going on," Maia said. "Two deaths, same house, two weeks apart? Like Mama, I don't believe in coincidences."

"I had my doubts when Talbot's drowning was first reported," Selene said.

"We all had our doubts," Mama added. "*And* there was no investigation, just a quick ruling by the coroner."

"Here's another thought." Selene finished spreading a hunk of goat cheese on a thick slice of bread. "We just saw the footage of a stranger leaving the mansion after murdering Harry Pepper. Maybe that guy killed old Mr. Talbot, too."

Appetite diminishing quickly, I pushed my salad dish aside. "Isn't it asking a lot to believe that a stranger came to town half a month ago to kill Talbot and then returned yesterday to kill Harry?"

"Not if he was a hired assassin," Maia said, picking through the bowl for a cherry tomato.

Case, a hired assassin? That was something I hadn't considered. Still, why wait so long before killing Harry? Why kill Harry at all?

"Or maybe," Maia added, "the killer was actually someone *inside* the house who had an ax to grind, like Sonny or Lila."

"I think we can all agree that Sonny disliked his father," Selene said.

"It was more like he hated the control his father had over him," Mama corrected.

"The same goes for his wife, Lila," Maia said. "She was always talking to us at the yoga studio about how much she hated the old man. Talbot controlled the purse strings in that house and she despised him for it."

"Those strings couldn't have been too tight," Selene said. "I never saw Lila carry anything but Louis Vuitton bags when she came into the hair salon for her mani-pedis. She drives a silver Lamborghini, too."

Maia took another sip of water. "Maybe Lila drowned the old man."

"Getting a divorce from Sonny would've been easier," I said.

Maia nearly spit out her water trying not to laugh. "But then she'd have to give up her pampered life. Besides, I heard her prenuptial agreement was airtight. She wouldn't get a dime if she divorced Sonny."

"You're saying she might have killed her father-in-law out of hatred," I asked, chewing on an olive, "and then killed Harry, too? What for?"

Clearly enjoying the whodunit game, Selene said, "Maybe Lila and the hired assassin were having a torrid love affair and Harry Pepper caught them at it."

"Or maybe Sonny hired the assassin for both murders," Maia said. "Maybe he's going to have Lila killed, too."

"That would be horrible," Selene said. "She's my best customer."

"Let's hope the killer's caught soon," Mama said. "It's a small town. Someone has to have seen the stranger in the news video."

That was all my nerves could take. I made a "time out" sign with my hands. "Can we talk about something else, please?"

"Here's a thought," Mama replied, casually leaning

her elbow on the table. "How about deciding what you want for lunch?"

"Sounds good to me," Selene said. "I'm starving."

"Seriously?" Delphi asked, glancing into the empty bowl as she slid into the booth. "You ate everything."

And with that, the discussion was over. But not the conflict in my head. Now I had even more to consider.

My conflicted feelings about Case came to a head as Dad and I were in the garden area figuring the layout of the patio tables around the *Treasure of Athena*. The door opened and two policemen stepped out, one of them my former high school classmate and old friend Bob Maguire, a tall beanpole of a man with stubby orange hair and elfin ears. I'd never seen the other man before.

"Athena Spencer," Maguire said in his most official-sounding voice, giving me a solemn nod. I had to hide my smile behind a cough. Maguire had been a class clown who'd hardly ever had a serious thought in his head. If I was in a bad mood, Maguire could always make me laugh.

"Yes, Officer Maguire," I said, mimicking his serious tone.

The other officer said to my dad, "Sir, are you Theo Karras?"

"No, I'm John Spencer, Athena's father. And you are?"

"Officer Gomez," he said, displaying his ID. "We understand Mr. Theo Karras purchased a statue from Grayson Talbot Senior, and we'd like to talk to him about that. We were told he was here."

Although my *pappoús* sometimes came down to sit in

the patio and eat, Mama would've known he wasn't here today. She must have sent the police here to protect Pappoús, knowing we'd figure out what to do.

"Why do you need to talk to him about the statue?" I asked.

"We're not at liberty to say," Gomez said.

"Bob, can you at least tell me whether it has anything to do with the murder?" I asked.

"Funny you should bring that up," Gomez said.

The way both officers were watching me, I knew instantly that I'd made a huge mistake by jumping to that conclusion. I'd have to come up with a way to keep Pappoús out of harm's way quickly or he could easily end up in the hospital. He'd been told by his doctor to avoid stress because of his heart arrhythmia. I couldn't imagine what being questioned by the police might do to him.

Before I could respond, my dad said, "Theo isn't here. He—"

"It doesn't matter where he is since *I* purchased the statue." And just that fast my stomach did a flip at the lie, which didn't do too much for all that feta cheese inside.

"It's *your* statue?" Maguire asked, gazing at me skeptically.

I was shaking inside as I said, "Yes. It's my statue. If you want to talk to someone about it, I'm your person."

"We'll have to take you to the station," Maguire said, giving me an apologetic look. "Detective Walters would like to talk to you."

"Let me get my purse first."

"Do you want Mama to meet you down there?" Dad asked me quietly. I knew he'd come with me himself, but Delphi couldn't manage the garden center alone.

"I can handle this, no problem, Pops. Remember, I was a reporter in Chicago. I had to talk to the police all the time."

There. Now both officers knew where I was coming from. Or at least that was what I hoped, because inside I was one big ball of nerves.

At the station, I was shown to the detective bureau on the second floor and introduced to Bill Walters, a middle-aged man with short gray hair, coffee-colored skin, and an expression that seemed set in stone. He asked me to have a seat beside his desk where he had turned his computer monitor to face me.

"Before we begin, would you like a cup of coffee or a bottle of water?"

"Neither, thanks." I didn't think my stomach could handle it.

"Okay, then let's get started. I'll be taping this interview." He hit a button on a small recording device. "Please state your name for the record."

"Athena Spencer."

"Miss Spencer, have you heard about Harry Pepper's murder?"

I realized I was winding a lock of hair around my index finger, a nervous habit of mine, and let it drop, sliding my hands under my thighs to keep them still. "Yes."

"I'd like you to view a short video and tell me if you recognize the man in it."

Trying to keep my voice from shaking I asked, "What makes you think I'd recognize him?"

"Because of evidence we've recovered from the crime scene."

He must have seen the look of shock on my face because he hastened to add, "You're not in trouble, Miss

Spencer, please don't worry about that, but you could be a material witness."

"What kind of evidence did you recover?"

Detective Walters reached across his desk for a plastic bag that had a wrinkled piece of paper in it. Placing it in front of me he asked, "Do you recognize this?" His dark brown eyes watched me like a hawk.

I leaned over for a closer look and felt my mouth go dry. I had to swallow before I could answer. "It's a copy of the sales receipt for the statue I bought at the Talbot auction."

"That *you* bought? Why does it have Theo Karras's name on it?"

"We always purchase things for my grandfather's diner with his credit card, then we pay him back," I lied. "He gets points that way that he uses to fly back to Greece to see his relatives, so the more we spend the more points he has to use." I realized that I was rambling on and stopped.

"Let me get this straight. You purchased the statue for your grandfather for his diner with his credit card?"

"And his blessing. And then I paid him back."

"But the statue isn't *at* his diner," he stated.

"He—that is—we thought he could use the statue inside the diner's entrance, but it ended up being too large, so we brought it down to the garden center instead."

Walters studied me for a long moment. "I see."

"Why do you need to know who owns the statue?"

"We're trying to piece together what happened. I found this copy of the sales receipt crumpled in the victim's hand, leading me to believe he was either trying to hide it from the murderer or leave a clue to the murderer's identity."

I stared blankly at the piece of paper as my thoughts raced through the events of the previous evening. Until that moment I truly hadn't wanted to believe Case could be the killer, but that wrinkled copy made me think otherwise. Could Harry have been trying to tip off the police?

The detective started the video and I had to force myself to watch it again. When a man's hazy image appeared on the screen, the detective hit the pause button. "Do you recognize him?"

I swallowed again, wishing I'd accepted that water. "The video is fuzzy, but it might be the man who came into the garden center yesterday to inquire about the statue."

He tapped the plastic bag holding the receipt. "The same statue named in this sales receipt?"

I nodded.

"Did the man give you his name?"

"Yes. Case Donnelly."

"Did he make any purchases?"

"No."

"Did he give you any personal information?"

"Just that he was from out of town."

"Did he say where?"

I shook my head, wondering if I looked as sick as I felt.

"Anything else you remember about him? Any scars? Birthmarks? Tattoos?"

"Not that I saw. He had a jacket on."

"A tan bomber jacket like the one in the video?"

I was feeling sicker by the minute, knowing I'd been alone with a man who might have killed someone. "Yes, but like I said, the video is fuzzy and I'm sure a lot of men own tan bomber jackets."

He stopped the recorder. "Thank you. That's all we need for now."

As I was driven back to the garden center, I heard an all-points bulletin being broadcast over the squad car's radio.

Because of my testimony, Case was now a wanted man. Would he suspect it was me who'd turned him in?

CHAPTER SIX

IT'S ALL GREEK TO ME
blog by Goddess Anon

Liar, Liar

Ask any Greek whether Greeks are good liars and you'll get a resounding yes. It's something they're proud of. Get stopped by the police and how does a Greek answer? It's the automobile's fault, Officer. This car wants to move. It would be a crime to not let it once in a while to clean out that engine, you know what I mean?

Well, I'm here to tell you that it isn't easy telling a good lie—or being Greek sometimes. Take yesterday for example . . .

Wednesday

The weather turned so warm by midweek that Sequoia was deluged with tourists. Sailboats and chartered fishing boats filled the harbor; restaurants, bars, and diners had set up their outdoor tables and were busy bustling food and drinks to chattering patrons; boutiques had rolled out racks of clothing for early sales before the big Memorial Day weekend; and we were so busy I was able to push my fears to the back of my mind.

That ended when I went into the office to grab a cup of coffee and found Dad seated at the desk reading the local newspaper, the *Sequoian Press*. "Did you see the paper this morning?"

"Not yet."

He held it up so I could read the headline.

SEQUOIA MAN DEAD: KILLER IDENTIFIED

My shoulders immediately knotted as Dad read the article out loud:

"*Harry C. Pepper, age seventy-two, Grayson Talbot Sr.'s longtime trusted assistant, was found dead inside the Talbot mansion early Tuesday morning. Police have ruled the death a homicide and are now seeking a suspect known as Case Donnelly, who was last seen on a surveillance video outside the mansion's first-floor office early Tuesday morning.*

"*Detectives were unwilling to give out any further information because of the ongoing investigation, but according to a statement given to the press by Talbot's son, Grayson Talbot Jr., the safe in his father's office had been opened and the contents were askew. 'We're offering a fifty-thousand-dollar reward to anyone with information about Donnelly's whereabouts,' Talbot said. 'The public can be assured that we will bring this perpetrator to justice.'*

"That ought to get everyone in town out shaking the bushes," Dad said.

He continued reading. "*When Talbot was asked whether he thought Pepper's murder had anything to do with his father's condominium project, he said he would address that subject during a press conference at five p.m., Friday, at corporate headquarters.*"

My ears perked up. Talbot was giving a press conference about the project *and* the murder? That snapped me out of my funk. "Someone from the GMA needs to go to that conference."

Dad set the newspaper aside and stood up to stretch his back. "Why don't you go, Thenie? With your journalism experience, you'd be the perfect one to attend."

I rubbed my temples, my head starting to ache. I was getting sucked in deeper and deeper each day. "Fine," I said with a resigned sigh. "I'll go."

When the base for the statue arrived late that afternoon, I was reminded of Case once again. As the deliverymen mounted the *Treasure of Athena* on the elegant black pedestal, I couldn't help but go over my encounter with him in the garden. The irony was that if not for our run-in, I would never have known Pappoús owned a valuable Antonius.

As soon as we closed for the day, my father and Delphi brought in every available patio chair to set up several rows facing the long oak table at the back of the barn. My mother cleared the table of its garden décor, while I set out the paper plates, napkins, utensils, and mineral water on it and started the coffee brewing.

It was supposed to be desserts only, so Nancy, the owner of Downtown Shabby, a shabby-chic clothing boutique, brought in two trays of brownies, and Barb, the owner of Got Glass?, brought in three dozen donuts. Yiayiá brought a large pan of moussaka, a platter filled with kalamata olives, chunks of feta cheese, and slices of thick, home-made bread, and a big pan of baklava oozing with golden corn syrup. If the meeting lasted into the next day, they were prepared!

Soon after eight o'clock, members of the Greek Merchants' Association began to trickle into the garden shop. There were twenty in all, counting spouses, but Yiayiá had come alone so Pappoús could clean the kitchen and get it ready for the morning breakfast crowd. She'd persuaded me to stay and sit with her in the front row, and naturally Kevin was right beside me.

After members had picked up their refreshments, my dad started the meeting by asking who was going to attend Grayson Talbot Jr.'s upcoming press conference. A few hands went up, including Donald Fatsis's, who was seated in the back row with a chair pulled in front of him loaded with food.

Before Dad could say anything further on the subject, Donald took the floor, still chewing a big bite of food, to give an impassioned speech about how we had to stand firm in our efforts to stop Grayson Talbot Jr. from ruining the downtown. I could see people giving each other disgruntled looks. They'd been fighting this for months. There was nothing new in what he was saying.

"Thank you, Don," Dad said, forcing himself to be polite. "I was just about to propose we set up another meeting with Talbot to try to forestall the project."

At that point, Kevin interrupted, rising from his seat. "With all due respect, John," he said, using his lawyer's voice, "we all know talking hasn't gotten us anywhere and we're twelve days away from demolition. As I pointed out at our last meeting with the Talbots, our best option was, and still is, to file a lawsuit and get a court injunction to halt the project until we can get a judge to hear our case."

When he began to explain what that would entail, Fatsis jumped up to veto the idea, his beefy face, even his bald head, turning red with barely concealed fury. "Do you have any idea how much that would cost? I don't know about any of you, but I don't have either the time or the money. Anyone here know a lawyer who'd work for free? Kevin? Oh, that's right, you're just a legal aide. Anyone else?"

"And what would *you* propose we do instead?" Kevin challenged, ignoring the barb.

"Who made you a member of this association anyway?" Fatsis shot back.

There was a moment of stunned silence. Kevin glanced around the room to gauge the other members' reactions, but they were studiously avoiding his gaze.

Mama rose and went to stand beside my dad. "*I* invited Kevin." She folded her arms and gave Fatsis a piercing stare. "He has the legal knowledge to guide us even if he can't take our case to court."

She and Dad were joined by Yiayiá in her long black skirt and blue blouse with a blue print scarf over her head. "Do you have a problem with that, Mr. Fatsis?" Yiayiá asked, pronouncing it the Greek way of *Faht-sees*.

At his muttered "No," Yiayiá said, "*Entáxei*." Good. "Now sit and eat your baklava."

"With all due respect, Mrs. Karras,"—Fatsis paused to mop his perspiring face with a napkin—"my proposal is that we don't spend a fortune trying to convince a judge who's probably already in Talbot's pocket to see our side. I *also* propose that you let *me* try to convince Talbot to stop the project."

That remark brought a distinct murmuring of disapproval.

"What makes you think Talbot will listen to you?" Nancy asked.

"Because I've dealt with him in the past," Fatsis retorted, "and he's always been fair."

"Fair?" Barb called. "Are we talking about the same man?"

"Remember, Don," Dad said, "we have only twelve days before demolition is scheduled to begin, and your shop will be first on the block to go."

"Which is why I've got the most at stake," Fatsis said. But somehow, he didn't sound too convincing.

Several people jumped to their feet to protest his proposal until Fatsis finally sat down and folded his arms across his heavy chest, pouting like an angry child. To end the dispute, Dad asked for a show of hands for those in favor of Fatsis meeting with Talbot, and not a single person's hand went up. Then he asked the same about having Kevin look into fees for filing the lawsuit and injunction, and only a few went up, no doubt due to the points Fatsis had made about the cost.

I'd been sitting there holding my tongue, trying my best not to be involved, but I finally had to say something. Rising, I said, "I have two suggestions. The first is to set up a fund-raising site to pay for the legal fees. I'll bet all the shop owners as well as everyone living in and around the downtown area will get behind it. No one wants to see that huge condominium go up and block their view."

There was a buzz of excitement at that idea, so Dad made a motion and it carried. Then came the tough question. Dad looked around the room. "Who would be willing to set up the site and manage it?"

Before anyone could respond, Fatsis was on his feet again. "I'll do it. I have the time and know-how."

Now, *suddenly,* he had time? That sure wasn't what he'd said moments earlier.

"Any discussion on Don running the site?" Dad asked.

No one spoke up. Finally, David Jennings, the owner of the men's clothing store, said, "I move that Don sets up the funding site and runs it."

The motion carried and Fatsis sat down, rubbing his hands as though he couldn't wait to get started. His eagerness to take charge made me wary, especially when he'd just professed to be against any type of legal action. But then, considering what I knew about him, I tended to look at everything Fatsis did with a skeptical eye.

In the short time I'd been back, I'd heard more than one person complain about purchases made at Fatsis's art gallery, claiming the items he'd sold as original works of art had turned out to be fakes. He'd also been written up a number of times by the Better Business Bureau. Both of those factors could explain why his sales had been steadily declining.

"Athena, what was your second suggestion?" Dad asked.

"Once we get the injunction, everyone in Little Greece uses whatever resources are available to spruce up their storefronts. Paint is cheap, trim isn't hard to remove or have installed. We all know people who would be willing to help. I drew up some ideas for The Parthenon that are on the refreshment table. If all of you get on board with this, Talbot can't complain about Little Greece being run-down and out of date. In other words, we stand together and work together."

I was applauded for that, and as I sat down, I could hear people discussing improvements they could make. Dad proposed another meeting for the following Wednesday night and it carried. Then everyone went back to the refreshments table for seconds and even thirds, until the food was gone.

As soon as the shop cleared out, we locked the door and then Dad, Mom, Yiayiá, Kevin, and I cleaned up and put the furniture back in place. I could see that my grandmother and parents were tired, so I sent them all home under the pretense of wanting to finish cleaning by myself, even shooing Kevin out to see them home safely.

Humming softly as I planned my next blog, I bagged up the trash and carried it out to the bin behind the shop. I even had the title: *A Forkful of Baklava Makes Everything Better.*

There's nothing like Greek food to make even the most stubborn individual soften, except in the case of certain fatheads who are so full of themselves that . . .

I heard a noise and saw Oscar sitting on a wrought-iron chair, watching me expectantly, as though waiting for dinner. I opened the trash bag, found a paper bowl that still had some moussaka in it, and walked carefully toward the table. He was used to my dad and Delphi but was still cautious around me. "Here you go."

Delphi had told me that he'd been coming around since he was big enough to climb over the fence. He was a cute little raccoon, either not fully grown or the runt of the litter. He had a pointy gray snout with a black nose, white whiskers, and black fur around his dark eyes, lined with white, giving him the notorious burglar appearance. But he was friendly and growing more accustomed to people. Even the customers liked him. Oscar had become our unofficial mascot.

He began to eat with his little hands, keeping one eye on me. When he'd finished, he washed his face like a cat and then hopped down from the chair and made his way toward the back of the property. I was tempted to follow to see if he'd made a bed for himself back there, but then I glanced at the time and headed inside.

Preoccupied, I didn't notice at first that someone was sitting at the long oak table. I turned, then gasped, startled to find Case Donnelly watching me, a smile on his face. For a second I froze. Except for a ceiling fan whirring softly high above us, there wasn't a sound in the room. I'd locked the front door myself. How had he managed to get in?

"Evening, Athena."

I reached for my cell phone in my hip pocket only to remember I'd set it on the table where Case now sat. My eyes darted toward the table, but the phone wasn't there.

He held it up. "Looking for this?"

CHAPTER SEVEN

I stared first at my phone in his hand and then at Case. He knew—*had* to know—that I'd turned him in. Why else would he have come back?

Determined to show no fear, I lifted my chin and forced myself to say in a firm voice, "What do you want?"

"A chance to redeem myself."

That wasn't what I expected to hear.

He stood abruptly, startling me. I glanced around, ready to flee. But he merely pulled out a chair adjacent to his and gestured toward it. "Please, have a seat."

"I'll stand, thanks. Just say what you want to say and get out."

"Have it your way." He reached inside his bomber jacket as though going for a gun. I flinched, holding my hands protectively over my face, expecting to hear a shot. Instead I heard a rustling noise and peered through my fingers to see him smoothing out what appeared to be a piece of ancient parchment paper. I tucked my hair behind my ears, trying to cover my embarrassing reaction.

"Take a look at this," Case said.

"That's okay. Just tell me what it is."

"Athena, I won't bite. I didn't come here to harm you."

"Then you won't mind giving me my phone back."

"I'll give it back if you'll please sit down and let me explain this document to you. It's what I intended to show you the last time I was here."

"So why didn't you?"

"As I recall," he said with a wry smile, "you were late for your dinner date."

He was right. I pressed my lips together and said nothing.

"Please?" He gestured toward the chair.

I weighed my options. Case was sitting at least three feet away. If I decided to run, I might be able to make it to the front door, unlock it, and be out in public before he could reach me. Maybe.

If I decided to stay, I wasn't sure what would happen.

But as I took a longer look at him, his appearance alarmed me. His eyes had dark circles beneath them, he hadn't shaved, his hair was unkempt, and he was wearing the same clothes I'd last seen him in—clearly a man on the run. The sight of him looking exhausted, desperate, and alone tugged at my heart. But could I trust him?

"I'll listen to what you have to say on one condition. You have to leave immediately afterward."

In reply, he pushed the document across the table toward me.

I sat down opposite him instead of adjacent and leaned over the fragile piece of paper. At the top in large, old-world font was the heading *Costas Mouseío Téchnis Kai Glyptikís,* with an address in Crete, Greece, on the next line. Below that were the words *Paralaví Tis Agorás.*

He leaned across the table to point to the main heading. "This says Costas Museum of Art and Sculpture. Costas was my mother's maiden name, and it was her grandfather, my great-grandfather, who opened the museum."

"So you're Greek?"

"A quarter Greek, a quarter Irish, and a mix of German and French." He pointed to the next line. "This is the address of the museum."

"And how does this involve me?"

"It's a sales receipt. That's what *Paralaví Tis Agorás* means." He pointed to a smaller heading farther down that said, *Treasure of Athena*, followed by a detailed description of the statue—*my* statue. He tapped the description. "Notice anything unusual?"

"That part's in English." I was starting to get a gut feeling about where this was going.

"Bingo. Now bear with me for a moment." Case pointed to a line below the description. "This is the price the buyer paid for the statue in drachmas. It would be the equivalent of five thousand dollars in US money, which was a small fortune back in the early nineteen hundreds."

He indicated a name and address near the bottom. "Here's the buyer's information. As you can see, he was from Manchester, England. From that and a lot of searching I was able to find out that the buyer subsequently sold the statue to an art dealer in London. I tracked the next sale to a buyer in New York, and finally found the *Treasure of Athena* right here in Sequoia in an auction notice. And that led me to you." He sat back with a smile, clearly proud of himself.

"Where are you going with this?" I asked warily.

"I'm trying to prove something to you. *Nothing* on an authentic sales receipt would have been written in English back then because my great-grandfather knew only one language—Greek."

Case pointed to a scrawled name just below the purchase price. "This is not my great-grandfather's signature, either. It's a forgery. This document was written by a crooked art dealer who realized early on that Antonius's sculptures were going to become exceedingly valuable. The dealer conned the museum manager into helping him steal the statue and then they split the profit. Both of them ended up going to jail, by the way, but by the time the law caught up with them, the statue was long gone."

"You're asking me to believe a six-foot-tall stone statue was moved out of the museum right under your great-grandfather's nose?"

"As incredible as that sounds, yes. Look, it's getting late, so I'll keep this brief. Let's just say my great-grandfather's trust in the museum's manager was misplaced, serious mistakes were made that resulted in the museum's closing, and a beautiful statue he'd bought to honor his late wife's memory was lost as a result. And by the way, my great-grandmother's name was Athena."

Once again, I felt a tug at my heart. I truly wanted to believe Case's story, yet I still had doubts. "How did you happen to find this forged document?"

"Through a long, involved process. I found an old newspaper clipping about the theft among my grandfather's papers when I was helping him clean out his belongings, so I asked him to tell me about it. And after I learned what the *Treasure of Athena* meant to my great-grandfather, and how long both he and my grandfather had searched for it, I promised my grandfather I'd do whatever I could to find it. Plus, I had the advantage none of them had—the Internet.

"My next step was to fly back to Crete to convince

someone in the police department's bureau of records to let me rummage through boxes of old files. My mother went with me to act as interpreter because I speak only a few words of the language. But it was worth our effort because the art dealer's criminal records were still intact, including his bills of sale. Luckily for us, Greeks rarely throw anything away."

I folded my arms across my shirt and gave him a skeptical glance. "Amazing how everything worked out."

He gave me a dimpled smile. "I agree it sounds like something straight out of a movie, but it really did happen that way."

I slid the document toward him. "Okay, so you've come a long way to find the *Treasure of Athena.* Now you've found her, and you can tell your grandfather the statue is in good hands."

"You don't understand. The museum could be reopened if—"

"No, *you* don't understand." I pushed back my chair and rose. "I listened to your story as you asked. Now you keep your end of the bargain and leave." I held out my hand. "My phone, please."

Case ran his fingers through his hair, visibly exasperated. "The whole purpose of showing you this document is to convince you that I came here to right a wrong done to my family. If I can at least take the proof of ownership back to Greece, there's a chance my family can recoup their loss in court. That would give them the funds to reopen the museum."

"But if you have the proof of ownership, what guarantee do I have that you won't try to reclaim the statue?"

"Please, Athena, believe me, I'm just an honest man trying to—"

"An honest man? You broke into our garden center Tuesday morning to steal that proof of ownership."

"Wait a minute. I'll admit I came back to look for the document, but the compartment was empty."

"And what would you have done if you'd found the document?"

"I would've asked you to lend it to me long enough for me to take it back to Greece. I wouldn't have kept it."

"So you say *now.*"

"The proof of ownership is supposed to stay with the statue. But you didn't have it, so the most logical place to look next was at the Talbots'. And by the way, I went there to *ask* for it—or buy it if I had to."

I sat down again, thinking about what he'd just said. "Explain to me why anyone would leave a valuable document inside a sculpture where it would be a prime target for a thief."

"It was Antonius's trademark. My grandfather said it was part of the mystique of owning one of his sculptures. And remember, his art didn't become valuable until after his death."

"So why wouldn't that document have been inside the sculpture when I received her?"

"That's exactly what I wanted to know." Case sat forward, his hands clasped, an earnest expression on his face. "Please believe me, Athena. I went to see Talbot for one reason only, to find out what happened to the proof of ownership, but I wouldn't have killed for it."

"Then why did the video show you running away from his office?"

"Because I made a gigantic tactical error. I was going to present myself at the front door and ask to see Grayson Talbot Junior. Then I saw the French doors standing open just a few hundred feet away and knew that's where

Talbot's office was located, so I stupidly headed in that direction instead."

"Whom did you expect to find there?"

"Talbot Junior."

"What made you think it was his office?"

"I found a virtual tour of the mansion on the Internet that his wife had posted after she did some redecorating. I didn't realize the two Talbots' offices were side by side."

Bragging on the Internet without a care to their safety did sound like something Lila Talbot would do. "Were you planning to just step inside and announce yourself?"

Case scratched his ear. "Let's just say it wasn't one of my better decisions."

"To put it mildly."

"I didn't realize I'd been caught on his security cameras until I saw my name and face plastered all over the news. Now everyone is convinced I'm a murderer and the whole town is being turned upside down to find me. But the God's honest truth is that I saw a man slumped over a desk and knew he was dead by his pallor, so I took off before anyone thought I was the killer. And until I saw a newspaper headline yesterday, I didn't know who'd been killed."

"What do you want from me, Case?"

He placed my phone on the tabletop and slid it toward me. "Help me find the killer."

Once again, he'd managed to surprise me. "I can't do that. I have absolutely no experience tracking down criminals. And I'm already involved in a battle with the Talbots. I can't jeopardize that by sticking my nose into a murder investigation involving them."

"Please, Athena? I have no one else to ask. I'd hunt for the killer myself, but the police surely have their dogs searching for me. I'd be arrested before dawn. I'm a stranger in town. They've got me on videotape. What chance would I have of getting a fair trial?"

Case was right. He wouldn't stand a chance against Sonny Talbot and his powerful connections. I tucked the phone in my hip pocket. "Let me think about it for a moment."

I paced around the room, trying to sort out my feelings.

The moment the coroner had ruled Talbot Sr.'s death an accidental drowning and failed to do an autopsy, my family had had their suspicions, mainly because of who the Talbots were—greedy, power-hungry people who were unabashedly proud of the influence they wielded in town. With the second death in the Talbot mansion coming so soon after the first, and a murder no less, I was having an even harder time buying the coroner's ruling on Talbot Sr.'s death.

Had someone paid off the coroner to skip the autopsy or was it just sloppy, hurried work on Dr. Kirkland's part? I remembered my dad saying Kirkland was a miserly man easily swayed by money and power who counted the rich in town as his patients. Dad had gotten Kirkland's number a few years back when his wife had hired Spencer's to landscape their new house.

But even if it were true that Talbot Sr. and Harry Pepper *had* been murdered, if Sonny himself wasn't doing any questioning, what could I do about it? Was it possible that Sonny was involved somehow? Could it be that he wanted to get rid of the two men who stood in the way of his condominium project?

If I could prove that Sonny was even partially responsible, I could shut down the demolition immediately. So perhaps helping Case clear his name would be beneficial to both of us.

One thing I knew for sure. I couldn't handle the investigation alone, nor could I ask anyone in my family to put themselves at risk to help me. And if I involved Kevin, he'd never be able to keep it under his hat. He'd have to brag about it to someone, and I simply couldn't take the chance of word getting out, especially since I was now involved in halting the condominium project.

My only option seemed to be working with a man whom I had to consider a suspect. But how could I do that when his face was plastered all over town? And there was still the question of who the rightful owner of the *Treasure of Athena* was. If I was able to clear Case of murder—and that was a big if—would I then have to fight him to keep my statue?

One of Dad's sayings popped into my head: Keep your eyes on the prize. To me that meant, regardless of my feelings about the man sitting before me, the ultimate prize would be to see justice done. I would just have to keep focused.

I glanced around at Case to see him watching me expectantly, a hopeful look in his tired eyes. His stubble was filling in quickly and his dark, disheveled hair was curling a bit at the ends. That gave me an idea. Perhaps there *was* a way for him to help.

I sat down at the table and folded my hands, my thoughts coming so fast I had to take a deep breath. "Let's find the killer."

CHAPTER EIGHT

Case's smile of relief reached all the way up to his tired eyes. In a voice choked with emotion, he said, "Thank you."

Even in his disheveled state—unshaven, ruffled hair, wrinkled clothes—I couldn't help but gaze into those golden-brown eyes and remark to myself how attractive he was.

Then I noticed him watching me and gave myself a mental shake. I wasn't about to let him think I was doing this as a favor to him. I had to put that to rest immediately. "This is about one thing, Case: justice. Don't read anything deeper into it than that."

He nodded. "I get it."

"Good. Then let me fill you in on what I know."

Case leaned back in his chair and folded his arms over his shirt. "Go ahead."

"About two weeks ago, Grayson Talbot Senior died from what was ruled an accidental drowning. No one in my family bought it then because of the way the coroner ruled so quickly without ever performing an autopsy."

"How did he get away with that?"

"Exactly what I'd like to know, along with why Talbot's son didn't demand one. And now that the elder Talbot's trusted assistant has been murdered, I'm even more skeptical about the first death being ruled accidental."

"How did Talbot drown?"

"According to his son, Talbot Senior had gone up to his suite for a bath after dinner as usual and sometime later must have slipped beneath the water. His daughter-in-law Lila found his body the next morning when he didn't show up for breakfast."

Case's eyebrows drew together. "His daughter-in-law found him? In his bath? That seems a little personal."

"That's the story Sonny gave the *Sequoian Press.*"

"Who's Sonny?"

"Sorry. That's my family's nickname for Talbot's son. When the news about the drowning first hit the press, it was presumed that the elder Talbot's discovery in the tub was just a matter of his daughter-in-law noticing his absence at breakfast and going to check on him. But now that you mention it, why *would* she go? Lila had let it be well known around town that she hated him. If he had been my father-in-law, I'd have told my husband to do the checking, or at least send a maid. They did have staff."

"Was the daughter-in-law ever questioned as a possible murder suspect?"

"If she was, it was kept hush-hush."

Case shook his head. "It's hard to believe Talbot's son didn't ask for an autopsy. I thought it was automatic."

"After a news reporter questioned him, Sonny explained it away by saying that the coroner had decided against an autopsy because of the information Lila had given him."

"Which was what?"

"That he must have fallen asleep in his bath, which explained why he'd slipped under the water. The coroner's ruling was based solely on Sonny's word, and no one questioned it. Not only that but he also held the funeral and burial immediately after his father's death."

"That part's not uncommon, but the lack of an autopsy makes me suspicious."

I leaned back against the chair and crossed my arms. "Sonny could have paid the coroner to skip the autopsy."

"It's hard to believe he holds that much sway over a county official."

"If you knew the Talbots, you'd believe it. It's also well-known there was no love lost between father and son. Anyone who had business dealings with them knew Sonny was urging his father to retire so he could run Talbot Enterprises his own way."

"At least Talbot's body wasn't cremated, so it *could* be exhumed." Case leaned his chin on his palm, a furrow between his brow. "Looks like we've got our work cut out for us. The first thing we need to do is talk to the coroner and try to get to the bottom of things."

"That could be a problem. Dr. Kirkland is a difficult man to deal with. It'd probably be easier to dig up the body ourselves."

Case gave a little half smile. "We could do that, too."

"I was *kidding*. Besides, *we* won't be doing anything just yet. You're still a wanted man, remember?"

"If you think I'm going to sit around twiddling my

thumbs while you do the grunt work and possibly put yourself in jeopardy, you're wrong."

"Believe me, I wouldn't go it alone. I just meant that we're going to have to change your appearance."

He glanced down at his clothing. "How?"

"Leave that to me. But first I need to find you a safe hiding place for the night so you can get some sleep. I'll work on a more permanent living arrangement tomorrow."

"What's wrong with staying here?" He glanced around. "All I need is that wicker sofa over there and a bathroom. You have a bathroom, don't you?"

"Yes, right next to the office up front, but staying here is too risky. My father sometimes comes in early when he can't sleep. He could easily catch you off guard." I chewed a hangnail on my thumb, trying to think.

Two rapid knocks on the front door brought us both to our feet. I met Case's alarmed gaze. Who would be at the shop at that time of the evening? It wouldn't have been anyone in the family. They had keys.

"Athena?" Kevin called. "Are you there?"

Damn! I'd forgotten about Kevin.

I whispered to Case, "It's my"—I hated what I was about to call him—"boyfriend. He must have come back to walk me home. Wait in the office until we leave, then give me about twenty minutes to get back. I'll figure out a place for you to stay in the meantime."

I felt a vibration and slid my cell phone out of my pocket, only then remembering I'd put it on mute for the meeting. I checked the home screen and saw two text messages and two missed calls from Kevin, all in the span of ten minutes.

He knocked again, louder this time. "Athena? Are you okay?"

"Be right there, Kev." I turned to Case and pointed toward the office. "Go!"

I walked as calmly as possible to the front, running my fingers through my hair and trying to compose myself. Glancing around to be sure Case was out of sight, I unlocked the door and opened it. "Hey, you surprised me."

"I wasn't about to let you walk home alone."

He wasn't going to *let* me?

"Why didn't you answer my text messages or phone calls?"

I gave him a nonchalant shrug. "I put the phone on mute during the meeting and forgot about it. I guess I just lost track of time. Stay right here and I'll grab my purse."

Before I could get away, Kevin snagged my hand and led me to the front door. "You've had a long day, darling. Relax. I'll get your purse. It's in the office, right?"

I grabbed his arm. "No!"

At Kevin's startled look I gave his arm a squeeze and said, "No need to look there. I left it in the outdoor center on a white wrought-iron bench. Why don't you go take a look?"

"Athena, you know you'd never leave your purse outside with Oscar around." And then he set off toward the office.

I scurried after him, my heart thumping in my ears as I called loudly enough for Case to hear, "You don't need to check the office, Kevin. I'm positive my purse isn't there."

I caught up with him just as he opened the door and flipped on the light. "Hey," he exclaimed, "what's going on here?"

I felt my forehead. It was hot to the touch. "Kevin, before you overreact—"

"Looks like *someone* got a new coffee maker and didn't tell me."

I almost collapsed from nerves.

As Kevin strode over to the side table to have a look, I peered around the room, but there was no sign of Case, not even behind the floor-length drapes covering the rear window. The only other place he could be was under the big oak desk. Thank God it had a solid front.

"I told you my purse wasn't here. Now how about checking the garden while I take a look around the shop." I tried to turn Kevin by the shoulders and push him toward the doorway but instead he pivoted and headed straight for the desk.

Dear God.

I squeezed my eyes shut as he stooped down.

"I *knew* it," he exclaimed. He held up my tan leather bag.

I reached for the console table to steady myself. Where had Case gone?

My hand was shaking as I took the bag and slung it over my shoulder. "You're the best, Kev. Now let's get out of here."

"I'm with you on that," he said. "You look *really* stressed, sweetheart."

"You have no idea."

As Kevin charged out the door, I glanced around one last time, let out a sigh of relief, then shut off the light and closed the door. But as I passed the bathroom on my left, I caught Case's reflection in the mirror over the sink, and my stomach dropped to my knees.

At the door, Kevin put his arm around me and gave me a gentle squeeze. "You know what you need? A glass of wine to relax you. How about we stop at our favorite piano bar? My treat."

Our favorite piano bar? We'd been there exactly twice. "That's sweet of you, Kevin, but I *really* have to get home to tuck Nicholas in bed. Maybe another time. It's been a long, tiring day."

And it was getting longer by the second. I needed to get home, but I couldn't very well leave Case hanging, so I'd have to come up with a plan fast.

"Then I'll walk you home," he said, giving my shoulders another squeeze.

I had an idea.

"Hey, Kev, I need to use the restroom before we go. Wait right here."

I handed him my purse and then scurried toward the bathroom. But on the way, I had another thought and my heart started beating like a drum. What if Kevin decided he had to go, too?

I shut the bathroom door and turned on the light, causing Case to blink at the sudden brightness.

"There's been a change in plans," I whispered. "You're going to have to spend the night here after all. There's a throw blanket on one of the wicker sofas, and protein bars and bottled water in the mini fridge in the office."

"And apparently," Case said in a low voice, "a new coffee maker."

Despite my nerves I had to laugh but faked a cough to cover it. Considering the rough two days he'd had, it was amazing Case had managed to keep his sense of humor.

I lifted the toilet lid, let it close with a solid thud, and then flushed, whispering, "I'll be back before seven in the morning. If Dad comes in early, he'll go straight to the office, so you can slip out through the rear door to the garden area in back." I waited a beat, then added with a slight smile, "But then I don't need to tell *you* how to come and go as you please."

This time it was Case who tried to hide a smile.

I ran the water so Kevin would think I was washing my hands. "You'll have to stay here until you hear me shut the front door and lock it."

"Give me your cell number so I can get in touch with you."

I was about to do so when I remembered the precarious position he was in. "You've got to ditch your phone. You're traceable with it."

"Damn. I hadn't thought of that." He pulled it out of his pocket and looked around. "Where?"

I grabbed it out of his hand, stuck it in my purse, then turned off the water. "I'll dump it somewhere on my way home." I was about to open the door when I remembered something else. "How did you get into town?" I whispered.

"I took a cab from the airport."

"Good. Then there's no car to worry about. What about your travel bag? I'm assuming you brought one with you."

"I left it in my room at the Hilton. I was afraid to go back for it in case I was recognized."

"It's probably been confiscated by now. After all the press over the murder, I'm sure someone at the Hilton recognized your name and called the police. I'll have to get some clothing for you."

I waited until Case had stepped into the stall, then I turned out the light and opened the door.

"Athena," Case whispered.

I paused to listen.

"Thank you again."

Thursday

I sat straight up in bed. I had it! Pappoús's old fishing boat. He hadn't used it in over a year because of his arthritic hips and probably would never use it again. There were even a couple of fishing outfits my grandfather kept there that Case could use.

I lay back with a relieved sigh. I'd racked my brain for an hour before falling asleep, trying to think of a hideout. Now, finally, I had a plan. I glanced at the clock, then threw back the covers. Six a.m. I had two hours to get Case to the boat, fix his disguise, then get back to the house in time to get Nicholas off to school.

I'd taken a shower the night before, so all I had to do was apply blush and mascara, clip my hair into a loose bun, and don a pair of jeans and a hooded sweatshirt. I tiptoed down the staircase that ran down to the front door, avoiding the creaky stairs, then scooted up the hallway to the kitchen in back. I grabbed a piece of homemade oatmeal bread from the refrigerator and toasted it while the coffee brewed.

With a full belly, a small thermos of coffee, and a few surprises for Case in my purse, I left the house and walked toward Sequoia Harbor three blocks west. My *pappoús's* boat was docked at the southern end of the harbor on the last of three piers along the wide, wooden dock, directly across from the shops on Greene that were to be demolished. I put up the hood on my sweatshirt and strode toward the boat, avoiding eye contact with the fishermen busily preparing for the day. With my height and lean body, I knew I could be mistaken for a young man out for a walk.

Pappoús's old blue boat was coated with grime, but I wasn't worried about the outside. I found the hidden key that unlocked the cabin door and went below. I hadn't been on board for years, so I was relieved to see that the interior was in fine shape—no leaks, no mold, and everything exactly as I remembered it. There was a blue vinyl built-in sofa across from the galley, with two plastic chairs and a small, square white Formica table in the middle that was bolted to the floor. Beyond that was a tiny bathroom followed by a cozy bedroom tucked into the front of the boat.

In the bedroom, I searched the drawers of the built-in dresser and found a pair of worn, denim pants and a navy-and-white–striped T-shirt emblazoned with the Greek word *Páme*, the name of Pappoús's boat. In another drawer I found a black fishing vest with multiple pockets, and a pair of blue boxers. I located a black leather Greek-style cap and brown boat shoes in a small utility closet by the cabin door, threw everything in a bag, then checked the time.

Six forty a.m. I could give the inside a quick dusting and beat it over to the garden center. On my way out, I glanced around to be sure no one was watching, then dropped Case's cell phone over the side, watching as it descended into the watery depths.

The downtown was deserted as I made my way up Greene Street to Spencer's. I opened the front door, shut it quickly behind me, and locked it again. Then, just to be sure no one surprised me, I threw the bolt, too, so they'd have to knock when they got there. They wouldn't be happy about it but, oh well. Mistakes happened.

I glanced around but didn't see any sign of Case. I even walked over to the wicker sofa, but it was empty. The office door was still closed, which meant Dad hadn't been there. Case must have hidden when he heard my key in the lock.

"Case? It's me."

He stepped out of the shadows near the bathroom, a

cup of coffee in one hand, looking a little worse for the wear but not quite as tired as the evening before. I held out the bag. "I brought you something to wear."

"Thank God. I need to get out of these."

Standing behind the counter, I set the bag on the floor and began to remove the clothing. "Were you able to sleep?"

"Off and on. Something kept rattling around in the garden area."

"That was probably Oscar. He's a young raccoon we've kind of adopted."

Case picked up the T-shirt and held it against his shoulders. "This isn't going to fit. Your grandfather must be a size smaller than me."

"It'll be tight but it's the best I can do on short notice."

"What does *Páme* mean?"

"You're not saying it right. It's not like the word *fame*. It's pah-may, the name of my *pappoús*'s boat. That's Greek for 'let's go.'"

He picked up the black vest and Greek cap. "You want me to wear these?"

"Yes, they're part of your disguise, and stop acting like there's something wrong with them. You're lucky my grandpa keeps spare fishing outfits on his boat, which is where you're going to be staying, by the way."

"On his fishing boat?"

"It's the perfect hideaway. The boat is docked at the far end of the harbor on the last pier all the way at the end where few people go. It has a cozy living area below deck and the best part is that you'll be safe there."

"What if your grandfather decides to go fishing?"

"He doesn't use the boat anymore because of his arthritis."

Case lifted the underwear as though it was a piece of bad meat. "Okay, there's no way I'm wearing another man's boxers."

I shrugged. "Then I guess you'll have to go commando."

Giving me a scowl, he picked up the clothes.

"They're clean," I said. "Get over it. You're a Greek fisherman now, Dimitrius."

CHAPTER NINE

Case's dark eyebrows lowered. "Demitrius? As in the movie *Demitrius and the Gladiators?*"

"That's the Roman version," I said as I led the way toward the bathroom. "A Greek version is Dimitrius with an *i*. To keep things simple, we'll use Costas as your surname since it's your mother's maiden name."

"But Dimitrius? Seriously, am I ninety? How about shortening it to something sexier, like, I don't know . . . Dimitri."

Why did he want a sexy name? Not that it mattered to me.

I stopped in the short hallway that led to the bathroom and kitchenette. "I happen to think Dimitrius sounds more dignified, but we'll use whatever you like."

Case glanced down at the clothes in his arms. "Dignified in this outfit?"

"It's temporary." I opened my purse and pulled out a pair of hair-cutting shears that Selene had given to me, snipping the air in front of him. "Now go get dressed and then we've got to get over to the boat. I need to cut your hair to finish your transformation."

Muttering under his breath something about *Sweeney Todd*, murderous barbers, and bossy women, he walked into the bathroom and shut the door.

When Case stepped into the office a few minutes later, I had to pinch my lips to keep from laughing. Gone was the smartly dressed stranger in his navy loafers, slim jeans, and suede jacket. In his place stood a pale-faced fisherman in a black vest covered with small pockets, a striped T-shirt that was stretched tight across the shoulders, baggy denim jeans that were too short, and bare feet stuffed into a pair of old leather boat shoes.

"I look ridiculous."

Trying not to laugh I said, "You'll only have to wear them long enough to get onto the boat. I'll buy something else for you to wear later today."

"Then I need to pay you." He took a wallet out of his pants pocket and pulled out some bills. "Here's a hundred dollars and change. If it costs more, I'll pay you as soon as I can get to an ATM. . . ." A look of shock and then of anger flashed across his face as he stared at the bills in his hand. "Damn it! This is all I have. I can't use my ATM card or my credit cards. They're traceable, too."

I could only imagine how helpless he felt—his phone gone, limited cash, no other way to pay for anything, and only one person, a stranger at that, on whom he could rely. "Keep your money. You might need it. There'll be plenty of time to repay me after we've cleared your name."

He gazed at me for a long moment, his deep-set eyes searching mine, as though saying, *You really trust me.*

But *did* I?

"Okay," I said lightly, "let's finish up here before someone shows up. We've got work to do and I have to get back home to get my son off to school."

"You have a son?"

"Yes, and that's all you need to know. Here's a bag. Let's pack up your clothes."

As soon as we'd hid all traces of his being there, we left through the back door and crossed the outside garden center until we reached the narrow lane behind the shops on Greene. I opened the garbage bin and had started to drop the plastic bag with his things in it when he grabbed it out of my hand. "Not happening. These clothes weren't cheap."

I thought for a moment. "Okay, then we'll hide them in the hold of the boat."

We walked up the lane for two blocks, then turned east on Pine Avenue to head toward the harbor. But just as we were approaching the traffic light on Greene, I spotted Delphi on the other side of the street waiting for the light to change. I couldn't imagine what she was doing out so early. She rarely rose before eight o'clock.

"My sister's across the street," I whispered to Case. "Get behind the lamppost. Maybe she hasn't spotted us yet."

"Do you really think a lamppost is going to hide me?"

"Do you really think you're ready to try out your new identity? I haven't even cut your hair yet. Mess it up, quick."

"Thenie, hi!" Delphi called, waving, as Case tried to hide while he ruffled his hair. She glanced both ways and started across, a perpetual flower child in her colorful peasant blouse and a long, flowing white cotton skirt with her favorite bright green flip-flops.

"Pretend you don't know me," I whispered, then

stepped forward to greet her. "Hey, Delph. You're out early this morning."

"My stomach woke me up so I'm heading over to the diner to have breakfast with Yiayiá and Pappoús. Want to join me?"

"I've already eaten, but tell them I said hi."

Her attention shifted to my right and a smile lit up her face. "Oh, hello."

I spun around in alarm as Case stepped up to the curb, his hair in disarray. "Good morning."

My sister stuck out her hand. "Delphi Spencer."

"Dimitrius Costas," he said in a husky voice, taking her hand. "But you can call me Dimitri."

"Hi, Dimitri," Delphi replied cheerily. She cocked her head to one side. "Don't I know you from somewhere?"

"I doubt it. I'm sure I wouldn't have forgotten a pretty face like yours."

I discreetly poked my finger into his back, making him wince. "Dimitri was just asking for directions to the harbor."

Case clapped his hand on my shoulder. "And this kind woman has volunteered to show me."

My sister tapped her finger against her chin, clearly trying to work things out. I expected her to ask what I was doing out so early but instead she said, "I could swear we've met before, Dimitri."

"Nope," I said, removing Case's hand from my shoulder. "He's brand-new in town. I'll see you back at the diner later, Delph. Let's go, Dimitri."

Fuming inside, I started across the street and didn't notice the light had changed. As an oncoming SUV came at me, Case grabbed my arm and pulled me out of the way.

"*Green* means go," he said. "*Red* means stop. Now let's *pah-may* before we get run over."

As soon as we were on the other side, I glanced back to see Delphi swinging her purse happily as she headed to the diner.

Case glanced back at her, too. "Looks like I passed my first test."

"No, you *flunked* your first test. What were you thinking, flirting with my sister? Are you trying to draw attention to yourself?"

"Sorry. I didn't mean to flirt. Old habits die hard."

Flirting was an old habit?

As we approached the harbor, I put my hood up. "We can't be seen together until I get you some different clothes, so give me to the count of thirty, then follow me. I'll head straight down the dock to the last pier, pier three. Turn right and head to the farthest slip. Pier three, slip twenty-five, got it? And don't make eye contact with anyone."

"Aye, aye, Cap'n."

When I reached the *Páme* I glanced around to be sure no one was watching, then hopped into the boat. The flat-backed stern had a blue vinyl U-shaped seating area surrounding a plastic table for outside dining. Up a step and toward the cockpit were the swivel seats for fishermen and beyond that the helm. A deck on either side of the boat led to the bow where a sundeck could be used for tanning or cooling off after a swim.

My *pappoús* had purchased the boat decades ago, and for years our family had enjoyed it for weekend getaways. As we grew older, the boat was mainly used by Pappoús for fishing. Now, due to his health, the *Páme* sat unused most of the time, yet he still refused to consider selling or renting it out.

I unlocked the door to the cabin and went below.

"This is incredible," Case said, following me down the short flight of stairs. "Not what I expected at all."

"I told you it was the perfect hideaway."

I gave him a quick tour, then showed him the hatch that led to the storage area in the hull of the boat. "This is the hold where we can hide your belongings. Keep this throw rug over it and no one will know it's there."

I stowed his bag, closed the hatch and slid the rug on top of it, then revealed another secret about the boat, a tall cabinet in the bedroom that blended in with the rest of the wood paneling. Unlike the built-in drawers, the cabinet had no handle and was only accessible by pressing on the right side. Inside were my *pappoús*'s waders and tall rubber boots.

I left him to explore his new living quarters while I went back to the galley to get down to business. I took my cell phone from my purse, pulled out a chair at the small plastic table, and sat down. "What size shirt do you wear?" I called.

"Large," he called back. "Sixteen-inch collar. For pants it's a thirty-four-inch waist and same for the inseam."

"Shoe size?"

"Ten."

"Boxers?"

"Nope, briefs. Medium."

"Got it." I finished writing down his info, then called, "Would you like some tea?"

"Sure."

I slid the phone back into my purse and filled the teakettle with water. While it was heating, I found cups in a cabinet over the counter and packets of English Breakfast tea in another. There was a box of tea biscuits nearby, so I called, "Want some cookies? I'm not sure how fresh they are."

I didn't hear anything, so I walked back to the bedroom and found Case sound asleep on the bed, his shoes lying on the floor as though he'd kicked them off and collapsed backward into a deep slumber.

"Hey, wake up," I said, shaking his shoulder. "You can take a nap later. We've got to finish your disguise. Go take a shower and meet me in the kitchen. You'll find everything you need in the bathroom."

He was muttering to himself as he walked up the hall and shut the tiny bathroom door, while I returned to the small galley kitchen and set up my ad hoc barbershop. When he had finished, I had him sit on a step stool; then I draped a towel around his shoulders. Standing in front of him I ran my fingers through his thick hair, lifting up the long top layer to see how it parted without all his hair product slicking it back.

"My hair's still damp. Does that matter?"

"No, it's easier to cut that way."

"Good. And don't worry. I dried the stall afterward, so no one would notice."

"Thank you. Then you found the cabinet where the towels are stored."

"No, actually I used the bath mat that was hanging over the shower rod." He gave me a wry smile.

I had to laugh as I pictured him trying to dry off with a small, shaggy blue chenille mat. Trying to look serious, I focused on the task at hand.

Before I could snip a lock, he grabbed my wrist. "You're not going to give me a crew cut, are you?"

"Of course not. You wouldn't look Greek with a crew cut."

I started again only to have him grab my wrist a second time. "Are you sure you know what you're doing?"

"My sister's a hair stylist. I've watched her give haircuts to everyone in our family."

He drew in a breath and blew it out. "Okay. Go ahead."

I started by trimming about an inch of hair off the top, then layering the top and sides so they were about two inches long. "We need a backstory for you. Where are you from?"

"Pittsburgh."

"Then we need to stay far away from there." I thought for a moment and an idea popped into my head. "You can be from Tarpon Springs, Florida. It has a big Greek community. Do you know how to fish?"

"I fished when I was a kid." He was quiet for a moment, then said, "I don't know the first thing about Tarpon Springs. What if someone asks me about it?"

"I'll bring my iPad down to the boat so you can research it."

With his hair product washed out and some of the weight taken off, his hair began to wave. I started scrunching it to bring out even more of its natural curl.

Case winced. "Easy. I don't want to go bald."

"Sorry. I was just thinking that we haven't come up with a reason for you to be investigating the murders with me."

"Did Talbot's assistant have family in the area?"

"None that I'm aware of. Harry never married, and I'm pretty sure his parents died a long time ago. He had a sister, but she was killed in a boating accident a few years back."

Case brushed hair clippings off his nose. "Where is Harry from?"

"I don't know. I've never asked. I assumed from Sequoia. He and my *pappoús* opened The Parthenon together."

"Is he Greek, too?

"Only part Greek."

"What if I were his long-lost cousin from Tarpon Springs?"

"A Greek cousin? Might be too iffy. Pappoús might know whether Harry had relatives there."

"Maybe he never mentioned them. Besides, if I say I'm here to find my cousin's killer, do you really think anyone will stop to question my lineage?"

"You don't know my family. They question everything."

"Okay, then I'll be a private investigator that Harry's long-lost cousin from Tarpon Springs hired."

"And what if someone asks to see your investigator's license?" I tousled his hair to see what it would look like, drawing some of it over his forehead.

"Then how about this?" Case asked, sounding annoyed. "You think of something."

Yep, he was definitely annoyed. "I will. Don't worry about it."

As I stepped back to examine my work, he heaved a sharp sigh. "Are you done yet?"

I pulled one lock of hair down a little more over the right side of his forehead, then carefully removed the towel from his shoulders. "Now I am. Go take a look."

He walked around the corner to the bathroom and in a disgruntled voice said, "Great. I'm twelve years old again. All I need are braces."

"The only thing that matters is that you look completely different than when you arrived. Now sit back down so I can finish."

"You said you were done."

"With your hair, yes." I dug through my purse and held up a tube of bronzing cream. "Voilà."

"Makeup?"

"It's just a cream to give you some color until you can

get some sun. You're too pale to be a believable fisherman. But this will also wash off when you shower, so you're going to have to apply it yourself until you can get a tan."

After he'd perched on the stool, I put a dab on my fingertips and showed him. "Start with this much and apply it to one side of your face at a time. Now hold still."

As I smoothed on the cream, I couldn't help but notice his features—the arch of his dark brows, his long black eyelashes, the fine texture of his skin, his firm lips, and that dark stubble that made me feel things about him I shouldn't.

I swallowed hard. We were so close I could even smell the soap he'd used.

I suddenly felt his gaze on me and realized I'd stopped working. I immediately started again, a hot blush creeping up my face. "Okay, we're done," I said lightly, and capped the cream.

He reached up to rub his chin. "I guess I should shave."

"No, don't shave," I blurted.

At his look of surprise, I said, "What I mean is, it's part of the whole"—I made a circle around my face—"Greek effect. Now let's put that leather cap on and see how it looks."

Satisfied that I'd done a good job, I promised to be back by three p.m. with new clothes and groceries, then I shut the door and headed home while Case rested.

Back at the house, Nicholas was already up and dressed and coming down the stairs. "*Kalí méra*, Mamá."

I ruffled his brown hair. "How about just 'Good morning, Mom'?"

"*Kalí méra* sounds way cooler. Yiayiá said she's going to start my Greek lessons after school on Monday."

"*My yiayiá?*"

"No, *my yiayiá.* Your mom."

"Did she now?" Great, that was all I needed—more Greek. "Nicholas, we need to call my mama something else besides Yiayiá, otherwise it's too confusing. Why don't we call my grandmother Yiayiá and my mama Grandma?"

"Okay. I mean, *entáxei.*"

"'Okay' will do." As we headed to the kitchen I asked, "Oatmeal toast with strawberry jelly this morning?"

"*Nai, Efcharistó,* Mamá.*"

Now it was even "Yes, thank you," too. I started to protest but Nicholas had such a proud look on his face that all I could do was say, "You're welcome, sweetheart," and give him a hug. It didn't hurt him to know both languages. In fact, I knew it was good for his brain development. But I'd always hoped he would learn French, like I had, or Spanish.

As soon as Nicholas was on the bus, I drove to the diner for my morning coffee, arriving before eight a.m., and found my mama and sisters once again huddled around the computer, laughing and nudging one another.

"Don't tell me you're reading that silly blog again," I said as I sat down at the counter beside Maia.

"You don't know what you're missing," Selene said.

"You know who that woman sounds like?" Mama asked, pointing to the screen.

I paused, holding my breath.

"Mrs. Gabris. She dresses just like a peacock, too!"

I let out a silent sigh of relief. Thank goodness they hadn't realized I was describing Auntie Talia.

"And the fathead," Mama said. "That could be Donald Fatsis."

"His head matches his belly," Maia said, and they all chortled.

"Thenie, where's Niko?" Mama asked. "You're supposed to bring him here for breakfast, remember?"

"I'll think about it," I answered.

Before she could argue, I finished my coffee, said hello to my grandparents, and left as one of my sisters planned the comment she was going to leave on my blog.

When I arrived at the garden center, the office door was open, which meant Dad was already there. As I walked in, he was sitting at the desk reading the newspaper and sipping coffee. He lowered the paper to give me a smile. "Morning, Thenie."

"Morning, Pops." I glanced around to make sure everything was spotless, then realized the cup of coffee I'd had at the diner wasn't cutting it. That piece of toast I'd had at six a.m. was long gone. I'd have to grab a protein bar from the mini fridge.

As I started to make my coffee Dad asked, "Were you here earlier?"

My heart gave a startled thump. "No, why?"

"You must have slid the bolt last night after we left. I had to come in through the garden entrance this morning."

"I'm so sorry." My hands shook as I pressed start on the machine. "It was late when Kevin came to walk me home, and he wanted to stop at the piano bar for a drink"—I was rattling on because of my nerves and couldn't seem to stop—"but I just wanted to get home to tuck Nicholas in bed, so I used the back exit which was closer to home."

"It's okay, honey," Dad said. "No big deal. Nothing to get flustered over."

My shoulders sagged. I picked up the cup of coffee, added creamer, and took a steadying sip.

"By the way," Dad said, "Delphi mentioned that she saw you out early this morning helping a stranger find his way to the harbor."

Without turning around, I said more sharply than I intended, "And?"

He paused. "Thenie, are you feeling all right? You're as jumpy as a cat today. I was only going to say that was kind of you."

Okay, I had to calm down! I turned and forced a smile as I tore the wrapper off the protein bar. "Sorry, Pops. I think I just need food."

"You and your sisters," he muttered, raising the newspaper again. "I've never seen girls with appetites like the four of you have."

I took my cup and the protein bar to one of the chairs on the other side of the desk and sank into it, breathing in the coffee fragrance. I was about to bite into the bar when I noticed the newspaper in Dad's hands. The banner headline read: MANHUNT CONTINUES. And in smaller caps below that: POLICE K-9s ON THE JOB.

Appetite gone.

CHAPTER TEN

I set the protein bar aside and pulled out my phone to check my calendar for the day. I had to make time to get Case new clothes so he could leave the boat without drawing anyone's attention. He'd stick out like a sore thumb in Pappoús's ill-fitting fishing outfit.

From behind the newspaper Dad said, "Looks like the police have their hands full. They've had innumerable people calling their tip line to report sightings of Donnelly—" He paused to reach for his coffee cup.

I held my breath.

"—but so far none have panned out."

A wave of relief washed over me. "I'm sure Donnelly's long gone. I mean, why would a stranger stick around after committing a murder?"

"True."

I went back to checking my calendar only to hear Dad say, "Thenie, listen to this. Sonny's story changed from the last article. First, he said he found Harry slumped over his desk. In this article he's saying he found Harry lying on the floor, face up."

That brought my head up. Case's version of finding the body had matched Sonny's original story. Why had he changed it? "Any comments from the police?"

"Only that it's under investigation." Dad flipped down the newspaper to say, "I'm surprised the reporter wasn't on top of it. I would've questioned the dickens out of Sonny."

Maybe I could do that for him at the press conference on Friday. "Hey, Pops, when you're done with the paper, would you slide it over here?"

Dad pushed it across the desk, then got up with a groan and took his cup to the coffee machine. "If I were the detective on this case, I'd be looking for the killer close to home. I've mentioned this to a few people, but no one wants to believe anyone in town is capable of committing such a horrible crime. But as we know, Talbot Senior made many enemies."

"Actually, I've been wondering whether Sonny or Lila had a hand in his drowning."

Dad took off his glasses to polish them. "Really?"

"All they'd have to do is slip a few sleeping pills into his drink during dinner. Who outside the family would be able to pull off a death by drowning?"

"Have you ever been inside the Talbot mansion?"

"No."

"You weren't here at the time, but about two years ago Talbot Senior started to intensify his holdings in downtown properties, gearing up for this condo project. So he began throwing extravagant dinner parties to wine and dine the Greek shop owners. Your *yiayiá* and *pappoús* wouldn't attend, so I went in their place. But as soon as I figured out what he was up to, I stopped going, as did almost everyone else. But there were a handful who kept attending. In fact, those few stuck it out right up until the moment Talbot announced his condominium project."

I began to see where he was going with his story. "Do you remember who those people were?"

"Maria Odem was one of them. She'd lost her husband about a year before the dinners started, and she made it clear that she'd set her sights on Talbot as a replacement. In fact, I'm fairly certain that she and Talbot were having a, shall we say, romantic *liaison* until shortly before his death."

"You're kidding."

Dad held up his right hand. "Swear to God."

The more I thought about it, the more I could see Marie Odem working her wiles on Talbot. At the age of sixty-five, the tall, silver-haired, attractive older woman loved nothing more than flirting with men and spreading gossip. And as the owner of Wear For Art Thou, a popular, upscale clothing resale shop, she had plenty of opportunities for both. "How long did that go on?"

"It ended after she hinted publicly that she might be the next Mrs. Talbot. He found out and fired back in the press that Marie was nothing but a fortune-hunting crackpot."

"Wow. A woman scorned. That would make a good motive for murder."

"You bet. He died not long after that came out. *And* she knew her way around Talbot's wing of the mansion. Then there's Donald Fatsis." Dad shook his head. "What a bootlicker. We could all see how he was ingratiating himself with Talbot, trying to become his best friend." My father shook his head. "Neither of the two realized that Talbot's best friend was his bank account."

"The condominium project must have been a rude awakening for Don."

"Right again."

"Considering Fatsis's temper, I could see him going off the deep end about losing his shop. But I don't see how it would be possible for either Marie or Fatsis, or anyone outside the family for that matter, to be able to drug Talbot and time it so he fell asleep in the bathtub."

Dad slapped the desk. "*That's* where I was going with my story. Talbot always ended the dinners by announcing it was time for his bath. Remember this, Thenie, he was a spoiled old coot and used to his routine. What's more, he lived in a separate wing from his son and daughter-in-law and even had a private elevator from his bedroom suite on the second floor to his office on the first. We were all given a tour of the place the very first time we met, so anyone in attendance could've arranged to meet him privately for an after-dinner drink and slip a drug into it, knowing he'd soon be on his way upstairs for his bath."

"So, basically anyone who attended those dinner meetings had the means and opportunity," I said, thinking out loud. "You said there were a handful who kept attending. Who were they?"

"Two other shop owners, one of whom has passed away since, the other who sold the shop when her husband was transferred across the country."

"So that narrows down the suspect list. But why would either Marie or Don want to kill Harry, too?"

Dad put on his glasses. "Maybe their deaths aren't connected."

That didn't help my feelings about Case at all.

"Morning, everyone," Delphi called, strolling into the office. "Hey, Thenie, I've been racking my brain ever since I saw you earlier. I know I've met that handsome Dimitri before." She set her purse on the table in the office. "I just can't remember where."

Knowing Delphi, she wasn't going to let this go. I folded the newspaper article and tucked it in my purse. "Do you have everything in place for the statue unveiling tomorrow? Have you contacted the press? Confirmed with the caterer? Checked how many responses we've had to our invitations?"

"Yes, no, and yes, but wait, something's coming through." She pressed her fingertips against her temples. "I'm getting a message that Dimitri and I met recently."

Oh, dear God, I had to get her off that track. Pressing my fingertips to my temples I said, "I'm getting a message that it's time to open the shop."

Dad winked at me and said, "Grab some coffee, Delph, and let's get busy."

On and off all morning Delphi pondered aloud where she'd met Case, each time stretching my nerves just a little bit more. Finally, when we stopped for a break during a mid-morning lull, I told her point blank to drop the subject.

"What's your problem?" she asked, swinging one leg in annoyance. She was sitting in the chair in front of the desk, eating a handful of peanuts. "So what if I think Dimitri's good-looking? So what if we've met before? Jeez, Thenie. Lighten up."

I rubbed my forehead. "Sorry. You know how hectic Thursdays are."

Some more so than others. And I still needed to set up a meeting with the coroner, plus come up with a plausible reason to slip away to shop for Case.

Then an idea hit me.

"Speaking of hectic days," I said, stooping to retrieve

my purse from behind the desk, "I just remembered I'm supposed to meet one of my old college friends for lunch. She called yesterday evening wanting to get together today."

"Which friend?" Delphi asked, watching me skeptically.

I raced through a mental list of my friends and blurted, "Cathy Williams."

Delphi gave me a quizzical glance. "I thought Cathy moved to Florida after college."

Damn! I'd forgotten that she knew Cathy, too. "Yes, she did indeed move to Florida." I tucked my notebook in my purse. "But she's back."

Delphi scratched her nose. "That's odd. She told me it would be a cold day in hell when she'd return to this part of the country. She hated winters here."

"I didn't mean back permanently. She's just in town for a few days to visit her parents."

Delphi reached down for a peanut that had fallen on the floor. "I can't believe you agreed to meet Cathy with all we have to do. Seriously, Thenie, what were you thinking?"

"Must you question me about everything?" I snapped. She threw the peanut at me.

I pointed to my sister. "Now *you* check back with the caterer—"I slung my purse over my shoulder—"and I'll see you after lunch."

I walked out the door, remembered something, did an about-face, and snatched my iPad from my desk. Then, before Delphi could ask me another question, I hurried out through the garden entrance to the lane with all intentions of heading toward the men's clothing store—only to come to an abrupt stop.

I couldn't go there. The only legitimate reason I had

for shopping at a men's store would be to buy a gift for Kevin, whose birthday was in three weeks. Neither Dad's nor Pappoús's birthdays were coming up, so if I did buy something, someone in my family would surely hear about it and ask questions. Nothing went unnoticed in my family.

But I *could* slip into the resale shop, Wear For Art Thou, because there was a constant turnover of young clerks, mostly college kids home for the summer, and the shop was always jammed with tourists looking for bargains. Best of all, the owner, Marie Odem, was on a cruise with her friends.

I headed for her store on Oak Street, which backed up to Don Fatsis's art gallery on Greene. On my way there I phoned Kirkland's medical office, hoping to speak to him in person. I guessed he wouldn't be too busy. He didn't have a large medical practice because he would only take patients with full insurance coverage—no Medicare or Medicaid patients at all, which eliminated a lot of people in Sequoia. I was transferred to his nurse, who asked my reason for calling. I told her I had to speak to him about his wife's new landscaping plans and was put on hold.

In a few moments I heard, "Dr. Kirkland here."

"Dr. Kirkland, this is Athena Spencer from Spencer's Garden Center. My father did the landscape at your new house."

"Yes, Miss Spencer, I remember," he said in a friendly voice. "What's your question?"

"I'd like to ask you for a favor. Would you meet with a friend of mine tomorrow to answer some questions about your duties as coroner?"

His voice suddenly lost its friendly tone. "What does this have to do with my wife's landscaping plans?"

"Nothing. Your nurse must have misunderstood."

"Why does your friend need to know about my duties?"

"That didn't come out right. The interview isn't specifically about *your* duties."

"Then what *specifically* is it about?"

Damn. Now he was wary. *Think, Athena! Give him something believable.* "Specifically, it pertains to murder cases. You see—"

Before I had a chance to finish, he said, "Let me do *you* a favor by suggesting that your friend can find everything she needs on the Internet."

"Actually, she is a he, and he's already researched the subject as far as he can take it. But I thought that talking to a professional—"

"If he's another prying reporter sniffing around for information on the Pepper murder, I'll have him forcibly removed from my office."

Interesting that the subject of Harry's murder came up. "If you'd just hear me out—"

"I've heard all I need to hear, Miss Spencer, and that's the last I'll say on the subject. Good day."

Arrogant jerk. He might think that was the last he'd say, but he didn't know who he was up against. Having grown up with three clever and sometimes devious sisters had taught me a few things.

"I apologize for taking up your time, Dr. Kirkland. And by the way, please let your wife know that my dad is available starting Monday for that weeklong garden-scape project that he drew up for her. In fact, he had an idea for a koi pond that she's going to *love*."

And every word of that was the truth. My dad *was* available starting on *a* Monday—if Mrs. Kirkland ever actually decided to do that renovation. And he *could* have a koi pond installed. All I had to do was reel the coroner in now, because there was no way he'd want his wife to spend that kind of money. Kirkland was so tight he squeaked.

After a pregnant pause I added, "Or perhaps you could meet with my friend and me tomorrow, say around noon?"

"That's not going to happen," he said abruptly. "I'll deliver your message to my wife and let her get back to you."

Obviously, I needed to do a little more persuading. "You know what, Dr. Kirkland? Since you're such a busy man, I'll do *you* a favor by contacting your wife myself. So have a good day. I'm hanging up now."

"Wait." There was a pause and then a heavy sigh. "Maybe there's a way I can help your friend."

And just like that his voice changed from arrogance to some semblance of humility. "What kind of specific information is your friend seeking?"

"He's—um—writing his first mystery novel and struggling with the death scene. Who better to advise him than an expert in the field?"

He sighed. "I suppose I can make room on my calendar."

"Perfect. A noon meeting works best for us."

"Fine. Tomorrow at noon at the coroner's office."

I ended the call and gave the air a high five. Quick thinking! Although a mystery writer wasn't the cleverest of ideas, it did the trick. That was one thing checked off my to-do list. Now on to the next item: clothing for Case, er, Dimitrius.

When I stepped inside the resale shop there was only one salesclerk on the floor. The young woman was ringing up a huge pile of merchandise for a group of tourists, paying no attention to who came in the door. With her occupied, I combed through the men's tops and within ten minutes found three almost new, short-sleeved, button-down shirts that looked just right for interviews. I also found two short-sleeved T-shirts for casual wear, and even a polo shirt with the original price tag on it. Then I moved on to the pants.

"Athena," I heard, and looked around to see Marie Odem coming toward me. In a panic, I quickly tucked the clothing behind my back and pasted on a smile, my thoughts going a mile a minute. What could my reason be for buying all these men's clothes?

Clearly, I wasn't cut out for espionage. "Marie! I thought you were on a cruise."

"I got back yesterday." She was wearing her usual slim, belted black dress, a look that set off her silver hair. "I hear you had a good turnout for the GMA meeting," she said, trying to peer around at the bundle in my arms.

"I did. It was a good meeting. I'm sorry you missed it."

After an awkward moment of silence, she finally said, "Whatever are you hiding?"

"Oh, these?" I had no choice but to show her the shirts. "They're just, um, early birthday gifts for"—the only person I knew who would fit into them—"Kevin. But if you see him, please don't say a word. I want them to be a surprise."

With a haughty lift of one eyebrow she said, "I'm sure they *will* be a surprise. I would've thought you were gathering clothes for the homeless. The shelter is having a drive right now, as you no doubt know."

That would have definitely been a better answer. Now I was going to have to hold back that brand-new polo shirt for Kevin, because there was no way Marie could keep a secret.

"Actually, Marie, most of the clothes are for the drive. So I'll take all of these"—I thrust the pile in her hands—"and look around for a few more items."

Ten minutes later I left the shop with a big bag and what I was positive was an ulcer forming in my stomach. I threw the bag in the back of my white Toyota SUV and headed to a discount store a mile away. There I was able to purchase groceries and men's briefs and socks without being spotted by anyone I knew.

I drove back to town, parked in the public lot near the harbor, put up my hood, loaded my arms with bags—minus the shirt for Kevin—and strolled casually down to the water.

Most of the boats were out in the lake, so I encountered only a few tourists ambling along the dock, taking photos. I hopped from the pier onto Pappoús's boat, glanced around to be sure no one was watching, then unlocked the cabin door and hurried down the stairs.

"It's just me," I called.

No answer.

I set the bags down and was about to head toward the bedroom to see whether Case was still sleeping when a shadow fell across the floor in front of me. I spun around to see him descending the stairs wearing only Pappoús's denim pants, which he'd rolled to mid-calf length. I couldn't help but notice his bare chest—muscular and covered with a fine sheen of sweat—and his lean waist, the old pants riding low on his hips.

"Hey," he said, wiping his forehead with a towel.

I suddenly felt light-headed and realized I hadn't drawn a breath in several seconds. I turned away and began to unpack the groceries. "Hey, yourself. Where were you?"

"Lying on the front of the boat soaking up the sun."

He walked over and peered into the grocery bag. "What'd you buy?"

He was so close I could feel the heat coming off his body. "Standard staples. Eggs, sliced ham, cheese, bread, oranges, bottled water, and a few other necessities."

"Like my phone?"

"Damn! I'm sorry. I was in such a hurry that I forgot it again, but I'll pick one up after work this evening."

He opened the bag of clothing and pulled out a shirt. The first thing he noticed was the resale tag. "You bought used clothes?"

"I had no choice. If these don't fit, I'll donate them and try again."

As he picked up the bag and headed for the bedroom, I opened the refrigerator and began to put the groceries inside. "By the way, we have an appointment to see the coroner tomorrow at noon. I'll have to meet you at City Hall, so I'll give you instructions on how to get there before I leave."

"What's my cover story?" he called.

"You're a mystery writer from Tarpon Springs who's struggling with the death scene in your first book."

"And to think I was a simple businessman before. Now I'm a Greek fisherman who writes"—he paused— "or am I a Greek writer who fishes?"

I smiled as I took my iPad out of my purse. "Why don't we say you're a novice mystery writer who's renting my *pappoús*'s boat while you're working on your novel? Then you don't have to use the fisherman excuse."

"I've always wanted to write a book" was his wry answer.

My stomach gave a warning growl. I checked my watch and realized it was time for lunch. "Do you want a sandwich? I need to eat before I go back to the garden center, and we still have to compile our questions for the coroner."

"Sure." Case came out of the bedroom dressed in the tan T-shirt and a pair of slim-fitting, faded blue jeans. He held out his arms. "What do you think?"

That I needed to remind myself I had a boyfriend. "Everything fits," I said cheerfully. I glanced at his bare feet and added, "I'll pick up a pair of shoes for you tomorrow, too."

I pulled out the cheese, ham, and bread and set them on the table. "Do you want water or hot tea with your sandwich?"

He sat down at the table and let his long legs sprawl out to one side. "What I really want is a cold beer—and a cell phone."

I tossed him a bottle of water. "You'll have to make do with water until tomorrow. I'll try to get the phone later today."

As soon as I had the sandwiches made, I took out my notebook and a pen and sat down opposite him so we could plan our strategy.

"Keep in mind that I told him you're having trouble writing the death scene in your novel, so we'll need to make it look like that's your primary focus. And we can't make your questions too specific, like by mentioning either Harry Pepper's or Talbot's death. If we want to extract anything useful, we can't raise his suspicions about you."

"Believe me, I have no wish to have handcuffs snapped on my wrists, but what does that leave us? Remember, I'm not really a novel writer."

"But I *am*, I mean *was*, a reporter for a Chicago newspaper, and I do know how to come up with questions."

"Okay, then, let's go," he said, and took a big bite of his sandwich.

For the next twenty minutes, we bounced questions back and forth. Then I noticed the time and jumped up. "I've got to get back. They're going to wonder where I am."

"I'll clean up here," he said, as I packed up my notebook and pen.

"Thanks." I watched for a moment as he began to clear the table, trying to imagine Kevin doing the same. Somehow, I couldn't picture it.

I shook that thought out of my head, took my iPad out of my purse, and set it on the counter. "This is for your Tarpon Springs research. I'll see you at the coroner's office at noon."

"When do we pay Sonny Talbot a visit?"

"That'll have to wait until next week, but I'll have a chance to question Sonny at his press conference tomorrow."

Case's eyes lit up. "He's having a press conference?"

"Yes, he's going to talk about his downtown condominium project, which the Greek Merchants' Association is fighting. He promised to address Harry Pepper's death then, too."

"Perfect. Where is he planning to build his condominium?"

"Step out onto the back of the boat and look right across the street. He's going to raze the entire block of Greene Street known as Little Greece. And that includes The Parthenon, the diner that my grandfather and Harry Pepper started."

"What time is the conference?"

"Five p.m., and don't even think about attending. With all the media that'll be there, it's too risky."

"Isn't that the purpose of my disguise?"

"Are you serious? Why would you want to test it in such a public place?"

"I can't think of a better way."

"I can. Stay away!"

Case rubbed his hands together. "Come on, Athena. It'll be fun."

Fun?

Tums. I had to buy Tums.

CHAPTER ELEVEN

Friday

From the moment we opened the doors for our grand unveiling of the *Treasure of Athena*, Spencer's was mobbed. A whole slew of our local customers and a lot of curious tourists turned out to see our original Antonius. There were so many people in the garden area that I could barely squeeze my way among them. Of course, it didn't help that I was seeing spots before my eyes. The reporter from the *Sequoian Press* must have snapped two dozen photos of my family and me posed by the statue with various customers.

But by eleven o'clock, the food had been gobbled up, the shop had emptied out as the crowd left in search of other pursuits, and best of all, the cash register was full.

While the caterers loaded food trays into their van, I flopped into a wicker chair and gazed up at the statue as Dad took a seat at the wicker table next to me. "That turned out a lot better than I expected," I said.

Delphi brought us cups of coffee, then perched on the statue's base. "Good job, guys."

"Thanks." I held up my coffee. "Same to both of you."

My father inhaled the coffee aroma and sighed with pleasure. "This is just what I needed. Thank you, Delph. That was sweet of you."

"I know," she said with a satisfied sigh, smoothing out her long, flowing skirt. She was dressed in a vibrant red peasant blouse and tie-dyed navy cotton skirt with her ever present green flip-flops and her curly black hair pulled away from her face with sparkling red butterfly clips.

My outfit, as usual, was more conservative—aqua boatneck top and white pants with white flats. In honor of the occasion, I'd swept my light brown hair back into a high, loose knot and left a few long strands hanging down in front of each ear, with round pearl earrings to complete the look. It had taken an extra fifteen minutes of fiddling, but I wanted to look more polished for the photographs than my usual plain self. Even Dad had dressed up today, wearing a button-down white shirt and blue-and-green–striped necktie with navy pants and black shoes.

"Anyone want to come down to the diner with me for an early lunch?" Delphi asked.

"Hey, bottomless pit," Dad teased, giving her a playful poke. "It's only eleven o'clock. How can you be thinking about food already?"

"It has to be noon somewhere," she replied.

That reminded me, I had forty-five minutes until my meeting with Kirkland and I hadn't yet thought up a reason for being absent at lunch.

Ah. I had it. I made a show of stretching leisurely,

then stood up. "I'm going to help you tidy up back here and then take a break from the diner for a stroll to City Hall Plaza to sample pizza from the new gourmet food truck."

Eat pizza—meet with the coroner—almost the same thing.

But then I noticed the look of interest on my sister's face and wished I could take back my words. *Bad idea, Athena!* More proof I was not cut out for espionage.

Before my sister could respond, Dad jumped in. "Not that anyone cares but *I'm* having lunch at the Bon Ami Bistro with a lady friend." He gave me a wink.

"A *lady* friend?" Delphi asked looking from him to me. "It's your sister Maggie, isn't it?"

Dad smiled slyly. "Wouldn't you like to know?"

"Your cousin Patty?" quizzed Delphi.

"Give up, Delph. I'm not telling." He got up and headed toward the office with Delphi following behind, still trying to guess the woman's name. I dropped my head against the back of the chair. Saved by Dad.

At noon, I paused outside the door to City Hall and looked around for Case. He'd promised to be there five minutes ahead of time. Where was he? What if he'd been spotted even with his disguise? I scanned the men passing by on the sidewalk, but there was no sign of him.

"Are you ready to play detective?"

I turned with a gasp to find not Case but the new Dimitrius directly behind me. Trying not to betray my anxiety I answered, "Of course I am." *Not.* I was shaking like a leaf inside. "Are *you* ready?"

"Naturally." He gestured toward my upswept hairdo. "Different. I like it."

"Thanks." Trying to act casual about it, I fiddled with one of my earrings. In truth, his remark made me feel . . . awkward, and slightly pretty. My sisters were the ones who got all the compliments. I was always the tall, pale one in the back row of the family photographs who stuck out like a sore thumb.

After an uncomfortable moment in which I realized belatedly that he'd been waiting for a return compliment, Case asked, "Do I look okay?"

He looked—I had to take a breath—great. I hated to admit just how great, but the only way I could describe his appearance was sexy—that dark, almost curly hair dipping down over his forehead, his expressive eyes, the thick beard now filling in across his firm jawline, the crisp blue plaid shirt tucked neatly into jeans that fit him like a glove right down to his navy sh—

The shoes! My eyes widened in shock. I nudged him over to the edge of the sidewalk and whispered angrily, "You wore your own shoes."

He whispered back, "You forgot to buy me new ones."

"Case, your photograph is all over town. What were you thinking?"

"Mainly that your grandfather's shoes made me wince when I walked."

"And you couldn't wear them for one lousy hour?"

"I'm not a big fan of torture."

Chewing my lip, I checked my watch. "It's too late to do anything about it now."

"Calm down. Lots of men wear navy loafers. Now take a deep breath—thatta girl—and let's do this thing."

As Case opened the door for me, I pressed my hand against my racing heart. I still couldn't believe he was out in public and not worried at all, although his disguise had really changed his looks. Still, he made Kevin's an-

noyingly prudent nature seem desirable by comparison.
Fortunately, the building was practically empty because
of the noon hour, so only a few people were in sight.

"The coroner's office is down the hall to your left," I
said quietly. "Remember, you're Dimitrius Costas, a
mystery writer from Tarpon—"

"I've got it memorized, Athena."

I had a sudden thought and stopped in alarm. "Wait!
How do we know each other?"

"I broke into your shop and tried to steal your statue.
Remember?"

With a scowl, I started walking again. "I'm being serious. We worked out your history but not how we met."

"Hey, I'm just trying to lighten the mood." As we ap-
proached the coroner's office he said, "How about this?
We dated one summer when your family came down to
Tarpon Springs on vacation."

"I'm still being serious."

"So am I."

I couldn't tell if he was teasing or not, so I teased him
back. "What makes you think I would've dated *you*?"

Case gazed at me with a tiny quirk of a smile. "Because women can't resist me."

"How about we're distantly related and we met at a
family reunion in Tarpon Springs?"

"Whichever works for you." He reached for the door-
knob. "Ready?"

Ready to leave *that* subject behind. "Wait," I said, digging in my purse. "We need to put our phones on mute."

"If only I had one," he said dryly.

Damn. I'd forgotten *again*. "I promise I'll get one for
you later." I clicked the mute button and squared my
shoulders. "Let's go."

When we entered the office's anteroom, there was

no secretary to greet us. I saw a frosted glass door with the words *County Coroner* on the right side of the small room, so we headed for it. After I gave two soft raps on the glass, I heard a man call, "Come in."

Taking a steadying breath, I waited until Case opened the door and then I stepped inside. Immediately, Daniel Kirkland rose from his black vinyl swivel chair and came around his desk to greet us.

"Miss Spencer," he said with a polite smile, shaking my hand, his heavy palm damp with perspiration. "Nice to see you again."

The coroner was a short, stout man with craggy features, a red-veined nose typical of heavy drinkers, and a head full of white hair. He wore a white long-sleeved, button-down shirt, yellow-and-brown–striped tie, and brown pants with a sharp crease down each leg. His brown leather oxford shoes had that spit-shined look of an army man.

The office had typical administration-cheap furniture—a large maple desk and credenza behind it, a row of maple filing cabinets, a window covered by white aluminum blinds on one wall that looked out over the parking lot, and a gray linoleum floor.

Trying to unobtrusively wipe my palm on my pant leg, I said, "Dr. Kirkland, this is Dimitrius Costas, the writer I mentioned on the phone."

"Costas," the coroner said, eyeing Case warily as he shook his hand.

"Dr. Kirkland, it's a pleasure to meet you," Case said with his disarming smile, even as he, too, slid his palm discreetly down his pant leg. "Thanks so much for agreeing to this interview."

Kirkland indicated a pair of standard-issue white plastic office chairs in front of his desk. "Have a seat. I need to tell you up front, however, that I'm going to have to limit our conversation to twenty minutes. I need time to eat and be back for a meeting."

"We appreciate any amount of time you can give us," Case said. His easy manner made my insides unknot appreciably.

We sat in front of Kirkland's desk while he relaxed into his swivel chair. I slid my notebook and a pen out of my purse and gave them to Case, who opened it to our questions. When Case handed me my iPad, however, the coroner sat forward and held up his hand.

"Stop right there. There will be no videotaping of this conversation. Is that understood?"

His defensive tone put me on alert. "I'm just going to be taking down your answers."

Kirkland jabbed a thick finger toward Case's notebook. "Then what's that for?"

Case held the small, spiral-bound book up for Kirkland's inspection and said nonchalantly, "These are my questions. Athena is using her tablet because she can type faster than I could ever hope to scribble anything legible."

As Kirkland pondered Case's answer, I held my breath and waited, hoping he wouldn't cancel the interview before it even got started.

Kirkland made a motion with his hand. "Proceed then."

I felt my shoulders relax.

"One more thing," Kirkland added.

And there went my shoulders.

"You make sure I stay anonymous."

"Absolutely," Case said.

The coroner sat back with a smug look and folded his thick fingers over his stomach. Case's casual banter had obviously eased his mind, but Kirkland's guarded behavior didn't ease mine. It just made me even more suspicious of him.

Placing my fingers on the keypad, I let Case take the lead.

"My first question is probably the most obvious," he began. "What kind of training is required for your job?"

"It depends on the county," Kirkland said, loosening his tie. "In my case, I had to complete a probationary period of on-the-job training with the former coroner."

As I typed his answer, Case placed a checkmark next to the question, then moved on to the next. "Do you have any medical training?"

Kirkland puffed up in indignation. "I'm a licensed physician, sir. I have a thriving medical practice."

"Excuse me, then. Being new to town, I didn't realize that." Case continued down his list, placing checkmarks beside each completed question. "Would you outline your duties?"

"In a nutshell, I lead investigations into the cause of a person's death."

"Do you remove bodies from crime scenes?"

"Not personally, no, but I oversee the removal."

"What happens once you arrive on the scene?"

"I perform a cursory exam to look for signs of trauma and identify the cause and time of death."

"What if there's no clear-cut reason for the death?" Case asked, as I typed furiously to keep up.

"That's what an autopsy is for."

Case paused, as though considering the coroner's answer, then asked, "Are you the one who decides whether an autopsy is needed? Or do the detectives make that call?"

"I make the decision."

"In the event of a murder," Case asked, "do you interview witnesses at the scene or is that something the police handle?"

"The detectives and I both do. Usually I'm on the scene first so I start the investigation."

"What was the official cause of death in the most recent murder?"

"Asphyxiation."

"In layman's terms?"

"Suffocation."

"Whom did you interview at the scene?"

Giving Case a wary glance, Kirkland asked, "How does that pertain to your book?"

I glanced over at Case in surprise. *That* question hadn't been on our list. I could feel perspiration begin to gather under my armpits as I waited for Kirkland's answer, and I could tell he was struggling to come up with it.

"What I think Dimitrius meant to ask," I said, "is how much time did you have to spend at the scene interviewing witnesses on that case? We'd been discussing Harry Pepper's murder on the way over and I guess that's still on his mind. Right, Dimitrius?"

"Right. Sorry if I gave the wrong impression."

Kirkland's answer was curt and sly. "I spent as much time as I needed to spend."

I saw the narrowing of Case's eyes as he studied the man and I knew he was about to dig deeper, something we had agreed not to do. "How many witnesses were there when you arrived?" he asked.

I gave Case's hand a painful squeeze, but he merely pulled it away.

"I'm not allowed to answer a question pertaining to an ongoing criminal investigation." The coroner glanced over his shoulder at a clock on the credenza behind him, as though hoping our twenty minutes were up.

"Okay, then, let's talk about another death that occurred in the same house," Case continued, "Grayson Talbot Senior. There's no ongoing investigation into that case, so perhaps you can tell me about his cause of death."

I squeezed Case's hand again and he pulled it away again. He had wrested control of the interview from me and there was no way I could take it back now without raising the coroner's suspicions.

Looking through a stack of files on his desk, Kirkland replied with studied disinterest, "It was an accidental drowning."

"I read in the newspaper that Talbot's daughter-in-law discovered his body submerged in his bathtub one morning and said that he'd simply fallen asleep during his bath, which is how you ruled his death. Is that correct?"

"I believe so."

Case glanced at Kirkland with a puzzled expression. "That's odd. The account I read online said that Talbot's son reported that his wife had given his father a sleeping pill before retiring for the evening, which had caused him to fall asleep in the bath and drown. Is that true?"

"I don't remember Mr. Talbot ever telling me his father had taken a sleeping pill," Kirkland replied stiffly, "but I'd have to look up the report to be sure."

"Have you ever prescribed sleeping pills for Lila Talbot?"

"That's confidential information."

"Thinking back on it," Case probed, "don't you find it questionable that there are two conflicting accounts of the man's death? Either he fell asleep naturally or was drugged and then fell asleep. It has to be one or the other."

"What difference does it make to your novel? You're the one writing it."

Point Kirkland's. I stayed silent to see how Case would respond. But instead, the crabby coroner stood and began stuffing files into his briefcase. "I have to leave now."

I nudged Case and indicated that we should leave, too. We weren't going to get anything useful from Kirkland now.

I closed the iPad and slipped it into my purse, ready to stand up, but Case wasn't done yet. "One more question before you go. I would assume that by virtue of your position of responsibility you'd have interviewed both Talbot's son *and* daughter-in-law after both deaths. Did you interview the household staff?"

Kirkland snapped his briefcase shut. "I'm sure I did but it happened a while ago and I have a busy medical practice in addition to this job. And again, what does that have to do with your story anyway?"

The deaths happened a *while* ago? That was his *excuse*? That did it for me. His evasiveness had to stop. "Dr. Kirkland," I said with rising anger, "we've had two suspicious deaths in less than a month in a town that hasn't seen a murder in over a year. How is it *possible* you can't remember whom you interviewed?"

The coroner's expression turned dark. "I think it's time you left."

At that my short-tempered Greek side reared its head. "What are you hiding, Dr. Kirkland? Are you protecting someone?"

"Protecting?" he asked, puffing up again. "What are you insinuating?"

"Why didn't you perform an autopsy on Mr. Talbot when it's required by law in cases where no witnesses are present?" I asked. Case turned his head toward me in surprise. Oh yes, I'd done my research. I hadn't been a reporter all those years for nothing.

His face turning redder by the second, Kirkland said, "That's my business, not yours."

"It was Talbot's son's decision, wasn't it?" I asked. "What's the payoff? Unlimited term in office?"

He grabbed his briefcase and strode to the door. "See yourselves out."

And then he was gone, slamming the door behind him.

CHAPTER TWELVE

"So," Case said slowly as he escorted me out of the building, "that went well."

"I thought we were going to limit our questions to your novel only. Why did you go on the attack?"

"You did a fairly good job of that yourself."

"I'd had it with Kirkland's evasive answers. He's protecting the Talbots and I wanted to know why."

"I'm not criticizing you. In fact, I'm proud of you. Give me a high five, Goddess Athena. You were on *fire*!"

I *had* been on fire! I slapped his palm, proud of myself for taking a strong stance. "I knew by his last answer that Sonny Talbot made that call on the autopsy. At least now Kirkland has been warned he's going to have to answer for it."

"On the other hand, now that he's on notice, we may never get the truth from him."

I tapped my chin. "Was it Shakespeare who said, 'The truth will out'?"

"Yep. And the truth is, Athena, Goddess of War,

you've got more Greek in you than you want to admit. Remind me never to cross swords with you."

I couldn't help smiling just a bit. If it came down to a fight over the statue ownership, Case also knew now whom he'd be dealing with.

I spotted the Italian pizza truck parked at the curb just across the plaza and my stomach growled in response. "I'm going to grab a bite of lunch before I head back to Spencer's, so I'll see you at the boat later when I bring your cell phone."

"Thanks for the invitation," he said, falling into step beside me.

"What invitation?"

"I have to eat, too. And we need to discuss our strategy for the press conference."

"I told you, Case," I said quietly, "it's too risky for you to attend the conference, and you probably shouldn't be seen with me. You never know who's going to be there."

"And I told you it would be risky for Case to attend but not for Dimitri. So here's what I was thinking."

I came to a stop. "We are *not* going to discuss this out here in front of the whole town."

Case glanced surreptitiously over both shoulders, then whispered, "I don't think the whole town is here, but if it'd make you feel better, we could buy a pizza to split, take it back to the boat, and discuss it there."

"You're not going to walk around here with those shoes on! People will see them."

"Oh, no! People will see *your* shoes, too! Maybe we should go barefoot."

"You know what I mean."

Starting toward the food truck he pointed to a man standing nearby. "Look, he has navy athletic shoes on."

He pointed to another man eating a slice of pizza at a picnic table near the truck. "And so does he. And that guy over there has navy leather shoes. See? He even has a cell phone, lucky bastard."

"I said I'll get you your phone today," I ground out.

"Good. Then we're going to have a nice calm lunch and talk about our strategy."

We stopped in front of the menu board on the side of the truck and I pointed to one of their selections. "The wild mushroom pizza with feta and spinach looks good."

"Maybe to a goat," Case said as we got in line. "Give me a good old pepperoni loaded with mozzarella and onions any time."

"Add a double helping of antacid to that and we've got a meal."

"Here's an idea. How about we each get our own pizza?"

"That works for me," I said.

"Athena?"

I glanced around and spotted Kevin coming through the crowd. He was hard to miss in his blue plaid blazer, matching blue shirt, blue-and-coral–striped tie, navy pants, and, as karma would have it, navy shoes.

I immediately moved away from Case, pasting on a smile as I walked forward. "Kevin! What are you doing here?"

"I was just about to ask you the same thing. I texted you twice about meeting me for lunch and never got a response."

Damn! Once again, I'd forgotten to turn the ringer back on. What was it with me and phones? "I'm sorry, Kevin. I keep putting my phone on mute and forgetting about it."

Kevin pointed to someone behind me. "Who's he? You had your heads together like you were old friends."

I didn't need to glance around to know who he was talking about, but I did anyway and saw Case standing at the order window. My mind instantly went into hyper drive, turning over several possible answers before deciding to stick to the story we'd invented. "He's a writer, new in town. In fact, I gave him directions on how to get to the harbor yesterday and we just happened to run into each other down here. And as it turns out, we have distant relatives in common."

"Distant, huh? And now you're having lunch with him?"

"What would make you think that?" Why was my voice coming out all tight and squeaky? And why, oh why, was Case coming toward us?

"I ordered our pizzas," Case said.

I stared at him wide-eyed until he got the message.

Without a moment's hesitation, Case held out his hand and flashed his dimpled smile. "Hi, I'm Dimitri Costas. You must be Kevin. It's a pleasure to meet you. I've heard a lot about you."

Kevin shook his hand, giving him a hesitant smile. "Thanks."

"I told Dimitri," I said to Kevin, my wheels still searching for a reasonable explanation, "that you might be able to give him some legal advice for the mystery novel he's writing." To Case I said, "Kevin's quite a fount of knowledge."

Kevin used his hand to describe an imaginary headline of a newspaper. "Local boy makes it big as a high-powered Manhattan attorney."

Case nodded as though impressed. "Good for you."

Kevin lifted his chin proudly. "I had one of the heaviest caseloads in the firm. Got my photo in the *Times*, too. Any time you need to tap my legal expertise, give me a call."

Case said, "Thanks. I will. What was your area of specialty?"

"Bankruptcy law."

"Ah. Do you have a business card?"

Kevin checked his pockets. "I don't have any on me at the moment. Give me your cell phone and I'll type in my personal phone number."

Case patted his own pockets. "I seem to have left my phone at home." He shot me a pointed look.

"I have one of your business cards, Kev." I pulled my wallet out of my purse, took out one of Kevin's cards, and handed it to Case.

He read it with a frown, as though puzzled. "This says you're a legal aide."

Kevin scratched behind his ear. "That's just temporary. I'm looking into a position with a new law office."

"You are?" I asked in surprise.

"It's hush-hush right now," Kevin said. "I don't want to talk about it and jinx myself."

This from the man who said I should discuss my personal problems with *him*.

"Athena," someone called from the truck, "your order is ready for pickup."

"Be right there," I called back.

"Hey, honey," Kevin said, "I'm not going to be able to meet you for dinner tonight, so do you want to split the pizza with me? I've got about fifteen minutes and then I have to get back to the firm."

Did I want to? No. Did I have to? "Sure."

Kevin pulled out his wallet. "I'll get the pizza. You get us a table. By the way, I won't be able to make the press conference today after all. I have to help my legal team prepare for a trial. Nice to meet you, Dimitri. Feel free to call me anytime."

"Will do. Thanks."

As Kevin headed toward the pickup counter, Case imitated him by using his hand to describe a headline. "Local boy makes it big as a high-powered Manhattan attorney, then returns home to work as a legal aide."

I whispered angrily, "He hasn't been able to find a position yet, that's all. But you heard him. Something is in the offing. And you should have kept your distance when you saw us together. I don't want him to know we're collaborating."

"Why not? He'll find out sooner or later."

"It'll be my decision when to tell him, not yours."

"What do you see in that preening peacock anyway?"

"For one thing, he isn't a wanted man."

"Touché. And for another?"

I rubbed my ear, muttering, "It keeps my mother happy."

Case could hardly suppress a grin. "Great reason."

"Dimitri," came the call from the truck, "your pizza is ready for pickup."

Kevin turned around and gave a nod to Case. "I've got it. My treat."

"There's another thing," I said. "He's generous." Knowing Kevin was watching, I said, "Well, it was nice to see you again, Dimitri. Good luck with your book."

"Thank you, Athena." Then he added quietly, "I'll see *you* later."

"Don't you dare come to that press conference," I whispered.

Case merely smiled.

"I mean it, Case."

"I don't doubt it. Try to remember to buy me a phone, okay? Oh, and one more thing. Tell your boyfriend I approve of his shoe color."

I gave him a scowl and walked away to claim a table.

The rest of the afternoon seemed to fly by because we had an unusual number of tourists and I was needed on the sales floor. I took a coffee break at four o'clock to prepare my notes for the press conference and then got so busy I ended up dashing out the door ten minutes before the conference was due to start, crossing my fingers that I didn't get stuck in traffic on my way.

But naturally I hit a major snarl and pulled through Talbot Enterprises' main gates at five minutes after five o'clock. The parking lot in front of the sprawling, two-story, Tudor-style building was completely full, so I had to park in the employee lot behind the building. I shut off the engine, grabbed my purse, and hurried around to the front lawn where a crowd of people were milling around, waiting for Sonny's appearance.

A podium loaded with microphones had been set up on a cement terrace several yards from the central revolving door while a TV news crew and a reporter accompanied by his cameraman jockeyed for a good position. Thankfully, I didn't see Case anywhere, which meant that he'd either taken my advice or been frightened off when he caught sight of the cameras.

I spotted GMA members Barb and Nancy and went to stand with them. "Sorry I'm late. I had to park in the employee lot."

"So did I," Barb said, "and I got here fifteen minutes early."

I looked up at the podium. "Any word on when Talbot's going to appear?"

"Nothing," Nancy said. "Watch him cancel."

"Want to hear something fishy, girls?" Barb asked.

"We're all ears," Nancy said.

Barb glanced over her shoulder, then whispered, "Don't look now but Don Fatsis is at the back of the crowd."

"And?" I asked.

"As I was parking around back," Barb said, "I saw him walk out of Talbot's building through the employee entrance carrying a briefcase and grinning like a fool."

"Did he see you?" I asked.

"No. I ducked down. Now what would Fatsis be doing inside the Talbot building before the press conference?"

"The bigger question is why was he leaving through the employee door?" Nancy asked.

"What do you say we go ask him?" I asked.

"Not me," Nancy said. "I can't stand the man."

"I'm with you, Nan," Barb said. "Forget about it, Athena. He wouldn't tell you the truth anyway."

But as the two women chatted about other things, I kept thinking back to what my father had said about Fatsis buddying up to the elder Talbot. Was that what he was doing with Sonny now?

I glanced back at him and saw him grinning like he had a secret. And then I had an inspiration. "Hold my spot, girls. I'll be right back."

I walked around the edge of the crowd and pretended to be just coming up from the back of the building. Putting my hand to my chest I said breathlessly, "Whew. I thought I'd be late. Any word on why the press conference hasn't started?"

"Not that I've heard," Fatsis said in his usual grumpy voice, his gaze fixed on the podium and his grin gone.

"And I've got better things to do than stand around waiting for that jerk to get it together."

Standing on tiptoe to see above the heads I said, "I was hoping to get a closer spot. I sure wasn't expecting this big of a crowd." I dropped back down on my feet. "Looks like you got here late, too."

He grunted yes.

"That was some traffic accident on the bridge, wasn't it? Did you see that mangled motor scooter in the center lane?"

Another affirmative grunt. Clearly, he didn't want to talk to me.

"Did you see what caused the accident?"

"A tourist," he said, his upper lip curling in distaste, "as usual."

I rose up on my toes again, then gave up with a sigh. "I'm going to try to get closer. Let's hope we can rattle Talbot's cage—if he shows up."

Fatsis merely grunted again.

"One more thing," I said. "How is the funding site going?"

"It's in development," he growled. "Don't worry. I've got it covered."

Why didn't I believe him? "Let me know when it goes live so I can help spread the word."

I slipped through the crowd and came up behind Barb and Nancy. "Okay, here's the scoop. Fatsis arrived here late because he got caught in the same traffic accident tie-up on the bridge that I did."

"He didn't get here late," Barb said.

I smiled. "And there wasn't an accident on the bridge, either."

"I *knew* he was up to something," Barb said.

Nancy, always playing devil's advocate, interjected,

"But remember, he did say he would try to talk some sense into Talbot about the upcoming demolition. Maybe that's what he was doing."

"Then why would he sneak out the back door?" I asked. "And why lie about the traffic accident? If he was here to meet with Talbot, you'd think he would've told me since we're all supposed to be working for the same cause."

Nancy craned her neck to see over the crowd. "Look! Here comes Talbot now."

Flanked by four men in dark suits, two of whom I recognized as Talbot's attorneys, both younger than him, and two uniformed security guards, Sonny crossed the plaza and walked up to the podium. Flashing an arrogant smile, he was dressed in a black cardigan sweater, blue button-down dress shirt, open at the neck, with black pants and shiny black leather shoes. Had I not known what lay beneath the surface, I would've considered him good-looking, with short-cropped brown hair that was slightly gray at the temples, a year-round tan, and a brilliant white smile.

He tapped the main microphone. "Can everyone hear me okay?"

"I'm going to get closer," I said, and wove my way forward. I glanced around again for Case and was relieved that there was still no sign of him.

"Thank you for coming," Talbot began. "I'm Grayson Talbot, in case anyone here doesn't know."

That got a light titter from the audience. I noted that he'd dropped the *junior* on his name. He was *the man* now.

"I've called this press conference to announce that Talbot Enterprises is going ahead with its condominium complex starting ten days from now. It's a move I promise will revitalize the downtown area, and I'll be explaining just how that will happen in just a few minutes."

There was an audible gasp from the crowd. Ten days to stop Talbot.

"You're going to revitalize the downtown by razing our shops and driving away tourists?" a member of the GMA called.

"No, by bringing *more* people downtown," Talbot replied. "The entire main floor of the block-long building will be dedicated to upscale shops, a restaurant, a wine bar, and space for business offices, as well."

"We like our old shops," another woman called. "They have character."

"The upper floors," Talbot continued, "will hold deluxe two- and three-bedroom condominiums with balconies overlooking the harbor."

"How many floors?" came a voice from the other side of the crowd.

"Seven. Four units per floor."

"That'll block people's view of the harbor for everyone living behind it," an angry voice called out, raising a lot of loud grumbles all around.

"What happened to our regulation height of a maximum of three stories?" another voice called.

One of Talbot's attorneys leaned toward the microphones. "We're working with the planning commission on changing that."

His comment was roundly booed. I was certain the planning commission had already given him a stamp of approval. He was, after all, a Talbot.

A man from the local TV news station raised his hand. "What about parking for all these new people who'll be living downtown? We all know parking is at a premium now."

"There will be ample parking under and behind the building."

"Mr. Talbot," the reporter called, "does that mean you plan to demolish the shops you own on Oak Street as well?"

Talbot and one of his assistants had a whispered conversation, then Talbot said, "Just the first building on Pine Avenue, where we'll put in a multilevel parking lot."

"That's where my shop is," a woman called in a shrill voice. "You promised me that building wouldn't be touched."

Talbot raised his hand to shield his eyes from the sun as he looked in her direction. "Who's speaking, please?"

"You know who I am."

I looked around and spotted Marie Odem wearing her standard belted black dress, her hands on her skinny hips, glaring at Sonny. Then she caught sight of the TV news cameraman filming her and turned toward them with a practiced smile. "Marie Odem, O. D. E. M., owner of Wear For Art Thou resale shop, and for the record, *both* Talbots, father and son, promised that my shop would be saved."

"Forgive me, Mrs. Odem," Sonny said into his mic, "but I don't recall any such conversation with you."

"Liar!" she cried. "Either you tell these people what you told me at that last dinner meeting or I will."

"You must be mistaken," Talbot answered smoothly. He gave a nod to one of the security men standing nearby and the man began moving toward Marie. "I've never had any such conversation with you."

"Don't think you'll get away with your lies," Marie shouted, as the guard tried to escort her away. "Your father made that mistake." She twisted her wiry arm out of the guard's grasp only to have the second guard grab her. "Leave me alone!" she shrieked as they escorted her away from the crowd.

Talbot waited until the murmurs died down, then said with a smirk, "Apparently, not everyone is in favor of Sequoia keeping up with the times."

"You call a granite monstrosity keeping up with the times?" a woman cried. "It will ruin the harbor view and destroy Little Greece."

"Even your father came to that conclusion," I called.

"Not true," Talbot retorted. "My father was as committed to this project as I am."

"Really?" I called back. "As many will recall, he told everyone at the Greek Merchants' Association meeting just days before his death that he was canceling it."

"He was merely trying to pacify them," Talbot replied confidently. "He had no intention of canceling."

"Excuse me," I said, as a newspaperman snapped my photo, "but he signed an agreement that would've halted the project."

"Then where is that agreement?" Talbot retorted.

"He took it back to his office with him to prepare it for filing with the court," Nancy called. "So why don't you tell *us* where that agreement is?"

"I've never seen any such agreement."

"Excuse me again," I called, "but I also remember hearing that you were so upset by his announcement, you walked out of the meeting. So please tell us again how committed to the project your father was?"

Talbot shielded his eyes again. "Who's speaking, please?"

The TV news cameraman turned to focus on me.

"Athena Spencer. My father is president of the Greeks' Merchant Association." I looked around at the crowd. "Please raise your hands if you were at the meeting when

Grayson Talbot Senior announced he would cancel the project."

Over a dozen hands went up. I saw the cameraman panning to catch them all.

"And how many of you saw him sign a document?"

The same hands went up.

"Does anyone know where the document is?" I asked.

"Like Nancy said," Barb responded, "Mr. Talbot took it with him."

I turned back toward Sonny. "Any further comments about the validity of the agreement?"

Talbot ignored me to point to the newspaper reporter. "You had a question?"

"Charlie Bolt from the *Sequoian Press*," the reporter called. "Mr. Talbot, are you stating that all these people are mistaken in what they heard and saw, and that your father purposely deceived the GMA?"

"Let's just say he took the document with him for a reason," Sonny responded.

"That's why we need to stick to our resolution to file that court injunction," Nancy called, and got an immediate round of applause.

"Wait just a minute," Talbot said, holding up his hands to still the angry buzzing from the audience. "My father was an upstanding citizen of this town—".

"Upstanding?" I called. "He deceived all the shop owners in Little Greece by signing a paper to halt the project, then—"

"—drowned in his own bathtub several days afterward," a man called over the fading buzz. "That timing was quite a stroke of luck on your part, wasn't it, Mr. Talbot? Perhaps your father intended to file the document himself, but we'll never know that, will we?"

The man's voice seemed to echo as the implications

sunk in. A hush fell over the crowd as the TV cameraman swiveled back to Talbot, who slowly lowered his
hand from over his eyes. Everyone waited for Talbot's
response, and all I could think of was, *Dear God. I know
that voice.*

As Talbot straightened his cuffs, clearly stalling for
time, the onlookers began to whisper among themselves. I raised myself up on my toes again and looked
around for Case, but somehow he'd managed to melt
into the throng before he was caught on camera—or by
the security guards, who were now combing the area
looking for him.

"My elderly father died in what can only be labeled a
tragic accident," Talbot answered, trying his best to
look and sound bereaved. "But I swear to you that he
had no intention of canceling a project that was so near
and dear to his heart. And thus, I vow to you today to
continue the condominium project in his honor."

He was roundly booed.

"Were there any witnesses to your father's death?"
the TV newscaster asked.

"We're getting off topic here," Talbot said. "Let's go
back to the—"

"Answer the question," someone shouted from the
front.

Sonny closed his eyes and placed his hand over his
heart. "He passed alone, sadly, and it grieves me to this
day."

His polished performance made me want to gag.

"Why wasn't an autopsy performed?" I asked loudly.

Talbot responded, "That's enough questions about
my father's death. That's not why I called a news conference."

"Are you afraid to answer Miss Spencer's question?"
Nancy called.

After a hasty conference with his attorneys, Sonny said, "I've been advised to say nothing further on the subject of my father."

"Sounds to me like you're afraid to answer her in front of the cameras," came a man's voice.

I froze. It was Case again. I, along with everyone else, turned to look, but he had vanished.

"I came here to talk about the condominium project," Talbot snapped, clearly angry. "Nothing else."

"You said on live TV that you would address Harry Pepper's murder today," another familiar voice called. As all heads swiveled in the speaker's direction, I glanced around and saw Dad standing two rows behind me. He'd come after all.

Talbot held his hands to his eyes. "The newspaper gave his death full coverage. I don't see the need to discuss it further."

"They didn't cover everything," Dad called, as the TV news camera rolled. "How is it that someone gained access to the mansion without setting off any security alarms?"

"We had a power outage that night, sir," one of the attorneys answered.

"A big mansion like that with no backup generator for the security system?" Dad shook his head. "Hard to swallow."

"It wasn't my decision to make," Sonny replied. "It wasn't my home at the time."

"Well, it sure is now," Dad said, and got some snickers from the audience. "You held that estate auction before his body was even cold in the ground."

There was a whispered conversation among Sonny and his aides, then one of the lawyers stepped up to the microphone. "This conference is over."

As people began shouting questions, I heard a voice

in my ear say quietly, "Miss Spencer, Mr. Talbot would like to see you after the press conference."

I turned to see who it was and saw a man in a black suit walking away, holding a cell phone to his ear. At the same time, Sonny, surrounded by his henchmen, disappeared into the building.

Dad immediately began making his way toward me. I glanced to my right and saw Case doing the same thing.

Help.

CHAPTER THIRTEEN

"Athena, there you are!"

It was Dad who reached me first. Case saw him and veered away, almost bumping into one of the security guards.

"What a press conference," Dad said, shaking his head in disgust. "Then again, I don't know why I expected anything different."

Keeping my eye on the security guard who was now giving Case a long, hard look, I muttered, "Yep. That sure was a disappointment." I felt my shoulders tighten as I watched Case speak to the guard, but the man merely nodded and went on his way.

"Thenie?" Dad snapped his fingers in front of my eyes. "You haven't heard a word I've said. Where'd you go?"

"Sonny wants to see me. I'll be right back."

I hustled around the retreating crowd up to the door of the building, where two guards now stood blocking the entrance. "My name is Athena Spencer. I was told to see Mr. Talbot after the press conference."

One of the guards placed a call on his cell phone, then said, "Okay, step inside."

I walked into a lobby of gray and white marble floors, gray walls, and crystal sconces and chandeliers. Sonny was huddled with his attorneys near a set of white double doors but looked up as I approached. He whispered something to his team, then walked over to me. "I didn't appreciate your questions about my father's death."

"I didn't appreciate your dodging the questions, either. It makes me wonder why. I also have questions about why you're going against your father's wishes about the condo project when you're quite aware that he signed an agreement to cancel it."

"Unfortunately, the document seems to be missing," Sonny said, "and the only two people who would know where it is are both gone. Now," he said, as his cell phone dinged, "I've got business to handle, Miss Spencer. I don't have time to discuss that issue with you."

"I'll bet you'll make time if I start talking to the press about the lack of an autopsy."

At that both of his lawyers bent in for a whispered conference. Obviously, *they* thought it was worth his time to talk to me because after their conference, Sonny sighed sharply. "Fine. If you want to meet with me, it'll have to be tomorrow."

"That works for me."

The second those words were out of my mouth I wished I could take them back. What was I thinking meeting with Sonny alone?

Wait. I had a partner now. My shoulders sagged in relief. All I had to do was figure out a reason for Case, or rather my cousin Dimitrius, to be there with me.

"I don't work at the corporate offices on the weekend," Sonny said, "so I'll see you at my home office at ten a.m. tomorrow morning."

I made a show of checking the calendar on my phone. "Okay," I said, trying to keep a cool expression. "I can do that." We shook hands and then I walked out.

It had been just that easy. But would it be that easy to get the truth from him?

I could hear my dad saying, *Keep your eyes on the prize, Athena. It's all about justice.*

Dad was talking to Barb when I got back. "How'd it go?" she asked.

"I've got a meeting with Sonny tomorrow at ten o'clock."

"Do you want me to come with you?" Dad asked.

"I think it'd be best if I went alone. He made it clear he wasn't in favor of meeting with me, but after I threatened to talk to reporters about the lack of an autopsy, his lawyers pressed him to do it. Remember, I've handled interviews before. I'm not a novice."

"You are when it comes to the Talbots," Dad said.

Didn't I know that. But neither did I want to admit that I had a backup: Case.

"Sonny Talbot puts his pants on one leg at a time, Pops," I said. "That's what you always used to say about bullies."

"You'll do fine," Barb said.

Out of the corner of my eye I caught sight of Case trying to signal something to me. He was standing next to the TV news van parked at the edge of the plaza, well away from the crowd. He pointed to his watch, held up six fingers, then three, then made a zero, followed by a wavelike motion. I tipped my head slightly to indicate I understood. Meet him at the boat at six thirty.

I realized suddenly that my father was waiting for me to answer a question that I hadn't heard. I felt a blush sting my cheeks. "I'm sorry, Pops. I missed what you said. My mind was somewhere else."

"It wouldn't have been on that good-looking man over there waving at you, would it?"

We both swiveled for a look but thankfully Case had slipped away. "What man?" I asked.

Turning back to me, he said, "Isn't that odd. He's gone now, and here I was hoping you'd introduce me to meet the brave soul who questioned Talbot's drowning." Dad tilted his head and looked over his glasses in playful skepticism. "You sure you didn't see who the man was?"

"Sorry. I was all the way up front. Couldn't see a thing." I could feel my voice starting to get tight and squeaky again, a dead giveaway that I was lying, so I decided to change the subject. "But I did get the crowd all riled up, didn't I?"

Dad put his arm around my shoulders and gave me an affectionate squeeze. "Yes, you did. You got Sonny riled up, too. That was quick thinking on your part, Thenie. I'm proud of you. I'll bet it'll make the ten o'clock news."

"Good. I want as much attention on the subject as possible." I glanced at my watch. If I didn't leave soon, there'd be no way I'd make it to the boat by six thirty and, without Case having a cell phone, I'd have no way to let him know I was going to be late. I *had* to get him a phone today, something untraceable, and there was only one place I knew that sold them. So back to the discount store I needed to go.

Tucking my arm through my father's I said, "Where are you parked?"

"The employees' lot."

"Me too. I'll walk back with you."

As we started off around the building I asked, "Pops, what do you think Marie Odem knows? She seemed pretty adamant about having some kind of information."

"It sounds to me like one or both of the Talbots cut a deal with her to spare her building, then pulled the rug out from under her. Maybe she was promised her building would be safe if she didn't join in the fight against his project."

"You know what struck me as odd? When Marie said, 'Don't think you'll get away with this. Your father made that mistake.' That sounded like a threat to me."

"Are you suggesting Marie Odem is a suspect?" Dad asked as we stopped by my SUV. "Somehow I don't see her as the murdering type."

"But think about it, Pops. Remember those TV shows we used to watch? It was always about means, motive, and opportunity. From what Marie said today, we can guess she had a motive, *and* she knew the layout of the mansion, so she would've had the opportunity. All she'd need is the means to carry it off."

"Let's not forget the man who was caught on the security cameras. We don't know whether he's tied to Talbot Senior's death, but we do know he had the means and opportunity to kill Harry. Whether he had a motive remains to be seen."

I knew what Case's motive would've been—to find the statue's papers—but I couldn't share that with my father. Could I imagine the Case I'd come to know killing Harry over them? I didn't want to think about it.

"I've got to run to the grocery store, Pops. I promised Nicholas his favorite treat tonight."

I hated missing dinner with my son because of our late Friday hours, but luckily, he had my family to eat with and he loved my sisters, who coddled him no end.

"Then I'll see you back at the garden center," Dad said.

As I climbed into my SUV, I pondered my father's words and came to one conclusion: Marie Odem was definitely worth investigating.

After a quick stop at the discount store to pick up a disposable phone, a pair of brown canvas deck shoes for Case, and a Ghirardelli dark chocolate bar for Nicholas, I drove back to town, parked in the public parking lot close to the garden center instead of at the harbor so no one would see my SUV near the boat, and put on the hooded sweatshirt I now kept in my vehicle. Then I set out for the three-block walk to the harbor.

It was a warm spring evening, and everyone was taking advantage of it. I couldn't help but feel a little rushed as I walked along the sidewalk incognito, passing shops and tourists, getting the odd glance now and then. I must have looked slightly out of place wearing a thick sweatshirt with the hood up over my head, partially covering my face, but it was better than being spotted by a nosy shop owner, or worse, a member of my family.

As I drew near the dock, I noticed a police car parked alongside the curb and then saw two policemen talking to a man in a boat docked at pier one. I recognized the first cop, Bob Maguire, by his beanpole body, freckled face, and stubbly orange hair, and his partner, Officer Gomez, by his short, sturdy body and dark olive skin. For a moment I thought there'd been some sort of mishap, but then I saw them show the man a flyer and I knew at once they were looking for Case.

My heart began to race. If the police were going boat to boat, would Case's new haircut, clothing, and fake tan be enough to fool them? Trying to tamp down my rising fear, I pulled my hood down farther and steadied my stride so as not to attract attention. At the far end I turned onto pier three and hurried out to the last slip where the *Páme* was docked.

I glanced back to see what the cops were doing but the other boats blocked my view. Crossing the gangway, I jumped down into the boat, hurried past the seating area on the upper deck, and slipped through the cabin door, locking it behind me.

I scuttled down the short flight of steps calling, "Case, it's me. We've got trouble."

There was no answer. I called his name again and still heard nothing. Quickly, I took my purse out of the bag, tossed it onto the vinyl sofa, then tucked the shopping bag with his shoes and disposable phone into the utility closet near the door. I pulled my sweatshirt over my head and stuffed it down into the bag to cover the phone, then, looking around the cabin to make sure there was nothing else to hide, I slid my cell phone into my back pocket and made my way toward the bow.

Before I could get there, heavy fists pounded on the cabin door. "Police! Open up."

I backed against the wall, my heart slamming against my ribs. They had just been at the first pier. Why were they here so soon?

I decided not to answer, hoping they'd think no one was home. After a moment I started silently toward the bow once again only to hear, "We know you're inside. Open up or we'll have to smash the door down."

"Okay, just a minute," I called, trying to gather my wits. I'd heard nothing from Case and hadn't seen any signs of his presence, so he must have seen the police and headed away from the harbor.

I took a few slow breaths, fluffed up my hair, pasted on a smile, and opened the door.

"Athena?" Maguire gazed at me with a startled expression before giving my outfit a thorough sweep. "What are you doing here?"

Officer Gomez, standing next to Maguire, was glancing around the interior as though expecting to see someone else there.

"I came down to clean Pappoús's boat so we can take it out this weekend. What are *you* doing here?"

"We're asking everyone to keep an eye out for this man," Maguire said, showing me the WANTED poster that was now pasted all over town. "Have you seen him since the incident at your shop?"

"No, not since that evening."

"We saw someone wearing a gray hooded sweatshirt enter this boat just moments ago," Gomez said. "Was that you?"

"Of course," I said, trying to sound lighthearted. "Who else would it be?"

"Just seemed odd to see someone wearing a hooded sweatshirt on such a warm evening," Gomez said in his humorless voice. He paused to let that sink in. "Don't you think?"

I seemed to be doing a lot of odd things lately, and, fortunately, a lot of quick thinking, too. Luckily, I was getting better at it. I rubbed my arms as though chilled. "It doesn't feel warm to me. But I've been a little out of sorts all day. Maybe I'm coming down with something."

That made them step back.

Gomez nodded toward the utility closet. "What's in there?"

"Just supplies." I opened the door so they could take a look, thanking my lucky stars I'd tucked Case's things beneath my sweatshirt.

As I closed the door, I asked Maguire, " 'What made you think this guy would be on my *pappoús*'s boat?"

"We've received reports of unusual activity around here and were asked to check it out," Maguire replied.

"What kind of unusual activity?"

"Someone reported seeing a stranger in the vicinity."

Case was going to have to be more careful from now on. I knew of at least two nosy couples who lived in houseboats in the harbor. "Trust me, Maguire. If I were to see any indication that a wanted man was anywhere near here, I'd be dialing 911 ASAP."

"Good enough," Maguire said.

"Hold it," Gomez said. "Who is this *pahpoo* guy you keep talking about?"

"That's the Greek word for 'grandfather,' " I said.

I thought Gomez's curiosity had been satisfied, but then he started toward the hallway that led to the bedroom, and I felt panic rise inside. I darted ahead of him and barred the way. "Where are you going? This is private property."

"We have orders to search the premises," Gomez said.

They had *orders*? I glanced at Maguire for help, but he merely said, "I'm sorry, Athena. There's nothing I can do."

"But I just told you I'd contact you if I saw anyone suspicious."

"Step aside, ma'am," Gomez ordered.

My heart was racing so fast that I felt light-headed. If Case were hiding somewhere on the boat he'd be discovered now for sure, and there'd be no way to explain my way out of it. What had I gotten myself into?

Then I remembered something Kevin had told me. Lifting my chin, I said defiantly, "I'm not moving until I see a search warrant."

Gomez pulled a folded piece of paper out of his jacket pocket and handed it to me.

My stomach did a three-hundred-sixty-degree flip

and all of my quick thinking came to a halt. These men were serious; they'd come prepared. I looked over the document, but my hands were shaking so hard I had a difficult time focusing. Even so, I could see a judge's signature on it.

"Would you please step out of the way now, Athena?" Maguire asked.

I had no choice but to move aside. As they began to search the boat. I thought I was going to be sick, so I walked back to the galley and grabbed a dishrag to wipe off the counter, trying to do something to calm my nerves.

My first thoughts were of my family. What would they think when they found out I'd been harboring a fugitive? In Pappoús's boat no less? And my fears multiplied from there. Would they think I'd lost my mind? What if I were hauled off to jail for harboring a fugitive? Would my reputation be ruined?

And finally, I started wondering whether this whole ordeal was worth it. I tried to focus on all the reasons why I thought it was so vital to get involved: I'd keep an innocent man (I hoped) from being accused of a crime; I'd find justice for Harry Pepper and Talbot Sr.; and I'd stop Sonny from ruining the downtown. But the thought of being hauled away in handcuffs made it hard to keep that focus.

A few minutes later, both officers returned to the galley, Gomez holding up the boat shoes I'd given Case to wear. "Who do these belong to?"

I had to sit on a chair so my knees wouldn't give out on me. Case had been wearing those shoes at the press conference, so he had made it back after all. That meant he was hiding somewhere on the boat.

I realized the officers were still waiting for an answer

and said as calmly as possible, "They belong to my *pappoús*. He keeps extra fishing outfits here."

"They're damp," Gomez responded instantly, his mistrustful gaze making me feel even more jumpy. "Has he used them recently?"

"If they're damp, I'm going to take a wild stab at it and say yes, he must have used them. But then I don't keep track of my grandfather's comings and goings. Should I be?" I knew I was running the risk of annoying him further, but being a jumpy, nervous wreck wasn't working in my favor, either, so what did I have to lose?

Gomez shot me a dark look, but surprisingly, I could see Maguire behind him holding back a smile.

"Mind if we look around above deck?" Maguire asked, casually motioning to Gomez to put the shoes down.

Did I *mind*? Did I have a choice was the better question. I shrugged nonchalantly. "Can I stop you?"

As they clomped up the stairs with their heavy shoes, I went to the sink to glance out the window. Where was Case?

I suddenly remembered the tall, thin cabinet where my grandfather kept his rubber boots and overalls. I waited a few seconds to make sure the police were above deck, then dashed to the bedroom and opened the cabinet door.

Rubber boots and overalls. No Case.

I sat down on the bed, head in hands. There was only one more place above deck that Case could be hiding. It would be just a matter of time until they found him there.

Hearing a light tap on the porthole on one side of the V-shaped room, I hopped off the bed and ran to the window, bracing myself against the sudden rocking motion caused by a passing speedboat. But I spotted nothing that could have caused the noise. As heavy footfalls sounded on the deck overhead, I pressed my nose against the window for a better look, yet still saw only the shimmering blue lake.

Suddenly a hand shot out of the waves, tapped the glass, and sank again.

Case was hiding in the water.

CHAPTER FOURTEEN

I pressed my hand against my heart to still its rapid beating. At least Case was on the port side, away from other docked boats. But what if he surfaced again and the police heard the splash? I knew he couldn't stay beneath the water forever. And if they found him, the water would've washed away his fake tan and slicked back his hair. Even with the thick, dark scruff on his chin, he would still resemble the picture plastered all over town.

I needed a distraction. Quickly.

I twisted a lock of my hair. *Think, Athena. What would get the cops away from the harbor?*

"Excuse me, ma'am?" said a voice behind me.

I whirled around to see Officer Gomez standing in the bedroom door. "Yes?" I said, stepping away from the porthole.

"We're all finished here."

Maguire appeared behind him. "Sorry to have bothered you, Athena. We'll let you get back to your preparations now. But please do me a favor and call if you see any—"

A tap on the glass stopped him mid-sentence. Both men looked straight at the porthole.

"What was that?" Gomez asked.

"What was what?" *Think, Athena. Fast!*

As Gomez made his way into the bedroom, an idea came to me. I began to smooth out the blue cotton coverlet to hide the fact that I was trembling inside as I said, "It must be the rope we use to tie the front of the boat to a pier. Sometimes it knocks against the side when another boat goes by."

Gomez looked back at Maguire as if trying to decide whether to believe me, then stepped up to the porthole anyway and peered out. I held my breath, feeling as light-headed as though I were the one underwater. Another tap and we were both caught.

The seconds ticked by as Gomez waited for the rope to swing past again. If Case were anything like me, he would be just about out of breath.

Then out of the blue my cell phone rang, and my breath came rushing out. I pulled the phone out of my pocket, saw Dad's name on the screen, and another light bulb went on in my head. I had a plan, in fact, the perfect plan. I had to cough to cover my smile.

Okay, high school drama class, don't fail me now! "Hey, Papa, what's up?" I asked, keeping my tone cool.

"Did you just call me *Papa*? Thenie, is everything all right? I thought you were coming back to the shop."

"Wait, Papa. Slow down. You're talking too fast. You saw *who* in the alley? Are you sure it was the guy on the poster?"

Both officers were listening attentively now.

"Okay, stay calm, Papa. I have two police officers with me right now and we'll be there soon."

"Why are the police there?" Dad asked, clearly not catching on. "What's going on?"

"Just sit tight. We're on our way. Trust me on this, okay?"

"I got it."

"What's the problem?" Gomez asked as I put my phone in my pocket.

I slid past the officers and headed for the kitchen, forcing them to follow me. "My father believes he spotted the man you're after in the lane behind Spencer's."

Snatching my purse, I led the men out of the cabin and shut the door with a bang, hoping that if Case had surfaced, he would hear us leave. We crossed over onto the pier with me talking all the while. "My father is rattled, and he has a heart condition. I'd be devastated if something happened to him. I'd really appreciate it if you could check out the lane for him and put his mind at ease."

"Is he certain the man is still there?" Gomez asked, as Maguire used his collar microphone to radio in what was going on.

"He didn't say, but my sister Delphi is there. She may have seen him, too."

Damn! Why had I said that? Delphi could throw a hitch into my whole plan. "Look," I said. "All I know is that there's a murderer on the loose and you need to find him."

I crossed my fingers and kept going, putting more and more distance between us and the boat. As soon as we reached the street, I let out a sigh of relief. Now I just needed the cops to take off so I could call Dad and explain.

As we approached the squad car, Gomez asked, "Where's your vehicle?"

"Parked by my shop. I walked down. It's only five minutes away."

"We'll drive you," Gomez said, opening the back door for me. "We can get you there faster."

Damn! Another hitch in my plan. And what could I do? Say no and make him wonder why I'd refuse to take the fastest route? It was clear that Gomez didn't trust me, and I wasn't entirely certain Maguire did, either. The only alternative I had now was to send Dad a text and hope it reached him before we arrived.

With my nerves shredding fast, I climbed inside, buckled up, and immediately took out my phone. As I began typing, Maguire activated the lights and siren and took off at breakneck speed. But before I could finish, we hit a bump and my phone went skittering across the bench seat to the opposite door. I tried to reach it without taking off my seat belt, but my arm wouldn't stretch that far.

Just as I was about to sidle out from under the chest strap to grab it, they pulled up in front of Spencer's with a screech of tires. The two cops hopped out, Gomez swinging my door open for me. And there sat my phone with its unsent text message on the other end of the seat.

Okay, so maybe it *wasn't* the perfect plan.

As we entered the shop my thoughts were spinning as fast as the red and blue lights on the squad car outside. I could tell by the closed door that Dad was in the office, but how could I get to him before Gomez did?

"Where's your back exit?" Gomez asked.

I pointed toward the rear of the store.

"You go around the front and I'll head out the back," Gomez said to Maguire, one hand on his revolver. "We'll get a statement from her father afterward."

As they headed off their separate ways, I felt sweat

beading under my arms as I imagined how it was going to play out. They would look around, find no one, and come back inside to question my dad. I rubbed my temples. How had I managed to turn one bad situation into two?

Then the office door opened, Dad came out and motioned me over.

"What's going on?"

I heard the back door close and knew they were back.

I fairly shoved him back inside the office. "Just play along with whatever I say. I'll explain later." I glanced around. "Sit at your desk and pretend you don't feel . . . Here's Officer Gomez now."

Gomez came inside and shut the door, watching Dad ease himself into his swivel chair as though he were an ailing ninety-nine-year-old instead of an active sixty-year-old. "Are you all right, sir?"

I jumped in right away. "Yes, you sounded so frightened after seeing that man out back, Papa, that I thought I'd have to take you to the emergency room. Did you see any signs of the man, Officer?"

"No, we didn't." Gomez got out a small writing tablet and flipped it open. "Sir, are you up to giving a description of this man?"

"Maybe after a sip or two of coffee. Athena, would you make me a cup?"

I hurried to pop a pod into the machine. As it brewed, I said. "Officer? A cup for you?"

He shook his head, so I set Dad's refilled cup on his desk. "Anything else you need, Papa? A moment to gather your thoughts?"

"That would be helpful, dear," he said, patting my arm. To Gomez he said, "When I get flustered, I have a dickens of a time remembering things." He took off his glasses to polish them with a tissue. "Can you give me a minute?"

"It's best to get the story while it's still fresh in your mind," Gomez said. "Are there any details that stand out about the man you saw?"

"Details." Dad put his glasses back on. "Let me take a sip of my coffee while I try to recall exactly what I saw." As he reached for the cup on the coaster, he somehow managed to push his long, yellow writing tablet forward, causing the tissue box near the edge to fall off the desk almost at Gomez's feet.

As the officer bent to pick it up, Dad raised his shoulders, giving me a flabbergasted look. That was my cue to jump in.

"Over the phone you said he was wearing a leather jacket. Isn't that right?" I asked, as Gomez set the box on the desk. "I think you called it a fancy suede jacket."

Giving me a glare, Gomez pointed to the chair next to the coffee machine. "Take a seat and be quiet."

Chastised, I sat down and clasped my hands together between my knees, trying once again to calm my jumpy nerves.

"Can you describe the jacket, sir?" Gomez asked.

Dad shot me a quick look for assistance. I was out of Gomez's line of sight, but what could I describe through a gesture? A zipper?

I'd started to mimic zipping up a jacket when Gomez turned to see what I was doing. I scratched my chin, then pressed my hands between my knees again, squeezing them even tighter. There was no way I could help Dad with Gomez watching me so closely.

"Sir?" Gomez said impatiently. "The jacket?"

"Frankly, young man," Dad said sharply, "I didn't think I ought to stick around long enough to take that close of a look. It was a jacket and it was suede."

"Color?"

I pointed to my hair.

"Kind of a light brown I'd say."

I sagged back into the chair in relief. Go, Pops!

Maguire opened the door and came inside. "The lane's clear, Mr. Spencer."

Dad rubbed his chest, acting frail again. "That's a relief. Are you fellows done now? I think I need to go home and lie down."

Gomez closed his notebook and rose. "That's fine. I'm done here." He gave me a skeptical glance as he joined his partner at the door.

"Athena, thanks for your help," Maguire said, holding up his hand in a parting gesture. To Dad he said, "I'm sorry for the trouble, sir. I hope you feel better soon."

As the cops made their way toward the front door, Delphi, who was now standing behind the counter, made sure Maguire noticed her and gave him a little wave. He flushed a deep red as he tipped his hat to her and tried to hold back a delighted smile.

Perfect. That would make his day and maybe he'd be someone I could tap for information later on. As soon as the officers were gone, I gave my sister a *V* for victory, then turned to see my father standing in the office doorway. I gave him a smile.

He wasn't smiling back. "Come into the office, young lady. You've got some explaining to do."

CHAPTER FIFTEEN

Dad settled into the leather desk chair, leaned back, and folded his arms, while I sat across from him feeling like a guilty ten-year-old.

"Tell me what's going on. Why did you send the police on a wild goose chase?"

"Well"—I scratched my forehead, trying to stall while I thought my way out of telling him the truth—"it's a long story, and it's getting close to closing time." I lowered my voice. "And I really don't want Delphi to know anything about it, so could we talk tomorrow morning before she gets here?"

He got up and locked the door. "Then give me the short version and we'll call it a day."

The short version. I took a deep breath. "Okay, here it is. The police were searching Pappoús's boat for the guy they think murdered Harry and I had to lead them away."

"Why on earth would anyone believe that a murder suspect was hiding on your grandfather's boat?"

I looked down at my shoes, not only feeling but now

acting like a guilty ten-year-old, wishing I'd never involved my father in this mess. "Because I'm hiding him there."

Given the shocked look on Dad's face, I was glad he didn't have a heart problem. "You're hiding a *murder* suspect on your *pappoús*'s boat?"

"His name is Case, and it was either there or here, Pops, so I chose there because I didn't want to involve Delphi or you."

"That didn't work so well, did it?" Dad sat down in his chair and took off his glasses to rub his eyes. "I'm betting there is no short version of this story, is there?"

"No," I admitted.

"You're protecting a murder suspect?"

"He *didn't* murder Harry, Pops. His name is Case Donnelly, he's from Pittsburgh, and he came to Sequoia to find a document that proves the *Treasure of Athena* was stolen from his family's museum decades ago. Case didn't know he was a suspect in Harry's murder until he saw his face plastered all over town on those WANTED posters. He did see Harry's body, though, through the office's open doors the morning he was killed, so Case left fast because he didn't want anyone to connect him to Harry's death. He didn't realize he'd been caught on security cameras."

"Then he *was* at Talbot's mansion on the morning of the murder. What was he doing at the office doors?"

"Making a big mistake."

"That's not very convincing."

"You really need to hear him tell the story."

Dad shook his head. "My naïve little Thenie, what have you gotten yourself into?"

"Not what I expected to, believe me. But before you pass judgment, please talk to Case."

"Okay," he said with a resigned sigh, "I'll hear him

out. But let me pose this to you. Do you truly believe that Case whatever-his-name-is came here solely to find his family's stolen statue and all he wants now is the proof of ownership?"

"Honestly, I don't know."

"Just understand that if he finds this proof, he may try to claim the statue."

"He could, yes, but if I help him clear his name, he'd better not. He also knows that Pappoús bought the statue fair and square and has a credit card statement to prove it. But that's not my main concern right now. What's important is to prevent an injustice from being done."

Dad sat back with a sigh and shook his head. "Athena."

"It'll be okay, Pops. I'm helping Case, and he's going to help us fight to save Little Greece. In fact, we started a murder investigation today by interviewing Dr. Kirkland about his quick ruling on Talbot's death. We got a few useful facts from him, but the more we asked, the more upset he got, until he finally told us to leave his office."

Dad made a "time-out" with his hands. "Case, a wanted man, went to the courthouse to talk to the coroner?"

"Well, actually, he's not Case anymore. I helped him change his appearance and his name. He's Dimitrius Costas now, the last name being his mother's maiden name. Fortunately, he's part Greek so it wasn't too hard to change his appearance. And the story we concocted is that he's here from Tarpon Springs to write a murder mystery and that we're distantly related. My challenge is to keep Delphi from figuring out who Dimitrius is, because she's seen Case."

"And to keep your mother from finding out that she has a new relative." Dad massaged his forehead. "I think we should have met in the morning. I'm getting a headache."

"I'm almost done."

He waved me on. "Go ahead."

"The only other thing you need to remember is that Sonny gave two different versions of how he found Harry's body. And you heard him evade all questions about his father's death at the press conference. So now I'm convinced that Sonny is connected to both deaths somehow. Hopefully, I'll find out more when I meet with him."

"And that's why you asked me those questions about Talbot's dinner guests and the layout of his house?"

"Exactly."

Dad put his glasses back on with a sigh. "You have to realize, Thenie, that by helping Case hide from the law, you can be charged with aiding and abetting."

"It's a chance I'm willing to take. I can't stand the thought of the true killer walking around freely while an innocent man sits in prison for a crime he didn't commit. What if Sonny committed the murders? Or Lila? Everyone knows Sonny pulls the strings in this town. Do we turn a blind eye to that like the authorities seem to be doing?"

"The authorities can put you in prison, too, Athena."

"Not if I'm careful."

"You could be putting yourself in danger by taking on Sonny Talbot."

"I'm aware of that and I'm taking precautions."

"What if it turns out this Case Donnelly is the murderer after all?"

"Just listen to his story. That's all I ask."

The doorknob rattled. "Hey! Why's the door locked?" Delphi called.

"Just a minute," Dad answered. He rattled the door-knob as though it was stuck, quietly unlocked it, and opened the door wide. "I've got to get that knob fixed. What's the problem, Delph?"

"It's almost closing time and all the customers are gone. Should we lock up a few minutes early?"

"Good idea," I said, glancing at my watch. I still needed to get back to the boat to talk to Case. Hope-fully, the cops hadn't returned to the harbor and he'd been able to get inside. "I'll close up, Delph. You and Pops can go on home."

Before they left, I squeezed my dad's hand and said near his ear, "Thanks, Pops."

I left my SUV where I'd parked it earlier and once again walked down to the harbor, being very careful to look and act normally. I even stopped at the frozen yo-gurt shop on the way for a carton of dark chocolate fudge, part of the food I was supplying for our supposed family outing.

When I reached the docks, I kept my eye out for any signs of the police. I even scouted for their black un-marked cars, which every local knew upon sight. Still, as I reached pier three, my heart pounded harder with every step I took toward the *Páme*.

The boat was dark, and even with the lights along the pier, I had to use the flashlight on my phone to see the lock on the cabin door. I opened it cautiously, listened a moment, then called, "Case?"

His voice came from far back in the boat. "Can I stop holding my breath now?"

At least he hadn't lost his sense of humor. "Yes. The coast is clear. Literally."

I locked the door, flipped on the kitchen light, and

put the sack with the yogurt in it on the table. Case walked out of the hallway clutching a blue cotton bedcover around his body, his hair combed back, his fake tan washed away. He was holding a pile of sodden clothing and shivering in the cool evening air. "What should I do with these?"

"You're freezing. Let me turn on the heat." I took the wet clothes from him and placed them by the stairs to put outside to dry, then hit a switch on a heater mounted on the wall. Trying in vain to hold back my laughter I asked, "Why are you wearing a bedspread?"

"Because I couldn't find any dry clothes in the dark and I had to wrap myself in something. Why is that so funny?"

"It's just that I'm not used to seeing a man wearing a—" I gestured toward the blue bedcover.

"I wouldn't be wearing this if I'd been able to turn on a light or make noise, but I didn't know where the police were." He pulled out a chair and sat down at the kitchen table. "Of course, if I'd had that cell phone you promised, you could've texted to let me know what was going on and then I wouldn't be wearing a—" He glanced down at the bedspread.

"Hey, I had to come up with a plan on the spot to save your life. It might not have been the greatest plan, but at least the police fell for it."

That seemed to sober him. "You're right and thank you for that. Another few seconds and I'd have either drowned or been arrested."

"That's exactly what I was afraid of. When I realized you were underwater, my only concern was to get the cops away from the boat." I walked over to the utility closet, picked up the shopping bag, and set it on the table. "And by the way, I was on my way here to deliver these when I spotted the police making their rounds."

He pulled out my hoodie and held it up. "I don't think it's my size."

I snatched it out of his hands. "That's mine."

He took another look inside the bag and his dimpled smile spread across his face as he removed the box with his new cell phone in it.

"There's something else in the bag, too."

He reached in and pulled out a shoebox. Opening it, he found his new deck shoes. "Thanks," he said, and bent down to slip them on. He rose, holding the bedspread around his waist. "Perfect fit."

As he sat down to open the cell phone box, I couldn't help but notice his bare shoulders, broad and strong, with sculpted arms and a line of dark hair that ran—

He glanced up and caught me staring. "What's wrong?"

"I—I was just about to point out that your tan washed off. You're going to have to make sure you reapply the cream before you go back outside." To hide the blush that was climbing up my neck, I got up to put the yogurt in the freezer. "Have you eaten anything?"

"Not since lunch."

"I haven't eaten either and I'm starving, so why don't you go take a hot shower and get dressed and I'll make us something yummy. You can set up your cell phone afterward."

As I pulled out the carton of eggs, a stick of butter, and packages of ham and cheese, I paused, turning toward the door. "Did you hear something?"

"Just my stomach growling."

"I mean above deck."

"No. What did you hear?"

I listened for a moment, then shrugged it off. "Probably just people passing by on the pier outside. I've been a little jumpy ever since the police burst in on me."

Ten minutes later Case came out of the bedroom wearing a fresh pair of jeans, a clean T-shirt, and a surprised expression as he watched me set two plates heaped with steaming omelets stuffed with melted cheddar cheese and smoked ham on the table.

"Wow," he said. "They look delicious."

"You sound surprised. Didn't you think I could cook?" I teased.

He came around to pull out my chair for me. "Not at all. What I should've said was that they look delicious *and* thank you for making them."

"You're welcome."

Case sat down across from me and propped his chin on his hand, his gaze lingering on me in a way that brought heat to my cheeks. "You're a woman of hidden talents, Athena."

No man had ever said that to me before. To cover my embarrassment I said, "You probably shouldn't say that until you've tried the omelet."

He laughed. "You're right. Let's dig in."

I picked up my fork and began to eat, watching covertly as he took a bite and chewed it, eyes closed, as though savoring every morsel. "Delicious," he said.

"Thanks." I checked my watch. "Good. We've got time to prepare for our meeting with Sonny in the morning at ten o'clock."

Case stopped eating. "What meeting?"

"At the end of the press conference, one of Sonny's men came up to me and said Sonny wanted to talk to me privately after the conference. When I met with him, I asked him the questions he wouldn't answer in front of the press. He got angry until I threatened to talk to a news reporter. That changed his mind, or his attorneys' minds, at least, so he agreed to see me privately tomorrow at the Talbot mansion since his office is closed on Saturdays. The thing is, I don't feel comfortable going alone, so I'd like you to come with me. We'll just have to give you a reason for being there."

"How about that I'm your boyfriend and we're heading out to go boating afterward?"

I thought about it for a moment. "We're better off sticking with the story we told the coroner. Kevin and I are kind of a known couple around town."

"Ah."

"Kevin! Oh, no. I was supposed to call him after work." I scooted back my chair and snatched my purse off the sofa, digging through it until I found my phone. On it were three text messages and a missed call.

"Hey, Kev. How are you?" Holding my phone between my ear and my shoulder, I took my plate to the counter and began to fill the sink with hot water and dish detergent. "What did you say?"

"I said I can hardly hear you. What are you doing?"

Being a horrible girlfriend.

Chapter Sixteen

Mortified, I shut off the water. "I'm just washing dishes after having a late bite to eat. Sorry I didn't call earlier, Kev. I had tons of work waiting for me at the shop when I got back from the—um—"

Case was reaching around me to put his plate in the sink, standing so close I could smell the soap on his skin and feel the heat from his body.

"From the what?" Kevin asked.

"Press conference," I blurted. "I'm so sorry I didn't call sooner. I had so many things on my mind I forgot."

"You're forgetting about me an awful lot these days," he said in an offended voice.

I couldn't lie and deny it. I had to make it up to him somehow. "How about this, then? Dinner at six and I'll fill you in on the conference."

"I'm way ahead of you. I've already made reservations for us at La Belle Cuisine at six, so I'll pick you up at five forty-five sharp."

Not that he'd thought to ask if I was free before setting up that reservation. Trying to drum up some enthusiasm I said, "Great. I'm looking forward to it. See you then."

I ended the call and heard a muttered, "Liar." I turned to see Case studiously working on his new phone.

"What did you just call me?"

"Not you. This phone. The directions say it's simple to set up. Ha!"

I wasn't sure I believed him—or maybe I was just feeling guilty. I put the clean plates in the drying rack and came to stand beside him, reading the directions over his shoulder. I noticed his hair was slicked back and before I realized what I was doing, I ruffled it.

Case caught my wrist and brought it down in front of him with a quizzical glance. "What are you doing?"

What *was* I doing touching him so familiarly? "Your hair," I said quickly, as heat flooded my face. "You had it combed straight back like the old Case. I was just trying to fluff it and bring it forward."

He studied me with his intense golden-brown eyes as he ran his thumb across my palm, turning my insides liquid. In a soft, almost seductive voice he asked, "You know what I want to do right now?"

I swallowed, my throat going dry as I imagined all sorts of scenarios. "What?"

He placed my hand on the table and picked up the directions. "Finish setting up my phone. It's hard to concentrate when you're playing with my hair."

Thoroughly humiliated by where my thoughts had taken me, I mustered up the indignation to say, "I was not *playing* with your hair. I was merely trying to style it so you wouldn't be recognized if you decided to step out this evening. So do yourself a favor and fluff it the next time you shower." And then I wouldn't be tempted to touch him.

I stuffed my phone into my purse and slipped on my hooded sweatshirt. "I'll see you tomorrow. It's getting late, and I promised my son a treat before he goes to bed."

Without looking up, he said, "I thought you wanted to prepare for our meeting with Sonny."

I stopped, my hand on the doorknob. Being so close to Case had completely thrown me off to the point that the meeting had totally slipped my mind.

"Let's have some of that yogurt," Case said, "and discuss quickly what we're going to say so you can get home to your boy. We've been through it with Kirkland. It shouldn't take long."

"Then I need to call Nicholas and tell him I'll be late." As I took off the hoodie and slipped my cell phone from my purse, Case pulled the dark chocolate fudge yogurt from the freezer and began to hunt for bowls and spoons.

"Nicholas, hi, honey. I'm sorry but I won't be home for at least another half an hour, so why don't you ask one of your aunts to read you a bedtime story tonight and I'll read you two tomorrow night?"

"Two? It's a deal," he said excitedly. *"Entáxei,* Mamá."

Entáxei again. Dear God. He was turning more Greek by the day. "Nicholas, could you do me a favor and just say 'Okay, Mom'?"

"I guess so," he said with a heavy sigh. "But then you have to do me a favor and stop calling me Nicholas like I'm a five-year-old wimp or something."

"But that's your name."

"Grandma calls me Niko and I like that better. It's way cooler."

"Let me think about it and get back to you. Good night, sweetheart."

"Kalinýchta, Mamá."

I put my phone away, feeling that same old dread of being sucked back into the family to the point where I was completely invisible again.

"Look what I found." Case held up an ancient ice cream scooper in a drawer and spooned out two big helpings of the creamy dessert. Handing me a bowl he said, "So what's going on with your son?"

"He's turning into a full-fledged Greek, something I was hoping to keep to a low roar. I purposely moved away from Sequoia to establish my own identity as a normal person, not as a *Greek* woman. Now I'm back and it's starting all over again."

"I get it. You're upset because your son is embracing his Greek heritage."

"Exactly."

"What's Nicholas's father's heritage, if you don't mind my asking?"

"He's a mutt, and I mean that in more ways than one. He's a mixture of English, German, Scotch, Dutch, and total jerk. And I'm being kind when I use the term 'jerk.' "

"I take it that's why you've gone back to your maiden name."

"Correct."

"So what your son needs is to balance out all the Greekness with your dad's heritage." Case tapped his chin with his spoon. "Spencer. I'm guessing it's English. Why don't you take Nicholas to London next summer and introduce him to your father's side?"

I smiled. "That's a great idea."

"So is this." He took a bite of yogurt and smiled back at me, flashing his dimples. "Dark chocolate. My favorite flavor. And one other suggestion that you can leave or take. If you don't like the name Niko and he doesn't like Nicholas, call him Nick. It sounds more grown-up. If I were ten, I'd feel like a baby being called Nicholas."

"That's exactly what he said." I sat in the chair across from him and dipped my spoon in the dessert, seeing Case in a different light. There was definitely more to him than met the eye, and that was saying a lot. "Thanks for the suggestion."

"All right," he said, "let's figure out our strategy so you can get home."

"First we need to get your cover story straight."

"I'm doing research for my mystery novel, aren't I?"

I took a bite of the yogurt, letting it melt on my tongue as I considered it. "The problem is that Sonny's a savvy guy. I really doubt it would work with him when it barely worked with the coroner."

"Then let's keep it simple. I'm your cousin Dimitri here for a visit and you're going to show me the town afterward."

"If that were the case, then why wouldn't I just pick you up after our meeting?" I took my bowl to the sink, thinking of the various versions I'd told. "Here's another problem. I told Kevin you were a stranger I met and gave directions to."

"Not realizing that we were distantly related and that I'd come to town to find my long-lost relatives, which you later learned you were."

I pretended to be having a conversation with Kevin. "Imagine my surprise, Kevin, when I found out Dimitri and I were distant cousins."

"There you go."

"And for our meeting tomorrow I can tell Sonny that the reason you came with me is because we're leaving immediately afterward to go to Holland, Michigan, for their Tulip Festival, something you've been wanting to see."

"Then we're back to the problem of why you wouldn't just pick me up after the meeting."

"Because"—I paused to take a bite and think—"Because we have lunch reservations at Boatwerks Waterfront Diner which is nearly impossible to get into during Tulip Festival." I banged my spoon on the bowl. "That's perfect. There's no way Sonny would find anything questionable about that."

"I seriously doubt he'd care." Case finished his yogurt and leaned back with a satisfied sigh. "Now on to the questions."

"Hold on. I just thought of something. When you spoke at the press conference, did Sonny or any of his assistants see you?"

"I made sure I stayed out of their line of sight."

"Good. What about the TV camera?"

"I stood behind it and I never let the newspaper photographer capture me, either. Why?"

"Because if you were in town for a visit, you wouldn't be at the press conference asking questions only a local would know."

"Got it." Case rubbed his hands together. "Then all our bases are covered. Let's get on with this."

I took my iPad out of my purse and we set to work, finishing in fifteen minutes. When I picked up his bowl to take it to the sink to wash it, he took it out of my hands.

"I'll take care of these," he said. "Go home to your son. It's not that late. Besides, I'm feeling a little waterlogged."

I couldn't help but laugh. "I'll bet you are."

I was still smiling as I headed for the door. How long had it been since I'd been around a man who made me laugh?

I slung my purse over my shoulder, then paused.

"One more thing. I don't want my SUV to be seen near here tomorrow, so you'll have to meet me at a safe place. Walk up to Greene Street, go north to the first light, and then head east on Pine Avenue for four blocks until you get to the Manchester apartments. You'll see my white Toyota SUV in the parking lot. Be there at nine thirty."

As I opened the door Case said, "So what about this Tulip Festival? Are we going?"

"It's just our cover story. Why? Did you want to go?"

He rubbed the back of his ear, almost as though he was the one now embarrassed. "I was just thinking it *would* be a good idea to get out of town after our meeting with Talbot so we can discuss the meeting. The boat doesn't feel safe anymore."

"Don't worry about the *Páme*. It's safer now that the police have checked it."

"True, but why not go to the festival anyway?"

"Why do you want to go to a Tulip Festival?"

He shrugged and sat back in his chair. "It's a festival, isn't it? It could be fun, and we're allowed to have a little fun, right? You can bring Nick and I might be able to charm our way into the Boatwerks. I'll even pay . . . you back when I can get to my money again."

I was confused for a moment, and it wasn't about money. In the middle of a manhunt, a murder investigation, and a phony identity, Case was thinking about having fun? But even more confusing—was he asking me out on a date? With my son?

"I'm not sure how much fun it will be, honestly, because of the crowds and the heat, but if you'd like to see what it's like, we can stop to pick up Nicholas—Nick—after the meeting and head north. I haven't been there in ten years, but I know we'll blend right into the throng of thousands of people."

"Great. Then it's a da—" He stopped abruptly.

"It's a what?"

He rubbed the dark scruff around his mouth and smiled. "It's a day away. See you in the morning."

Halfway back to my apartment, I heard a beep signaling an incoming text. I waited until I'd pulled into the driveway of my parents' home, then took out my phone to read it.

Dimitri: *Thought you might need my cell number. And BTW, thanks again for everything.*

Athena: *How did you get my number?*

Dimitri: *Wouldn't you like to know? Kalinýchta, Athena.*

Athena: *You're speaking Greek now, too?*

Dimitri: *Kidding. Looked it up on a translation website. How about I leave you with some Shakespeare?*

Athena: *Sure.*

Dimitri: *"I feel within me a peace above all earthly dignities, a still and quiet conscience."*

I sat there staring at the text. It was beautiful. I couldn't imagine Kevin or my ex ever sending anything like that.

Athena: *Thank you. That was lovely.*

I was about to put away my phone when it dinged again.

Dimitri: *Good night, Athena.*

Athena: *Kalinýchta, Dimitri.*

Despite all the day's frights, flights, and nervous flutters, I got out of the Toyota with a smile, a feeling of hope for tomorrow, and a quote for tomorrow's blog.

CHAPTER SEVENTEEN

Saturday

At ten o'clock on the nose, I leaned out the window of my SUV, pressed the buzzer mounted to one side of the Talbot gates, and announced my name. I was a bundle of nerves, while Case was casually reading through our list of questions as though we were headed to a ball game instead of a meeting with a potential killer.

I turned to study Case one last time. In his crisp red, blue, and white plaid shirt and blue jeans with his new boat shoes, he even looked like he was going to a ball game. It was a respectable enough look for every day, but in this instance, a pair of dress pants and a solid-colored shirt would have been the better choice for meeting with a Talbot.

But at least his thick beard was filling in nicely and his hair was perfectly scrunched so that it was almost curly. His tan wasn't quite as dark as I'd hoped, but he definitely didn't look anything like the man on the WANTED posters.

Moments later the massive wrought-iron gates with their gold T insignias began to creak open.

"Ready?" he asked.

I gave myself a quick once-over. Black blazer over a red and black print top, with black pants, shiny black flats, and my hair fastened into a loose bun. I pulled down the visor to check my lipstick, flipped it back up again, and took a deep breath. "Ready."

I drove through the gates and up a long, curving drive lined with beautiful old Sequoia trees, making the grand reveal of the mansion even more impressive. As I pulled up to the portico, with its thick white columns, a young man in a gray zip-front jacket and white pants stepped forward and held out a hand to help me from the vehicle. "Your keys, please, miss," he said.

"Wow, a valet even," Case said, as we watched the Toyota disappear around the back of the mansion.

Another man dressed in a slim-fitting black suit admitted us into the grand foyer, a two-story entrance with a black marble floor, winding marble staircase, and the largest crystal chandelier I'd ever seen hanging from a domed ceiling far above us.

"So this is what a mogul's home looks like," Case said quietly.

"When you enter through the front door."

"Ha. Very funny."

A set of French doors on our right opened and a stocky, forty-something blond-haired man dressed in a navy blazer and tan pants stepped out and came to meet us. Looking like he'd be more comfortable with a surfboard under his arm, he informed us that Mr. Talbot would see me in a few minutes. Then, with a scowl, he gave Case a thorough once-over. "You'll have to wait outside. We were expecting Miss Spencer to come alone."

"Seems rather presumptuous of you to expect a young woman to enter a strange home unaccompanied," Case said.

"And you are?" he asked.

"Dimitrius Costas," Case said, giving him a hearty handshake. "Who are you?"

"Thaddeus Eastgate, one of Mr. Talbot's attorneys," he said, as though this were a magical title, "and you needn't worry about Miss Spencer. We'll take good care of her. In the meantime"—he pointed to a wide opening on the left side of the foyer, where I could see a curved, white leather bar with matching white leather stools—"I think you'll find the bar a very comfortable place to wait."

"Would you explain why he can't come with me?" I asked, standing close beside Case.

"Because this is a private meeting," Thaddeus said stiffly.

"But *you'll* be there, right?" Case asked.

"Of course. I'm Mr. Talbot's legal advisor."

"And I'm Miss Spencer's legal advisor."

I caught myself before I gave Case a surprised glance. There went the story we'd crafted.

"Then I'm assuming you have a law degree," Thaddeus said with a smug smile.

"I'm assuming you have one, too," Case said.

Thaddeus's gaze swept down Case's casual outfit. "May I see your State Bar Association card, please?"

"You show me yours and I'll show you mine."

Thaddeus immediately retrieved his wallet from his back pocket, slipped out a card, and showed it to us.

Case patted his jean pockets, and said, "I seem to have left my wallet at home."

"Isn't that convenient?" Thaddeus said sarcastically. "Well, Mr. Costas, unless you can prove you have the credentials to represent her, you'll have to remain outside. So please have a seat at the bar."

I glanced at Case in dismay.

"Okay, look," Case said, an angry note in his voice I hadn't heard before, "I'm here to support my cousin because she doesn't feel comfortable walking into that meeting alone against Mr. Talbot and his legal team. So you tell your boss that if he wants to have this meeting, he's going to have it with both of us. And I suggest you let him know right now that we're ready to see him or we are walking out of here and heading straight for the local newspaper office."

I gazed at Case with new appreciation and stood up straighter beside him.

"Well, hello," I heard, and glanced over my right shoulder to see Lila Talbot descending the spiral staircase, her blond ponytail swinging girlishly, showing off enormous black diamond teardrop earrings. A former Miss Sequoia beauty pageant winner, the forty-year-old had on a black yoga top that barely covered her lacy black bra, tight-fitting leopard-print stretch pants that showed off her toned curves, and gold thong sandals that glittered under the light of the chandelier.

She walked up to us and held out her hand to Case. "I'm Lila Talbot. And you are?"

"Dimitrius Costas," he said, flashing his dimpled smile as he took her hand.

"It's a pleasure to meet you, Dimitri," she said in a sultry voice, putting her other hand on top of his almost as though she were claiming him.

"I'm Athena Spencer, by the way," I said, and held out my hand so she'd have to let go of Case's.

She did let go but she didn't shake mine. "Oh, right, you're the yoga instructor's sister." With a dismissive glance she turned back to Case and practically purred, "So what brings you here on a Saturday?"

"Athena has a meeting with your husband."

I glanced at Case in surprise. *Athena* has a meeting? Hello?

Lila's catlike eyes lit up. "And that leaves you with nothing to do but come have a cocktail with me."

I smelled a setup. "Actually, Lila," I said, "that meeting is with both of us. And don't you think it's a little early to be drinking?"

She threaded her arm through Case's and led him toward the bar, calling back, "It's never too early for a mimosa, darling. Come, Dimitrius, I'll show you what I have to offer."

I stood there with my mouth open as they walked away.

"Miss Spencer," I heard, and turned to see Thaddeus standing in the office doorway. "Mr. Talbot will see you now."

As I looked back at Case in shock, I could hear Lila say, "Dimitrius sounds so formal. Do you go by anything else?"

"Why don't you just call me Dimitri?"

That rat! He had deserted me without so much as a backward glance in my direction. Now what was I going to do? Our whole plan revolved around him handling the tough questions.

"Miss Spencer?" Thaddeus said again.

I drew in a deep breath and let it out. I couldn't very well leave now.

And with that the French doors closed behind me.

* * *

I found myself in a big conference room with walls covered in cherry paneling and framed opera posters. A long cherry table sat on a black, burgundy, and tan oriental carpet in the middle of the room, surrounded by at least a dozen burgundy-colored leather chairs.

Sonny, seated at the head of the table, stood up to greet me, making me come to him instead of the other way around, no doubt his way of taking the upper hand. He was wearing a gray plaid vest over a white shirt adorned with gold and diamond cufflinks, and gray pants, looking every inch the slick multimillionaire he had become. His brown hair had some gray at the temples, but otherwise the fifty-nine-year-old could easily have passed for forty-five. He was trim, tanned, and freshly shaved, his skin as smooth as mine.

"Miss Spencer," he said, shaking my hand. "A pleasure to see you again."

"Mr. Talbot," I said.

"Just Grayson, please," he replied with a smile. He was being extremely gracious, more so than he had been at the press conference.

He turned to Thaddeus on his right and placed his hand on his shoulder. "You've met Thad already, so I'll skip the introductions there." He turned to a twenty-something, skinny, brown-haired, twitchy sort of man on his left. "This is my assistant, Dale Pinkus, who'll be taking notes. He can provide you with a transcript if you'd like."

"Thanks, but I've brought my own notepad," I said.

Sonny indicated the chair to his left. "Please have a seat."

I was surprised he didn't have his other attorney

there to make it three against one. But perhaps Sonny didn't consider this meeting a threat, which was a benefit to me because I was already starting to feel my insides shake, especially without Case there to back me up.

Buck up, Athena. You've handled interviews for a major Chicago newspaper. You can do this, too.

"Can I offer you anything to drink?" Pinkus asked. "Coffee, tea, a cocktail?"

"I'll have a glass of water, please."

As I took out my iPad, Pinkus hurried to a low cherry console that served as a bar, opened a built-in fridge, filled a crystal glass from a water bottle, and placed it in front of me. "Mr. Talbot, sir?"

"Nothing for me, Dale. Thank you." Sonny waited until his assistant was seated beside Thad, at Sonny's right, then said to me, "Let me begin by stating why I invited you here. Certainly, we have our differences of opinion on the downtown condominium complex, but after you hear what I have planned, we can work through them in a way that will benefit both of us."

"Both of us? I'm here to represent the shop owners, not myself."

"Please let me finish," he said. "The Downtown Merchants Association is a pivotal and powerful force in this community, so when one of its members tosses out derogatory comments about a project designed to—"

"Excuse me?" I said, my back stiffening in anger. "Are you referring to my comment?"

Sonny made a temple of his fingers. "Yes, Miss Spencer, I was, and I hadn't finished speaking."

"First of all, Mr. Talbot, I represent the Greek Merchants Association, which is an off-shoot of the Downtown Merchants Association. Secondly, the Downtown Merchants are in complete agreement with our position, and thirdly, there was nothing derogatory about me reminding everyone about the agreement your father and the GMA reached to cancel the project."

"Please let me finish, Miss Spencer, then you may have your say."

I took a deep breath and sat back, unclenching my fists beneath the table. If I was going to get anywhere with this man I had to calm down and pull up my professional self. "I apologize for the interruption," I said. "Please continue."

Sonny straightened his tie. "Getting back to what I was saying, when adverse comments about our project interrupted the press conference, along with questions about my father's death, which, by the way, have no bearing on the project—"

"No *bearing* on the project?" I sputtered, my journalistic professionalism flying out the window. "Your father's death certainly *did* have a bearing on the project because he'd made an agreement to *cancel* it, which he signed in front of witnesses."

Sonny folded his hands and placed them on the table, taking a long time to answer as though trying to control his temper. "Sadly, Miss Spencer, you and the others heard what you wanted to hear, an old man trying to pacify your committee in any way he could while continuing forward with his plans. And as I stated at the press conference, my father was as committed to this project as I am."

"What about the document he signed?"

"Yes, what *about* that?" he asked coyly. "Why do you suppose he took it with him?"

"I was told he wanted to prepare it for filing with the court."

Sonny leaned back, his elbows on the arms of his

chair, looking very smug. "Unfortunately, Miss Spencer, I haven't seen the agreement since that meeting. That makes it your association's word against the Talbot Corporation's."

That was the moment I realized he had me over a barrel. We had no document to back up what Talbot Sr. had promised. Another thought flickered through my mind, but before I could follow it, Sonny broke into my thoughts.

"Now," he said, "*if* you will abandon any plans you have to file that court injunction, which, by the way, will merely delay the project and cost your GMA a lot of money, I firmly believe we can put aside all this bad blood between us and come to a mutual understanding that will benefit the entire town."

The court injunction. Had Sonny suggested we meet in private so he could sway me to drop it? Costly or not, it had to be a hitch in his plans or he wouldn't have brought it up. I smiled to myself. Maybe he didn't have me over that proverbial barrel after all.

"Explain something to me," I said. "How will your project benefit Sequoia if you demolish an entire block of shops and restaurants that are popular with tourists to build a giant condominium complex for some up-scale tenants who *won't* be spending their money at the tourist shops? And by the way, The Parthenon, the diner that's been owned by my grandparents for thirty-five years, is on that block, so don't think I won't fight this with every resource I have."

"You're not getting the picture, Miss Spencer," he said. "My project *will* benefit the town—or at least those *in* town who choose to be a part of it. So if you'll give me a chance to explain exactly what those benefits will mean to you"—he made a show of studying his fingernails—"I think you might come around to a new appreciation of the project."

I pressed my lips into a hard line, wishing I didn't have to answer. "Go ahead."

"The entire first floor of this deluxe building will be open to the tenants that I hand select. What if I were to offer your grandparents prime space for a brand-new family restaurant, with a big, modern kitchen, plenty of room for tables, an area for outside dining, and a budget big enough to allow them to decorate it in any way they choose—within our guidelines of course?"

His words echoed inside my brain: new diner, modern kitchen, as much money to decorate as they needed . . . I could see it all. I could also imagine the sheer rapture on my grandparents' faces, and for a brief moment I even found myself considering it for their sakes. But a hand-selected few? How could I sell out on the others?

"That still leaves them without an apartment and a lot of shop owners out in the cold," I said.

"Forget the other owners for the moment and picture this." Sonny held his hands as though to frame imaginary windows. "A twenty-four-hundred-square-foot corner condominium overlooking the lake. In fact, make that the top-floor unit, with a balcony. And it's just one elevator ride down to their main-floor diner."

I could indeed picture my elderly grandparents, who'd scraped to get by their whole lives, living in grand style, with comforts they couldn't begin to imagine and had never before experienced—or expected to. Sonny had no idea how tempting it sounded to be able to give Yiayiá and Pappoús such a golden opportunity.

"What do you think, Miss Spencer?"

"That they'd never be able to afford a place like you're describing."

"Ah, but that's where you come in, my dear." He leaned toward me on one elbow and pointed his index finger at me. "You, Athena Spencer, can make that happen, and all it will take is one nod of your head."

Chapter Eighteen

Sonny leaned back, his smug smile in place, thinking he'd won me over, so I decided to play along. "What would that nod mean?"

"That your family would get everything I promised, and in return, you'd convince the GMA to drop the idea of a court injunction."

Then I was right after all; his game was bribery. But I could play that game, too. "I'll need a few moments to think it over."

"Take your time."

I took my glass of water over to the window and sipped it, gazing out at the mansion's rolling green lawn, letting him think I was seriously considering his offer. From the corner of my eye I caught Sonny giving Thaddeus a quick thumbs-up.

Okay, Athena, you've got them right where you want them. Now's the time to strike back. Athena Spencer, big-city journalist, was coming to life.

"All right," I said, returning to my chair, "here's what

I propose. I'll do my best to convince the others in the association to hold off on filing that injunction—"

"Great," Sonny said with a pleased smile. "Then we have a deal."

"You didn't let me finish."

"I'm sorry, go ahead," he said, obviously taken aback.

I placed my hands on the table and leaned toward him. "I want you to give the other shop owners the same deal you're offering my grandparents—shop space and a condo unit at a very reasonable rate." I knew no one would go along with it. Not only did most of the owners have their own houses, but they were adamant about saving Little Greece. Still, it was satisfying to see how far Sonny was willing to go to get his deal.

Thaddeus gave him a subtle "no."

"We can accommodate both requests only if the other shop owners can afford the rent," Sonny said.

"That's why I said I wanted them to have the *same* deal you're giving my grandparents."

"Not possible," Thaddeus said. "They will certainly be welcome to talk to a sales associate once the building is under construction. And I know some of them own houses, so they wouldn't even need a condo, which renders your proposal ridiculous. Therefore, I'm asking you flat out, are you prepared for a court battle?"

I shrugged. "Are *you* prepared for a court battle?"

Sonny's hand fell flat on the table. "I don't get it, Miss Spencer. Don Fatsis is already on board. He even signed a lease for his new space. So why turn down this golden opportunity for your grandparents in order to fight what's going to happen anyway?"

That rat Fatsis had cut a deal with Talbot and hadn't mentioned a word to us about it. Was that why he was at the Talbot headquarters before the press conference?

"What do you say?" Sonny asked. "Are you going to take care of your grandparents or are you going to empty the bank accounts of your fellow GMA members to fight the Talbot Corporation?"

"I'll need a few moments to consider it."

I could tell by the tensing of Sonny's eyebrows that he was losing patience. After a quick conference with his attorney, he leaned forward, all business now. "Okay, what else do you want?"

"The answers to a few questions that were raised at the press conference."

Sonny rubbed his forehead as though it were aching. "I don't remember what was asked. I fielded a lot of questions that morning."

"Just tell me whether you're open to answering some questions raised at the conference."

He consulted with Thaddeus again, at which point the attorney said, "Our answer is yes, but my client reserves the right to decline to answer certain questions."

That was lawyer mumbo-jumbo for *maybe so, maybe not.*

I took a deep breath and referred to my notes. Now that I had to bring up the murder, I was starting to lose my nerve again. Damn Case for abandoning me!

Okay, Athena, become the warrior goddess. I tucked my trembling fingers beneath my legs so he couldn't see them and said boldly, "If you reserve the right to decline to answer certain questions, then I reserve the right to decline the deal."

Thaddeus started to whisper something, but Sonny pushed him away. "Damn it, Spencer, ask your questions then. I want this meeting over with."

The nerves in my stomach were fluttering so hard it took all my willpower to stick with it. This was where

Case was supposed to take over, get tough, and get answers but, thanks to that turncoat, it was all up to me now.

"Why wasn't an autopsy performed on your father?"

"*That* again," Sonny said, giving me a disgusted look. "I suggest you take it up with the coroner."

"I did, and Dr. Kirkland said you declined to have one done." Which was not what Kirkland had said, but I wasn't about to let Sonny evade the question again.

Thaddeus said something in a whisper, then Sonny said, "Okay, fine. Here's my answer." As though he had the lines memorized, he said, "Kirkland made it clear that my father had fallen asleep, slipped under the bathwater, and drowned. It was as simple as that. Therefore, I chose not to ask for an autopsy because I took the coroner's word that there was no need for one."

"So, basically, Kirkland let you have the final say."

Thaddeus said instantly, "We decline to answer that."

Fantastic! I'd just gotten Sonny to admit he'd swayed Kirkland's decision. As I typed his answer I thought, *Too bad I don't have a witness.* Clearly, Miss Leopard Skin Pants was more important than my concerns were.

Reading from my notes I said, "Then the coroner went along with your decision even though the law clearly states, and I quote, 'in a case of death when no one is present, an autopsy must be performed.' " I glanced at Thaddeus. "Isn't that right?"

The attorney blinked at me with wide eyes, clearly caught off guard. After a hasty conference with his boss, Thaddeus said, "Yes, in certain situations."

"In *certain* situations?" I repeated, making sure Thaddeus understood that I knew he was dodging the truth. "I would think that law would apply to *any* situation that met the criteria, especially given Grayson Talbot Senior's standing in the community." Turning back to Sonny I drove home my point. "What you're saying is that Kirkland broke the law for you."

Neither of them said a word. Pincus's fingers halted on his keypad.

I smiled to myself. Who had whom over that old barrel now?

"Without an autopsy," I asked, "how would you know your father's death wasn't caused by a heart attack or a stroke"—I was going full steam now—"or someone wanting to do him harm?"

Sonny's eyes turned ice cold, matching his voice. "The fact of the matter is that he drowned, and we had to deal with it."

"Very quickly, too, I noticed. If he were my father, I'd have demanded answers to assure myself that he died of natural causes instead of rushing to have him buried."

"I didn't rush—"

"Seriously, didn't you even *wonder* if there was a possibility of foul play?"

"Of *course,* I wondered, but my wife—"

"We're going to decline to answer that," Thaddeus said, cutting him off.

Sonny banged the table with his fist. "Would someone let me finish a sentence, for God's sake?"

No one said a word until Sonny said, "I didn't rush to have him buried. He wasn't in any condition to wait around after soaking in a tub all night."

"Then you held the estate sale what, two days later?" I asked, watching Sonny's face get redder and redder. "What was your hurry?"

Thaddeus said, "We're done here. Mr. Talbot has another meeting to attend."

Sonny put his hand on Thaddeus's arm. "Hold on, Thad. Let's not be too hasty. Remember, we're trying to cut a deal. Yes, I did wonder about my father's death until the coroner put my mind at ease. As for the estate sale, that was in Harry's hands. It was his decision when to hold it."

And naturally Harry wasn't there to defend himself.

"In all honesty, Miss Spencer, my wife was the last one to see my father alive and the first to find him dead, and that does make one wonder at times."

Now he was being honest? He'd just thrown his wife under the bus. "Are you saying it's possible your wife had something to do with your father's death?"

Thaddeus jumped up. "My client will *not* answer that question."

Sonny glanced at his watch, and I could see a tiny smile playing at one corner of his mouth. That his wife had something to do with his father's death was exactly what he was saying, and what he wanted me to believe.

"Mr. Talbot," Pinkus said, "we need to cut this short."

"Just five more minutes," I said, "and this is about Harry Pepper's death. Do you remember who Kirkland and the responding police officer interviewed at the scene?"

Before Sonny could respond, Thaddeus said, "Mr. Talbot agreed to answer your question about his father's death, not about Mr. Pepper's."

"Actually, when your boss announced that he was having a press conference he promised to address Harry Pepper's death, which he failed to do, and afterward he promised to answer my *questions*, not question. And one more thing, I didn't put any qualifications on what those questions were. Perhaps Mr. Pinkus can read that back from his press conference notes."

I was on *fire* again!

"It's all right, Thad, I'll answer them," Sonny said. "Five people were interviewed. Me, my wife, the housekeeper, the gardener, and Thad. And in anticipation of your next question, both Dr. Kirkland and the detectives agreed Harry's death occurred as a direct result of a *home invasion.* Someone broke in looking for something and murdered Harry after finding it or when he couldn't find it. Now that someone has a name and a face, he will be found and prosecuted."

The guilty party would be found and prosecuted all right. "In one newspaper account," I said, "you were quoted as saying that the safe in your father's office had been opened. Was anything taken?"

"It held many documents, Miss Spencer. It'll be months before I can answer that."

"What do you think the killer was looking for?"

"I don't know. I'm leaving it for the detectives to solve."

I glanced down at my list. "Grayson, why did you give the newspaper two different accounts of finding Harry's body?"

The attorney started to protest but again Sonny restrained him. "I withheld information to protect my wife from being considered a suspect because her discovering both bodies might have seemed suspicious. It wasn't until sometime after the first newspaper article came out that Lila told me I had the position of Harry's body wrong, so I corrected it in the second one."

"Why did she get it wrong the first time?"

His hand tightened around his pen, his knuckles turning white. He really wanted to make a deal with me or he'd never put up with all these questions.

"Because she was nervous. She said the first thing that came to mind."

"And the first thing was that he was slumped over the desk. Then later he was on his back on the floor with a receipt in his hand. That's quite a difference."

Sonny tilted back on two legs of his chair, his hands on the arms. "That's my wife for you."

It was odd that the first version of Harry's discovery happened to be the way Case remembered finding him. "How did you explain your mistake to the investigators?"

He sighed sharply. "I told them the truth, that finding both bodies was too much for Lila's mind, which was fragile already and became more so because of the way my father emotionally abused her." Sonny looked toward the window, shaking his head sorrowfully. "I'll forever blame myself for not putting a stop to it. But he had us both on tight leashes."

Sonny on a leash? Lila fragile? I wanted to laugh. Clearly, Sonny could tell the detectives anything and they'd accept it because of who he was.

Sonny sighed as though the weight of the world rested on his shoulders. "She's under a doctor's care now. She suffered greatly because of my father's disdain for her, so naturally his death affected her in several ways, one of which was relief. And then for her to discover Harry's body? What are the odds of her finding both men dead? That could have sent her over the edge."

I studied Sonny for a moment. What *were* the odds? Perhaps he'd wanted to send her over the edge to get rid of her. And why wasn't I buying his grief-stricken act? I'd seen Lila with my own eyes and if she was under a doctor's care, it was probably a plastic surgeon's. I had a feeling Sonny's act was more about wanting me to connect the dots between his wife and the murders than to feel any pity for her.

"Where were you when Harry's body was discovered?"

Sonny's hand came down hard on the table, making

me jump. "Enough about the murders. Are we here to talk about a deal or are you here to poke into things that are none of your business?"

"If you want me to cut a deal with you, Grayson, then I need to be able to go back to the GMA and say in all honesty that I trust you to be fair with them, and so far, you haven't given me that assurance."

He glanced at the expensive gold watch on his wrist, then pushed back his chair and stood up. "You know what? I'm done trying to placate you and your greedy Greek friends. The deal is for your grandparents alone, not for the entire block of shop owners. Now you've got five minutes to decide their fate." Starting toward the French doors he called, "Thaddeus, come get me when you have her answer."

He was calling *my* family greedy? "I'll give you my answer right now," I said, halting him before he reached the door. "The deal is dead."

CHAPTER NINETEEN

Rising, I slid my iPad into my purse, put the strap over my shoulder, and walked past him into the grand foyer.

I heard the French doors slam behind me and only then did I let out my breath. My legs were shaking so hard I thought I'd have to sit on the steps so I didn't faint, but then I saw Case perched on a barstool and forced myself to keep going across the marble floor toward the bar. It was only when I reached his side that I sagged onto the closest stool and put my face in my hands, so relieved it was over that I wanted to either cry or punch him.

"Are you okay?" he asked, putting his arm around my shoulders.

I jerked away and gave him a glare. "No, I'm not okay, and thanks for deserting me."

"What you need is a mimosa to calm you down." He hopped off his stool and went around behind the bar as though he owned it.

I needed to calm down all right. I slid off the stool and marched out of the room, pushing my purse strap back onto my shoulder.

Case caught up with me as I waited for the valet to bring up my car. "Athena, I'm sorry about what happened."

"Yeah, right."

"We need to talk."

I was too upset to speak, so I said nothing. When the car came around, I got behind the wheel and Case slid into the passenger side.

"Let me explain," he said.

I started the engine. "Go right ahead. I'm dying to hear why the meeting that we were supposed to attend together suddenly became all mine. Oh, wait. I know the answer. Lila showed up." I put the Toyota in gear and stepped on the gas. "So much for your big show of not wanting me to go up against the Talbot team alone."

I said nothing as I drove through the open gates, leaving Case to sit in silence and ponder his actions. There was simply no excuse for him to abandon me the moment the sexy heiress stepped into the room. I turned onto the main road, not knowing exactly where I was going. But the fact was that we *did* need to talk, and I certainly wasn't going back to the boat and take a chance of being seen with him.

"I'm sorry," Case finally said. "I made a quick decision and that wasn't fair to you."

"You deserted me to go with Lila without even a second thought. Would you have been in such a hurry to leave if one of Sonny's butlers had offered you a drink?"

He gave me an incredulous glance. "Is that why you're angry? Because Lila offered me a drink? You wouldn't be jealous of Lila, would you?"

He caught me so off guard I almost swerved into the

oncoming lane. Jealous of Lila? Was that how I was coming across?

"I have a boyfriend, remember? And Lila's a married woman, in case you've forgotten." I stopped for a traffic light, my head throbbing with tension from the grueling session with Sonny. "You have some nerve making up an excuse for your behavior. I needed you there and you were sitting at their bar sipping a mimosa."

"Athena," he said gently, "I knew I wasn't going to get anywhere with Junior Attorney, so when Lila showed up, I decided to make the best of a bad situation and try to get information from her. We needed to question her anyway. And guess what? I got some very useful information. So can we please go somewhere quiet to discuss it? I'm sure you've got things to share, too."

I said nothing for a long moment. Now that my nerves were calming from too much adrenaline in my system, I could see that he was right about Sonny's attorney. With Thaddeus standing guard, Case wouldn't have gotten through the conference room door. Maybe he'd made the best decision after all.

"I'm sorry, too," I said begrudgingly. "I shouldn't have snapped at you. You're right. You wouldn't have gotten into the meeting."

"Why don't we stop somewhere out of town and have lunch? We can discuss everything then. Oh, wait. I forgot. You wanted to take Nick to the Tulip Festival."

"But so did Selene and Maia, and they wanted to get an early start to beat the crowds, so Nicholas—Nick—went with them. He loves being with them."

I thought for a moment. "I know a diner about thirty miles east of here where we can talk in private."

"A diner? After what you went through? Why don't we go somewhere nice, somewhere we can have an expensive glass of wine and a good meal?"

Before I could even think of a nice restaurant out of town, he added, "My treat."

"You don't have any money," I said.

"Damn. Then you decide."

"There's a nice restaurant outside of town in the other direction that should be pretty empty today."

"Let's do it."

I adjusted the rearview mirror and merged onto the interstate. Twenty minutes later I pulled into a Hilton Garden Inn and parked by the restaurant attached to it. We asked for a quiet table at the back and were seated at one tucked well behind the bar area. As I predicted, the restaurant was nearly empty. Only the bar was full.

Feeling unusually hungry, no doubt because of the meeting, I ordered a glass of cabernet and an open-faced roast beef sandwich and mashed potatoes smothered in gravy. Case ordered a ham and sharp cheddar cheese sandwich, fries, and a beer.

While we waited for our food to arrive, I pulled out my iPad and went over my meeting with Sonny. "And guess who else Sonny offered this golden opportunity to? Don Fatsis, who accepted it without ever saying a word to us about it, the fathead. But I'll come back to him later. Anyway, I couldn't persuade Sonny to offer the same deal to the other merchants, so I ended the meeting, but not before I got some information from him about the murders."

"Did you learn why the coroner didn't do the autopsy?" Case asked, as the waiter delivered our drinks.

"Sonny said he chose not to ask for one because Kirkland assured him there was no need for it. After I pushed him a little, I got Sonny to admit he'd influenced Kirkland's decision."

Case raised his hand to give me a high five. "Major victory."

"Not quite. The only witnesses to his admission besides me were his own employees."

Case lowered his hand. "Again, Athena, I wish I could've been in there with you."

"Me, too. Anyway, in my mind there's only one reason for Sonny to sway Kirkland away from doing an autopsy. He didn't want the truth about his father's death to get out."

The waiter chose that moment to deliver our food, and after he gave me an odd look, I had to remind myself to keep my voice down. I was so hungry I took a bite of roast beef before continuing. "When I asked Sonny why he changed his story twice about finding Harry's body, he changed it again. Now he says that *Lila* found Harry, not him, but since she'd also found his father, he told the investigators a lie to protect her, fearing that finding both bodies would make her look suspicious."

"Did you ask why Lila had given two versions of finding the body?"

"Yep. He said finding both bodies had been too much for her fragile mind. Apparently, that caused her to forget how she found Harry's dead body."

"Fragile mind?" Case laughed. "Tough as nails would be a better description of Lila. If he's trying to protect her, why is he sharing such private information with you? Did he think that would make you want to cut a deal with him? Didn't he realize you would tell others in the Greek community? Or is he trying to create a division in your group by singling out a few for his special offer?"

"That's why I wanted you there, Case, to ask those kinds of questions. I was so surprised by what he was saying that I couldn't think of everything."

"Athena, you didn't really need me there. You did an excellent job. You got the information you needed."

I couldn't help but smile. "I did, didn't I?" I paused for another bite. "I still can't decide what Sonny's agenda is. If Lila really is responsible for the deaths of either or both men, why is he claiming to protect her while undermining her at the same time?"

"Lila had a different account of Harry's death." He paused for a bite of his sandwich, then washed it down with a drink of beer. "She said she was about to leave for her ten-thirty yoga class when Sonny texted her to check on Harry, his reason being that he was tied up in a meeting in his home office. Lila found it odd because he usually holds meetings at their corporate headquarters. But she was on her way downstairs to leave anyway so she gave him the benefit of the doubt and obliged him.

"Here's where the twist comes in," he said. "On her way to check on Harry, Lila peeked into her husband's conference room and no one was there. That was her first clue that something was amiss."

"Was she certain that Sonny had texted from home?"

"After she'd called the police, lo and behold, there was her husband coming down the staircase dressed for a golf outing. That was when she decided that he'd set her up to find Harry's body, just like he'd done with his father's body."

I smacked my hand on the table. "I *knew* he wanted me to connect Lila to both deaths. I really don't understand why she didn't tell Sonny to go check on his father himself. After all, he was Sonny's father, just as Harry was his employee, not hers."

"I asked her, but she was being very manipulative with the information she was sharing with me, implying that he wants the estate to himself."

"But why would Sonny need to frame Lila for murder? If he wants the estate to himself, all he has to do is divorce her."

"Unless she has some dirt on him," Case said.

"That's a possibility." I took a moment to enjoy a bite of mashed potatoes and gravy. "On the other hand, if Lila has enough evidence on Sonny, he could go to jail and she'll get to live in the mansion and enjoy all the perks of being a Talbot."

"He could still divorce her from jail."

I sighed. "True again. And he probably would unless, as you say, she has some dirt on him. In fact, given who he is, she's bound to have something to hold over him. If I were her, I'd be looking over my shoulder."

"Lila also offered up the information that only her father-in-law, Sonny, and Harry knew the combination to the safe, and that Sonny could have rifled through the safe to make Harry's murder look like a robbery gone bad."

I stared at Case in awe. "You really did get some good information from her."

"I told you so."

"So she's pushing Sonny forward as the killer and he's doing the same to her."

"Yep. And when I suggested that perhaps someone else had gotten into the office and forced Harry to open the safe, she scoffed. Then she downed her mimosa and said she had to leave for her yoga class."

"Obviously she wants you to think that Sonny is the killer."

"It would help to know what the detectives found when they entered the office," Case said. "If Harry was on the floor, then someone moved the body. I'd like to ask Kirkland, but I highly doubt he'll see us again."

"But I know a cop on the police force who I might be able to persuade to give me more details."

"He's not one of the cops who searched the boat, is he?"

"Well, yes, he is, but we were friends in high school and I *think* he has a crush on Delphi, so maybe he'll talk to me. Also, my sister Maia teaches Lila's yoga class, so I can check to see if Lila made it to yoga the morning Harry was murdered. It would be pretty cold-blooded of her to kill someone, then show up for yoga."

"On the other hand, it could help make Lila look innocent." Case scratched his ear. "After talking to her it was clear that she had a grudge against her father-in-law, so she does have a motive. What we still need is a motive for her to kill Harry."

I rubbed my temples. "This is getting convoluted, Case. Right now, it seems like Sonny and Lila are pointing fingers at each other and maybe neither one had anything to do with the deaths. Maybe we should focus on our other suspect, Donald Fatsis."

"Remind me again how he fits into the picture."

"He owns the art gallery on the block to be demolished"—I lifted my wineglass but set it back down again as a light went on in my head—"and *now* I understand why Don wanted to be our spokesman for the condo project. He didn't want anyone to know he was working with Sonny. And get this. My father told me that Fatsis had been dealing privately with old man Talbot right up until his death. So when Talbot Senior canceled the project, Fatsis must have been furious."

I started thinking out loud. "Knowing that Sonny wanted to go forward with the project, Fatsis might have wanted to get rid of Talbot Senior and befriend Talbot Junior to cut a deal."

"How does that help us solve Harry Pepper's murder"—Case itched his stubbly chin—"because my being at the top of the Most Wanted list is getting as old as this beard."

"If Harry was in charge of Talbot's affairs, he surely

would have known where that signed agreement was. Maybe Fatsis went there after it and ended up fighting with Harry. Fatsis is a huge guy. Poor little Harry wouldn't have stood a chance against him. And by the way, I like your beard."

"You do?" He smiled, his gaze meeting mine.

Feeling a blush starting, I quickly switched to the topic at hand. "We have to consider Fatsis a strong suspect in both murders because he knows how to get to Talbot's suite without being seen, where his office is, and when Harry would've been there."

"Then let's talk to him next," Case suggested. "And you know what just hit me? Sonny gave you all that information in a private meeting while Lila was doing the same with me. It could be that they're in on this together and are playing us."

"I thought that at first, but there was no way they could've known that you would come with me to that meeting."

"Good point."

I glanced around as I took a drink of wine and then nearly choked. "Case, look over your right shoulder."

He turned toward the bar.

"See the white-haired woman in the black dress and strappy red shoes? She's the one talking to the man in the navy suit sitting on the stool beside her."

"Talking to him? She's almost sitting in his lap. Who is she?"

"Marie Odem. She owns the resale shop where the condominium parking lot is supposed to go. Do you remember her from the press conference?"

"Isn't she the one who threw a fit about Sonny breaking his promise to her?"

"Which he denied doing," I said. "Yes, that's Marie, and boy, is she dressed to kill, pardon the pun. She's the last person I'd have expected to see here, especially at the bar sloppy drunk. She's practically sliding off her stool."

I finished my meal and wiped my fingers on my napkin, thinking over what had transpired at the press conference. "Remember Marie yelling to Sonny 'Don't think you'll get away with this. Your father made that mistake.' That sounded like she was threatening Sonny."

"With murder?"

"Why not?"

Case glanced over at her again. "Athena, look at her and tell me you believe that scrawny older woman could have caused a smart man like Talbot to drown."

"She might be scrawny, but she's wily and she attended those private dinners, too."

"She'd get further with a lawsuit."

"Stop being so cynical and just listen. Marie was having an affair with Talbot Senior, with designs on marrying him until she gossiped about it. He found out and made it publicly known that she meant nothing to him, which ended her plans abruptly. That doesn't mean she couldn't have gone back one evening to have a glass of wine for old time's sake."

"And then did what, watched him take a bath and pushed him under?"

"Yes! And suffocating Harry is something a woman could do, too."

"I don't think Marie's strong enough to smother a man, even a small man like Harry. He'd fight back. And what would her motive be?"

"Harry might have known she was there the night Talbot Senior died."

Case leaned closer and said quietly, "Tell you what. Let's invite Marie over for a drink and see what we can get her to tell us about Harry. Maybe she'll reveal something."

"I don't know if we'll get anything useful. She's had a few too many drinks already."

"Exactly why it's the perfect time to talk to her. She's drunk, and there's no one around to overhear us."

"But then she'll see me with you, and it'll get back to Kevin or someone in my family and I'll have a mess on my hands."

"Chicken."

I took a sip of wine. "I'm okay with that."

"Come on, Athena, we've got a believable story concocted about being distantly related. Just stick to that and we'll be fine—if she even remembers any of it tomorrow."

I twisted a lock of my hair. "I can already hear my mother's fingers on the computer doing an ancestry hunt."

"You worry too much. I'll bet there's a Dimitrius out there somewhere in your family tree."

"It *is* a common Greek name. But I still think it'd be better for me to talk to Marie alone. If you insist on having it *your* way, however, *you* go invite her over."

"She doesn't know me."

"But she does love to flirt. And you can use your charms on her just like you did on Lila."

He gave me his dimpled smile. "Promise you won't get jealous this time?"

"I was *not* jealous of Lila." When he smiled again, I said, "Just shut up and go."

CHAPTER TWENTY

"Marie," I said, rising from the booth as Case ushered her over, "I'm so glad you could join us."

She looked puzzled for a moment, then pointed a skinny finger at me. "Athena Spencer."

"Right."

Steadying herself on the back of a chair she pointed from me to Case. "You and Dimitrius are—?"

"Distant cousins," Case said. "Please have a seat."

Marie gazed at him as though he were dessert. "I suppose I could join you for one quick drink."

"There's no such thing as one *quick* drink," Case said. "Not in the company of such beautiful women." Case held her arm to support her as she wobbled down onto the plump leather seat across from me. "What would you like, Marie?"

She covered her mouth to hide a hiccup. "Another Bloody Mary, please."

"Nothing for me," I said. "I'm still working on my wine."

Marie turned to watch him walk over to the bar. "Dimitrius is quite the charmer."

"Yes," I said, glancing over at him, "he is that."

She propped her elbows on the table and set her chin in her hands, gazing at Case with unfocused eyes. "I can see a resemblance to him on your mother's side—those dark good looks and curly hair." She heaved a pitiful sigh as she turned her bleary gaze back on me. "Poor dear, you really are the odd duck of the family, aren't you?"

"Excuse me?"

"Drinks should be up in a minute," Case said, sliding onto the seat beside me.

"Tell me more about you, Dimitrius," Marie said, fluttering her eyelashes at him.

"I came up from Tarpon Springs to work on my novel, and my cousin here"—he put his arm around my shoulders—"is giving me a tour of the town."

I glanced at Case. "That reminds me. We promised to be back in time to meet Kevin for dinner, so we have to keep an eye on the time." Ignoring the perplexed look on Case's face I turned back to Marie. "Dimitrius and Kevin have really hit it off."

"How nice." She pushed herself upright as the drinks arrived.

I smiled to myself. That should put an end to her making us a gossip item.

After she'd taken a noisy sip of her Bloody Mary, nearly jabbing herself in the eye with the celery stick, I said, "That was quite a press conference yesterday. I didn't realize your shop was going to be demolished, too. You should've brought it up at a meeting."

She set her glass down so hard her drink sloshed over the sides. "It wasn't supposed to be demolished. That's why I never said anything." She hiccupped. "That dirty liar promised me it wouldn't be touched."

"Who promised you?" I asked. "Talbot Senior or Junior?"

"Both of them." She pulled the celery out of her glass, bit into it, and chewed angrily. "I don't want to talk about either one of those liars." She tore off another bite of celery. "Men. You can't trust them." She turned her head to gaze at Case, her body swaying dizzily. "Tell me you're not like other men, Dimitrius."

"I'm not like anyone you've ever met, Marie," he replied with a smile that could melt butter, "and you can call me Dimitri."

"I know what you mean about trusting men," I said, drawing her attention back to me. "Talbot is lying about the condominium project. We're trying to find the truth."

"He lied to me, too!" She attempted to hit her fist on the table for emphasis and missed. "But I know secrets about the Talbots. He got the message. *Now* he knows you can't mess with Marie."

"What was your message?" I asked.

"Never you mind. He got it, that's all. He wouldn't dare tear down my building now." She pointed to her face. "I could see the fear in his eyes."

And I could smell the alcohol on her breath. "Maybe you can give me some tips to pass along to the others. You're aware that Talbot offered a bribe to Don Fatsis, right?"

She gave me a puzzled glance. "Gray tried to bribe Fatsis? He told me that deal was for me alone."

"Who is Gray?" Case asked.

"That was my pet name for Grayson."

I was talking about Sonny and she was talking about his father.

"Oh, Gray was a charmer," she went on. "He told me I was the one for him. I thought he meant he was going to marry me." She started to tear up. "After I told my friends and word got out—it was even printed in the paper's gossip column—he called the newspaper and told them I'd made it up and to retract it. It was retracted the very next day."

She began to weep and dug for a tissue in her purse. "I was so humiliated, I didn't want to leave my house. I couldn't eat or sleep—" She covered her face and cried harder. "I had to go on anti-depression medication."

"I'm sorry, Marie," Case said. "That must have been shattering."

"But that didn't do the trick, so the doctor ordered sleeping pills for me." She sniffled. "I was afraid to take them though, so I put them away." She lowered her voice to say, "But don't tell him. Dr. Kirkland gets very angry when I don't follow his instructions."

She had sleeping pills! I glanced at Case to see if he caught it and got a nod.

Marie blew her nose, pulled herself up, and reached for her glass. "You know what got me back on my feet? My shop. And now that damned Talbot boy wants to demolish it." After taking a long drink, she set it down hard, sloshing more over the edge, then said with a sneer, "No one messes with Marie and gets away with it. Not Gray Talbot and not his son, either."

"How about Harry?" Case asked.

Still on a rant she continued, "That Talbot boy. Now he's sorry he humiliated me in front of everyone. I still can't believe he denied meeting with me."

Humiliation was clearly the trigger that set her off.

As she finished her drink, Case said, "I keep telling Athena not to trust him. You obviously learned your lesson the hard way. How did you feel about trusting Harry?"

"I trusted Harry. He left the office doors open for me so no one would see me enter."

"When was the last time you went to see Gray?" I asked.

At that Marie seemed to pull back into herself. With a faraway look in her eyes, she said in a slurred voice, "Secrets and lies. So many secrets and lies." Her expression saddened. "Poor Harry. He was a kind man, but way too loyal to Gray. Bad things happen to people who are loyal, you know." She drifted off for a moment, then said, "Even Harry had secrets."

"Will you tell me one of his secrets?" Case asked.

Leaning toward Case again she said in a whisper that was fortunately loud enough for me to catch, "Harry wasn't supposed to tell anyone about keeping the office doors unlocked at night." She glanced over her shoulder, then added, "Not even Gray's son."

"But?" Case prompted.

She picked up her empty glass as though to take a drink, stared at it for a second, then looked around. "Do you know where the ladies' room is?"

"It's that way," I said, pointing behind me.

Case helped her out of the booth, then sat back down as Marie wobbled toward the restrooms.

"Well," I said, "what do you think of her as a suspect in both men's deaths now?"

"She certainly had the means, motive, and opportunity to kill Talbot," Case said, "but I still can't figure out a reason for her to kill Harry."

"How about this? If anyone started asking questions about Talbot's death, Harry would have told the police about Marie having access to Talbot's suite. And that would've made her a suspect."

Case sat back. "Okay, Sherlock, why would she wait two weeks to kill him?"

"She had to find the right opportunity."

Case glanced around at the door to the ladies' room. "When she returns, help me steer the conversation back to Harry."

"I'll try, but the way she staggered off, I doubt we'll get much out of her now."

Case reached for his beer glass to take a drink. "You give up too easily, Athena."

I glanced at my watch. "I really do have to get home."

"Were you serious about us meeting Kevin for dinner?"

I gave him an incredulous look. "I said that just to stop Marie from spreading gossip about us."

"Are *you* meeting him for dinner?"

"Yes," I said with a heavy sigh.

A tiny flicker of a grin appeared on one side of his mouth. "You do realize Kevin is going to find out about us sooner or later. Us collaborating, that is."

"Not tonight, so let's cross that bridge when we come to it."

Case stood up as Marie returned to the booth.

"Anyone else thirsty?" she asked, barely able to focus on us.

"I'm afraid we need to get going," I said.

"Then *I* shall walk *out* with you," she said in a queenly manner. When she had to grab onto the table to steady herself, Case jumped up and put his arm around her waist.

"We don't want you to have a traffic accident," he said. "I'll drive you home in your car and Athena can follow me. But first tell me who you think killed Harry."

She grabbed the table for support, then leaned forward to say, "Harry had a secret, that's why he died. Secrets and lies. Nothing but secrets and lies with the Talbots."

"What was Harry's secret?" Case asked.

Marie hiccupped, then leaned close to Case to whisper loudly, "He had a confidant."

"That was his secret?" I asked.

She scoffed at me. "No. I heard him talking on the phone to someone and they were planning something. And obious—*obously*, he wasn't talking to Gray's son or daughter-in-law." She held her finger to her lips. "Don't say anything, but I heard Harry say he didn't trust either one of them."

"When was this?" Case asked.

Marie gazed at him longingly and breathed into his face, "You're so handsome."

"Marie, focus," I said. "When did you overhear Harry's phone conversation?"

"At the Talbot house after the funeral dinner." Marie sighed in exasperation. "Can we go home now?"

"Absolutely," Case said. "Just one more thing. Did Gray's son know Harry had a confidant?"

"He didn't until yesterday," she said, lifting her chin. "That'll show little boy Talbot, I said to myself. No one messes with Marie and gets away with it."

Then Sonny knew everything Marie knew, including that Harry had a confidant.

She put her hand to her forehead. "I feel sick. I want to go *now*."

Case put his arm around Marie to support her and began walking her toward the front of the restaurant. "Where's your car?"

"By the hotel. I didn't want anyone to see me." She shook a finger at Case. "But you spotted me, you naughty boy."

"You're a hard woman to miss, Marie," Case said.

"I'll go get her car," I said to Case. "Give me your keys, Marie."

She thrust her purse at me. "Couldn't find them if I tried." She suddenly pushed away from Case, her hand over her mouth. As I turned to head into the parking lot, she stumbled toward a group of boxwood shrubs near the door, where she emptied her stomach.

"At least she got it out before her car ride," Case said.

I tapped my foot nervously as I waited for Case to return from Marie's house. I'd parked around the corner from her small bungalow and checked my watch. I still had to drive Case back to the marina, then go home to change and be back in time for my dinner with Kevin, which I found myself dreading like the plague. At least I didn't have to worry about Nicholas. He'd be having a ball with my sisters all day.

But working on the murders with Case was seeping into my blood like a drug and I found myself wishing I could keep investigating. Being with stolid Kevin for two hours was only going to make me squirm with boredom. Yet I didn't see any way I could cancel now without making up another lie. As my mother liked to tell us, "Oh, what a wicked web we weave when first we practice to deceive." And deception had become the name of my game.

The passenger door opened, startling me. Case got into the car with a frown on his face. "I couldn't get her to tell me any more about Harry's confidant. I'll have to try again when she's not drunk."

"Do you really think she'll admit the truth if it implicates her?"

"If I do it right, yes. She's a wealth of information." Case fastened his seat belt as I put the car in gear and pulled away from the curb. "She's also desperate for male company, and I just happen to be free for dinner Tuesday evening."

"You're actually going to take her to dinner?"

"You bet."

"You and Marie." I had to laugh. "I can't wait to hear about it. Maybe she'll even invite you in afterward for a nightcap."

Case was silent for a moment, then muttered to himself, "Secrets and lies."

"Everyone has them," I said.

He turned to study me. "Tell me a secret about Athena the Warrior Goddess."

"She's a mythical character."

"I mean the real Athena. Why do you stay at the garden center after everyone goes home?"

"Why do you want to know?"

"As they say, confession is good for the soul."

"I write a blog," I said matter-of-factly. "It helps me keep my sanity."

"A blog. How about that? We're both writers," he teased. "What do you blog about?"

"What I know best. My crazy family."

"What do you call it?"

"Don't tell me you're going to read it."

"I might. I have a lot of time on my hands these days."

"It's called *It's All Greek to Me.* I use the pseudonym Goddess Anon and I actually have a lot of followers, including my own family." I couldn't stop a smile from spreading across my face. "The funny part is that they don't know it's about them."

"Secrets and lies," he said with a smile. "Everyone has them."

I pulled into a parking lot near the marina. "Okay, here you go. This is as close as I want to get."

"I can tell."

"You can *tell*? What is that supposed to mean?"

"You didn't ask *me* for a secret."

I shut off the ignition and turned to face him. "I don't have time to play truth or dare. All I meant by saying 'as close as I want to get' is that I don't want my SUV seen too close to the marina."

"And here I thought you meant you didn't like to get too close to people."

"I have a son. I think that qualifies as being close to someone."

"A child. Your heart is safe with him. First husband must've really done some damage, and your big family gets in your face, right? Making you crazy? So you write the blog to let out your frustration, and you keep people at arm's length to protect your heart from ever being trampled on again."

I rolled my eyes. "Okay, Dr. Freud, you've got me all figured out, including that I'm afraid you're going to trample on my heart. Now get out and stop analyzing me."

"You don't have to get prickly. I was just teasing."

"Grow up with three sisters like mine and you'd grow prickles, too. Now go."

Just as he reached for the door handle, I glanced in the rearview mirror and saw Delphi on the other side of the street. Fortunately, she hadn't noticed my SUV or me. "Get down," I said, and leaned toward the center of the vehicle.

"You just said to get *out*."

I grabbed the neck of his shirt and pulled him toward me. "Delphi is on the other side of the street. I don't want her to see us."

I waited a beat, then slowly peered over the back of the seat. She was still there but was on her cell phone walking toward the diner, so I ducked back down. "That was close."

"Speaking of being close."

Realizing we were almost nose to nose, I sat up. "Good-bye, Case."

"Athena, about what I said earlier," he said, straightening his shirt, "it was rude of me to pry into your private life."

"You're right, it was rude. I don't pry into yours."

"And that's exactly what I mean. You keep your distance."

"Let me remind you why we're working together. One is to clear your name. The other is to stop the Talbots from tearing down Little Greece. The third is for justice's sake, to find out who caused the two deaths and prevent him or her from getting away with it."

"Let me remind *you* why I came here in the first place," Case said. "To find the statue and proof of authentication."

I inhaled slowly, pushing down my irritation.

"Before you come back with a rebuttal," Case said, "I told you from the beginning that that was why I was here. Now let's plan our next move."

"Fine," I answered sharply. "First of all, we have four potential suspects with motives for wanting Talbot Senior dead. We have two with motives for Harry's death. So we need to dig deeper to see if either of our other two suspects have motives for killing Harry. That means questioning Lila again, but this time I'll talk to her."

Case pointed his finger at me. "See? There's that jealousy thing again."

"It's not—I'm not jealous! I just feel I'll get further if she doesn't have anyone to flirt with."

"And I say *I'd* get further because she likes me, but go ahead. Give it a try."

"Thank you. Then I need to talk to Marie again when she's sober and confront her with what she told us today." I began to count on my fingers. "I also need to talk to Bob Maguire, the police officer I mentioned, to see if he'll give me any new information on the case. I need to ask my sister if Lila showed up for her yoga class the mornings both men were murdered. And I need to question Fatsis."

"Look at you go! You're really into this, aren't you?"

"I guess I am. My plan is to start with Don Fatsis. I'm going to his shop just before noon on Monday to catch him before he heads out for lunch."

"You mean *we're* going to his shop."

"Not *we*, Case. Just me. I don't want him to feel cornered, which he would if we both came at him." I rested my forehead on the steering wheel, trying to figure out how to approach Fatsis. "I know. I'll tell him I need advice about the condominium project. Maybe I can pretend to be outraged by Sonny's bribe and see if he says anything about his offer."

"Suggest buying him lunch at The Parthenon and then I can accidentally run into you."

I stared at him as though he'd grown horns. "How about I jump off the pier and swim across to Chicago?"

"Okay, scrap The Parthenon idea. Crazy family. I get it."

"Not crazy family this time. Crazy you. You have to stay away from the diner so you don't raise anyone's suspicions. And tomorrow, you need to lie low, too. Hang out on the boat, get a tan, and keep growing out that beard."

"This beard is staying short. No mountain man look for me."

As he opened the passenger door I said, "Wait. There *is* something you need to help me with."

He rubbed his hands together. "Great. What is it?"

"Meet me at the garden center at seven a.m., Monday morning."

"Because?" he asked skeptically.

I scratched my eyebrow. "Remember when I said my plan to get the police off the boat wasn't the greatest?"

Case gave me a sidelong glance. "I don't think I'm going to like where this is going."

"I had to involve my father to get the police to stop focusing on the marina. And then naturally I had to tell him about you being on the WANTED poster. So I had no choice but to tell him an abbreviated version of your story. Now he wants to hear the whole thing from you."

CHAPTER TWENTY-ONE

I raced home to find Nicholas in the backyard with Pappoús and Uncle Giannis, who were overseeing the installation of an above-ground swimming pool. Uncle Giannis, my mother's brother, lived just four houses away. He and Aunt Rachel had two sons, both taking pre-med courses. Greeks were notorious for urging their children to become doctors or lawyers. Thank goodness my father had been different. He didn't care what we girls did as long as we did something that made us happy and enough money to live independently. Mama didn't care what we did as long as we *married* someone with money.

"We're getting a pool?" I asked as Nicholas ran up and threw his arms around my waist.

"Grandma says it'll be good for me to learn to swim."

"I'm sure it will," I said, ruffling his hair, even though I was annoyed that *Grandma*, otherwise known as Meddling Mama, hadn't checked with me first. My mother came out through the back door just then—she had a view of the yard from her large kitchen window where she'd always kept a close eye on us as we were growing up.

"It seems we're getting a swimming pool," I said.

"We thought it would be good for Niko's development," Mama said.

"*We?* I'm Nicholas's mother, Mama. I should have been consulted."

"You would have said yes. And it *is* our backyard after all."

"That's not the point," I said, as my grandfather joined us. "You said this was for Nicholas. So next time, consult with me first, please."

She reached over to put a strand of my hair behind my ear. "You seem frazzled, Thenie. What have you been up to?"

"She always has a way of diverting the subject, doesn't she, Pappoús?"

"That's my Hera," he said, his voice hoarse from age.

Theo Karras was a small, wiry older man with a dark olive complexion, a little black still showing in his white hair, strong arms, and a back that was slightly bowed from standing over hot stoves all day. But even though he had a small build, his strong personality more than made up for it.

"To answer your question, Mama, I had a meeting with Sonny Talbot about the condo project and then I met a friend for lunch."

"Did you get anywhere with Sonny?" Mama asked.

"Nope. He wanted me to persuade the GMA to give up the fight and in return he would give Pappoús and Yiayiá a condo on the top floor of his building and space for a new restaurant on the ground floor."

"What about the other shop owners?" Pappoús asked.

"He offered it to only one other shop owner—Don Fatsis—who accepted."

My mother gasped, her hand to her throat. "That *prodótis*."

I glanced at her for a translation and she said, "A traitor, Thenie. You should have stuck with your Greek lessons."

"Pah," my grandfather said, then spit on the ground. "As if we would turn our backs on our friends. I hope you give Fatsis a piece of your mind."

"You bet I will, Pappoús. In fact, I learned that Fatsis never intended to help us fight the Talbots. He just wanted us to believe he did."

"Just wait until the others find out about him," Mama said. "His name will be mud in this community."

My grandfather spit to the side again. It was a Greek thing.

"Don't say anything about Fatsis to anyone until I talk to him, Mama. I want to make sure I have the facts straight. After all, they did come from Sonny."

She tucked another lock of hair behind my ear. "For you and Niko I would do anything, even put up this swimming pool in my backyard."

"Speaking of which," I said, "are you going to hire a swimming coach for him or just throw him in and see if he comes to the surface?"

She threw back her head and laughed. "Thenie, you girls learned to swim by jumping off the side of the boat—in life jackets of course." She brushed his hair back as my son came to stand by her side and said lovingly, "We're all strong swimmers. We'll teach you, Niko."

"I can't wait," Nicholas said, clapping as he jumped up and down.

"See?" Mama asked, as Uncle Giannis came striding over. "He's been cooped up in the big city far too long.

He needs to get rid of all that energy out here where the air is clean and there's room to play."

I couldn't argue with that.

"The pool should be up by this evening and they'll start filling it overnight," Uncle Giannis told us. "By midday tomorrow, Niko will be swimming."

"It won't be that fast, Uncle Giannis," I said.

"Ha!" he retorted. "You have a smart boy. He'll pick it up like a baby fish. Now, are you ready for some fun, Niko?"

"What kind of fun?" I asked warily.

"Uncle Giannis is going to teach me how to climb a tree, Mama. He told me he taught his boys to climb and he even taught you. Please, can I go with him now?"

"Can you believe this boy has never climbed a tree?" my uncle asked.

"We lived in a high-rise," I said. "No trees."

"We're going to remedy that, aren't we, Niko?" Giannis said. "I have the best climbing tree in town. Ask your mama. She used to climb way out on one big fat limb and toss water balloons onto her sisters when they passed underneath. Scared them half to death."

Nicholas looked happily amazed. "You did that, Mama?"

"A long time ago," I said. "Your aunt Delphi did it, too. And if you want to go with Uncle Giannis, it's okay with me."

"Come, Niko," my mother said, "let's go put on some climbing clothes. Thenie, why don't you get ready to meet Kevin for dinner? And for God's sake, wear a dress for a change. Show him you have legs."

I glared at her retreating form as she and Nicholas walked toward the back door together, holding hands.

Show my legs. Now she was telling me how to dress. And how did she know about my date with Kevin anyway?

IT'S ALL GREEK TO ME
blog by Goddess Anon

Check, please!

Did you ever go out on a dinner date and end up listening to the conversations around you—and finding their conversations way more interesting than your date's never-ending monologues? Hey, buddy, how about my *day?*

Why do I put myself through this again and again? Because if I call it quits with Mr. It's All About Me, my mother will simply find another "good Greek boy" for me to date, fall madly in love with, marry, and have a brood of children. Yeah, right. Not this chica.

Waiter? Check please. Hurry!

Sunday

Sundays were all about family, and when I say family, I mean FAMILY, and that meant that Spencer's Garden Center closed on Sundays because family came first.

Today was no exception. At one o'clock, after everyone had changed out of their Sunday finest, Uncle Giannis, Aunt Rachel, their sons Drew and Michael, and my aunt Talia, Uncle Konstantine, and their three Labradors showed up. Counting the seven of us Spencers, plus Yiayiá and Pappoús, we were fifteen in all. And lest we forget, there was also the star of the show, *the pool.*

There was one difference in today's gathering, however. Demolition day was coming up in eight days and we seemed no closer to halting it, which threw a pall over everyone but Nicholas. He was playing in the water, trying out the badminton game Uncle Konstantine had brought, romping with the dogs, and showing off the scrapes he got climbing Uncle Giannis's giant oak tree.

Mama had filled a long table on the patio behind the house with food and set up enough card tables and chairs for everyone. There was grilled lamb on a spit; pastitsio (one type of Greek lasagna); whole chickens roasted with crispy, lemony potatoes; a cucumber, feta cheese, kalamata olives, and tomato salad; and spanako-pita (tiny spinach and feta triangle-shaped pastries). I had to admit it was all delicious.

After stuffing myself and growing tired of all their gossiping, I slipped away to my room to write my blog. But then I found myself leaning on the chair's back legs, daydreaming about escaping the chaos below and going somewhere quiet, specifically the *Páme*, where I could lie on the bow listening to the lapping of the water against the sides, soaking up the sun and smells of the lake, and, oh yeah, there was Case, wearing only cut-off jeans, and bringing me a glass of iced tea.

My chair legs hit the wooden floor with a resounding *thunk*. No more of that kind of daydreaming. I needed to write a list of questions to ask Fatsis.

I worked for half an hour and had almost finished when Delphi strolled in wearing a purple and green tie-dyed sundress, green flip-flops, and her dark hair pulled back with a purple ribbon. Luckily, I'd already posted my blog about that yawn-of-a-dinner with Kevin, so I didn't have to scramble to hide it from her.

She flopped down onto my bed. "Mama told me to come shag you out. You're being antisocial."

"I needed a break."

"You had a ten-year break. Niko is having a blast, by the way. You should see how he's taken to the water."

"I hate that everyone changed his name. It's Nicholas, or Nick."

"Now you're being anti-Greek, too, Thenie. Niko

suits him, and he likes it. What's wrong with calling him that?"

I searched for a way to explain that I wanted to get away from all that *Greekness*. Finally, out of frustration, I said, "What if I started calling you Delphinium because I decided it suits you better than Delphi?"

She wrinkled her nose. "Delphinium? With all these dark curls and this Greek nose? Exactly how does a delicate summery flower suit me?"

"They're showy and they come in purple with lots of green leaves."

"I'm showy?" She stood up and glanced at herself in my dresser mirror, preening as she said, "I *am* showy. Stay up here and hide then, but what do you want me to tell Mama?"

"That I'll be down in ten minutes. Bye, Delphinium."

She turned to go, then paused at the doorway to say, "By the way, I think I figured out who the mystery man is."

My heart started to beat harder. "Are you talking about Dimitrius?"

"I prefer Dimitri, but whatever."

I swiveled to face her, putting my hands on my knees, pretending to be entirely bored by the subject. "Okay, let's hear your theory."

"I think he's been a customer at our store before, and not so long ago, either." Delphi put her fingertips to her temples and closed her eyes. "Wait. Something's coming through."

I turned back to my computer and read over my list of questions for Fatsis.

"I'm also seeing that he had a crush on me." Delphi opened her eyes with a smile and tossed her hair. "But that's to be expected. I have that effect on handsome Greek men, being a flower and all. And I know what you're going to say. Something snide about if that's the case, then why don't I have a boyfriend? To tell you the truth, I don't want to be tied down. I like flirting too much. I've got years ahead of me to think about marriage and kids and all that goes with it."

"Are you rehearsing a speech for the next time Mama tries to fix you up with someone?"

"Mama's heard it already. Besides, she's busy working on finding Selene a new hubby. Oh, by the way, she's about to serve baklava and homemade ice cream that Aunt Rachel brought. You'd better come down or she'll send a whole contingent up to get you."

"I'll be down as soon as I close this file."

As she left, she said, "Who knows? Maybe Mama will fix Dimitri up with Selene. Maybe it was predestined and that's why he showed up when he did. We'll have to invite him over. I'm sure Selene will be delighted."

"Selene's too old for him." Why had I said that?

"How old is he?"

Foot-in-mouth moment. "I don't know but definitely not thirty-six."

"I'll have to have Mama contact her relatives in Tarpon Springs and find out more about him."

That was why I'd said it. "I'm sure he has a girlfriend," I blurted.

Delphi stopped and spun around, a skeptical look on her face. "I don't think so. For a man with a girlfriend, he sure flirted with me a lot."

"That's just his way. He's very friendly." And he and I were definitely going to have a talk about that flirting.

My sister studied me for a long moment, a shrewd look on her face. "I think you want him for yourself."

"I have Kevin, remember?"

Delphi stuck her finger down her throat. "Yuck." She walked out of the room calling, "Better you than me."

Monday, 7:00 a.m.

Case stood outside the garden center checking his reflection in the glass window panel. "Do I look Greek enough?"

"You look fine." More than fine, actually. *Strikingly handsome* were better words, with his golden-brown eyes, semi-curly dark hair, and that dark stubble on his chin. "Remember, my dad knows about your disguise. He'll be looking for the real you, so be totally up front with him about everything. Now let's get this over with because my sister will be here in less than an hour and you need to be gone before she arrives."

"Because?"

"She thinks you like her. And if you keep flirting with women the way you have been, they'll think you like them, too." Ignoring his smile, I unlocked one half of the double barn doors to get in, then closed and locked it behind us.

"Lead the way," he said.

CHAPTER TWENTY-TWO

My dad was reading the newspaper at the big oak desk in the office, so I rapped lightly on the frame and said, "We're here."

He rose and indicated the two chairs in front of the desk. "Have a seat." His tone was all business.

"Dad, this is Case Donnelly, now known as Dimitrius Costas."

Dad shook his hand, taking Case's measure. "Under the circumstances, I don't think it's right to say it's a pleasure to meet you, but thanks for coming in so early."

"I'm an early riser, so it's no problem. And it *is* a pleasure to meet you, Mr. Spencer. Athena has spoken very highly of you."

"Let's get right to it so we don't run out of time. Athena's version took a long time to tell."

"Then I'll make it as brief as possible."

While Case told Dad about the chain of events that led him to our store and what happened in the days that followed, I made them coffee and brought refills.

When Case finished talking, Dad took off his glasses and polished them with a cloth he kept in his top drawer, obviously thinking things over.

"Well, I have to say, you certainly don't resemble the man on the WANTED posters, Dimitrius—and that *is* the name I'll be calling you." He put his glasses back on. "By the way, Thenie, you did a good job of changing his looks. Now what I want to know is this, Dimitrius. What happens with the statue issue when the murders are solved? Given that you're cleared as a suspect, of course."

Case thought for a moment. "I return home knowing the statue is in good hands."

It was an ambiguous statement and I could tell Dad had caught it, too. "Even though you claim your documents show that the statue belongs to your family, are you willing to leave it here without a legal battle?"

"That's not my concern right now, sir. I'm more worried about my future as a free man."

"Why not simply go home?" Dad asked. "Take a bus. No one will stop you."

"I don't have any identification and very little money. I wouldn't even have a safe place to stay without your daughter's help—and yours, now, too. I did consider hiking up to the next city and thumbing a ride at first. But given all the media attention, I didn't think that was smart."

"A wise move," Dad said.

"There's another reason I decided to stick around. Athena's passion for justice raised something in me. Her concern for the Greek community struck a chord, as well, since I've been trying to help my Greek side of the family. So when she agreed to help me find Harry's killer, I decided to help her fight to save Little Greece and hopefully put a stop to the Talbot's control, as well."

I glanced at Dad and waited as he considered Case's predicament.

After a moment he said, "It's admirable that you want to help, but I worry that someone's going to trip up your story, and I hate to say this, but it may be someone from my own family."

"I'll have to take my chances. I gave Athena my word that I'd help and I'm a man of my word. Besides, I've always been good at beating the odds."

"Is that so?" Dad asked. "What's your occupation?"

"For the past year it's been doing research to track down the family statue."

"And before that?"

"I'm self-employed. Researcher-for-hire."

"I didn't know there was a need for that type of work."

"You'd be surprised, sir."

"College degree?"

"Political science."

With an eye on the time I said, "Dad, Delphi's going to be here any minute. Can we talk about Dimitrius's history some other time?"

"Sure, but I'm not worried about her," Dad said. "It's your mother who worries me. You know how she gets when she's curious. Like a dog with a bone." He rose from his chair. "I've got to get to work. Thenie, you'd better take him out the back way. Thanks for coming in, Dimitrius."

They shook hands. "Thank you for listening to my story."

"One more thing. Don't ever put my daughter in harm's way."

* * *

Five minutes before noon, I dashed down to Fatsis's Acropolis Gallery and caught him writing something at the counter. He had no customers. "Don, do you have a minute?"

He glanced up at me, then went back to writing. "What do you need?"

"Some advice on Talbot."

He studied me for a moment as though trying to decide if I had an ulterior motive, then checked his watch.

"How about lunch?" I asked. "My treat."

"I'm not sure I have the time."

"Please? It's important."

"I need to be back at twelve forty to meet with a private customer. But maybe if we make it quick, like at The Parthenon . . ."

Exactly what I was trying to avoid. But I forced a smile. "Well, I can certainly guarantee speedy service there." As well as ears trying to hear our every word.

He turned the sign on the front door over to CLOSED, locked up, then we walked three doors down to my grandparents' diner. My mama greeted Fatsis as though they were old friends and then seated us at a table close to the family booth where Selene and Maia were already eating. Both sisters shot me questioning glances, but I ignored them.

We made small talk about the tourist season being one of the biggest ever due to the warm temperatures, and then, after Don's platter of gyros with hummus and pita bread and my Caesar salad arrived, I got right to the point. "I wanted to fill you in on the meeting I had with Talbot."

Fatsis started to dip his pita bread into the tzatziki dip but stopped to look at me. "I didn't know you had a meeting with Talbot."

"He offered my grandparents a prime location in his new building for their restaurant and a luxury condo on the top floor if I can get the GMA to back off."

Fatsis paused, his food halfway to his mouth. "Did they accept?"

"Not yet. What did you tell him when he made you the offer?"

Fatsis started to choke on his food and quickly grabbed his Greek beer to wash it down. He used his napkin to wipe the tears from his eyes. "What are you talking about?"

He was playing dumb. Not a stretch for him. "Don, Talbot told me he made you the same offer. You don't need to pretend he didn't. I mean, it's a pretty sweet deal after all. So what did you tell him?"

He took another huge bite of gyros, mumbling, "That I'd have to think about it."

"He said you accepted it." I stabbed a forkful of salad and put it in my mouth.

Fatsis stopped chewing, clearly realizing he'd stepped into my trap. "You're taking Talbot's word over mine?"

"He had proof, Don." Or so I wanted him to believe.

Fatsis glanced around, then leaned toward me and said quietly, "Listen, Athena, not everyone's going to get into that building. First come first serve. My advice is for them to accept the offer. No one needs to know but us and your grandparents."

I could almost hear my mother's blood boiling somewhere behind me.

"What happens when the shops are demolished, the building goes up, and you and my grandparents are the only ones out of the whole group who moves in?" I asked. "The truth is that my grandparents would rather close up their restaurant than to turn their backs on their friends. *No one* but you wants to see those shops torn down."

"That's not true," he said, his big face bright red. "Marie Odem made a deal with old man Talbot, so I'm not the only one who doesn't care what happens to Little Greece."

I sat back shaking my head. "But Talbot Junior didn't offer Marie the deal. She was banking on Talbot Senior marrying her, and that's how she was going to save her shop."

"She didn't want to save her shop," Fatsis said snidely. "She wanted to marry the old man so she'd never have to work another day in her life. And think about this before you defend her again. After the old man put the kibosh on their marriage, she might have put the kibosh on *him*, if you get my drift. You know what they say about a woman scorned."

"I didn't ask you here to talk about Marie. I was hoping you'd change your mind and back the rest of us, but I can see your mind is made up." I folded my arms and shook my head in disgust. "I wouldn't plan on attending any more GMA meetings if I were you."

Fatsis wiped his greasy mouth with his napkin. "Talbot has all the power on his side. He's going to win no matter what we do. I've already checked into it. So here's some more advice. Stop fighting Talbot and use him like he's using us."

"And the others? Do we just sit back and watch as their livelihoods are taken away?"

"They can make their own deals with Talbot. They'd be better off working with him than with his old man, who was ready to tear down Little Greece a month ago, until he had a sudden change of heart, which personally I think Harry Pepper influenced."

My surprised look must have given Fatsis cold feet because he immediately said, "Forget I said that. I don't know what influenced the old coot."

"Something made you say that. What do you know about Harry, Don?"

"Nothing."

"What are you afraid of? Or should I say who?"

"All I know is that Harry and your grandfather were friends a long time ago, so maybe Harry felt bad that your grandfather was losing his home and diner and talked to his boss on his behalf. Whatever the reason, Talbot canceled the project."

As Fatsis stopped to take a bite, I had a sudden thought. What if my grandfather was Harry's confidant?

Fatsis checked his watch. "I'm going to have to go, but let me give you one more piece of advice before I do. Talbot's son has no sympathy for us, so we're better off cutting a deal with him and getting whatever we can."

As Fatsis stuffed his mouth with the rest of the gyros I said, "I really thought you were geared up for a fight to save our downtown, Don, and as determined as the rest of us not to let the Talbots run this city."

"You just named my reason for taking the offer, Athena. The Talbots have been running this city for a long time. We're simply one small block of shop owners who rent space. We don't have any clout. We'd be in for a long, drawn-out fight that would cost plenty more than any funding website could raise."

"Which I suppose you haven't set up."

Fatsis looked at his watch again and didn't answer.

"Then my next report to the GMA is going to be that you joined forces with the Talbots and you believe the rest of us should just bow down to the tyrant."

"Hey, if you want to look at it that way, be my guest. I'd prefer it if you told them to think of it as taking advantage of Talbot while we can."

"What do you think happened to the agreement Talbot Senior signed?"

"He took it with him, that's all I know."

"You don't have any guesses what happened after that? Like perhaps someone rifled through his safe and found it?"

He glared at me, his big, beefy face puffing up further. "Are you insinuating that I had something to do with it?"

"What did I say that would make you think that?"

At that moment, Case slid into the booth beside me, startling me.

"I thought I'd find you here, Athena."

That was definitely *not* in our plan.

CHAPTER TWENTY-THREE

Before the shock could register on my face, I forced a smile. "C—Dimitrius, what are *you* doing here?"

"I wanted to tell you about what I found out today about Talbot's secret deals." Case reached his hand across the table toward Fatsis, who had gone pale at Case's announcement. "Hi. Dimitrius Costas, Athena's second cousin several times removed."

"Don Fatsis," the big man said warily, his lips greasy with food.

"Ah, the gentleman who owns The Acropolis, the premier art shop in town."

Fatsis puffed out his chest. "You can't get art anywhere in town better than mine."

"That's surprising considering that you were about to file bankruptcy."

"What?" Fatsis's mouth opened in shock.

"What?" I reiterated, staring at Case.

"What?" my mother asked, appearing suddenly tableside. When we turned to stare at her she said to Case with a blush, ". . . would you like to drink?"

"Nothing for me, thanks. I'm only staying a few minutes."

"Don, Thenie, you need anything?" she asked.

"We're fine, Mama," I said firmly. When I didn't make a move to introduce Case, she gave me a glare and stalked off.

Case turned back to Fatsis. "You've been operating in the red for quite some time, haven't you?"

"How—what—?" he stammered.

"In fact," Case continued, "you recently made an inquiry into what kind of bankruptcy you'd need to file."

Fatsis's heavy face turned an angry red. "How would you know that?"

"It's amazing what people at the courthouse will tell you."

"I beg your pardon," Fatsis said, trying to act indignant, "but all I was doing was checking into it for someone else. Thank you for lunch, Athena, but like I said, I have a private client coming in."

"That client wouldn't be Talbot, would it?" Case asked.

The big man rose and tossed his napkin onto the table. "You don't know what you're talking about."

Case sat back smugly. "Those huge loans you took out on your business? Talbot Senior made arrangements to pay off your debts in return for you supporting his condo project, didn't he?"

"You," he bellowed, pointing to Case, causing every head to swivel toward us, "don't know what you're talking about."

And with that he stormed out.

I stared at Case in wonder. "What did you just do?"

"Put him on notice that we're onto him. I found out that Fatsis made a deal with old Mr. Talbot to support the condo project in exchange for having his debt of several hundred thousand dollars paid off. He had changed sides way back and no one knew it."

My mouth dropped open. "What a traitor! He has no idea what a pariah he'll be now in the Greek community."

"Did you really think he'd tell anyone in the GMA about working with the Talbots?"

I shook my head, still in a state of disbelief. "Mr. Talbot's change of heart must have really pulled the rug out from under him."

"But only until Sonny made it clear how he felt about the project," Case said, "then Fatsis knew he had to get in Sonny's good graces quickly."

"Fatsis is definitely becoming a stronger suspect," I said. "He knew the old man's evening routine and how to get up to his bedroom. Marie already told us Harry didn't lock the office's French doors at night. She might not have been the only one who knew that."

"Or she spilled that information to Fatsis after a few drinks," Case said, "and he's certainly big enough to hold an old man down under the water." He sighed in frustration. "But all we have are conjectures."

"Here's something I forgot to tell you. Fatsis reminded me that Harry and my grandfather were old friends. Perhaps Harry convinced Talbot Senior to build the condominium somewhere else for Pappoús's sake."

"Do you really believe a powerful mogul would care enough about Harry's old friend to scrap a multimillion-dollar moneymaker in the heart of the downtown area? Face it, Athena, Sonny might have been telling the truth when he said his father was just going through the motions to placate the GMA and never intended to file that document. Otherwise, why would he take it back home with him? He probably had Harry destroy it."

"But what if Harry *didn't* destroy it? What if he feared for his own life after Talbot drowned and handed it off to his confidant, just in case? He knew how important it was to the Greek community and especially to his former partner, Theo Karras, my *pappoús.* Case, it's possible that my grandfather is Harry's confidant."

"Wouldn't your grandfather have given the document to the GMA to stop the project?"

It was my turn to sigh in frustration, resting my chin on my palm. "You're right. But I still believe Harry's death has something to do with that signed document. I'll have to talk to Pappoús and see what he has to say about it."

I felt eyes on my back and glanced around to see that my sisters were watching us like hawks. I gave them a glare and turned to Case. "How did you learn about Fatsis's finances?"

"I told you I'm an expert researcher." He rose.

"Where are you going?" I asked.

"I'm going to slip outside to follow Fatsis to see who he's meeting with. I have a feeling he's going to run straight to the Talbot headquarters to see Sonny. And you're going to deal with your family, who is about to descend on our table. Let me know what your grandfather says."

And with that Case was gone, striding toward the door like a man on a mission. I turned back to my salad only to have Selene, Maia, and my mother pull out chairs at the table and sit down. The family descendeth.

"Okay, Thenie," Mama said, crossing her arms over her ample bosom, her heavy bracelets clattering. "What's going on?"

I wasn't sure what my mother was referring to, so I went with a sure thing. "We were discussing Donald Fatsis being a turncoat."

"You were discussing GMA business with a stranger?" Mama asked as though I'd committed a sin.

"He's not a stranger anymore. He's a friend who's trying to help us save Little Greece."

"A friend, is he?" She had a shrewd gleam in her eye. "And what does he get in return?"

"Yes, tell us, Thenie," Selene said, grinning like the Cheshire Cat.

"I'm helping him with his mystery novel, and that's it," I said. "He's writing a fictionalized account of the murders."

Maia looked at Mama and shook her head. She always had been the tattletale of the group. "Thenie makes it sound so innocent. The truth is that our Athena, girl reporter, is playing detective with a handsome stranger. And she's not just helping him with details. They're both actively looking for the murderers. They even went to see Sonny Talbot Saturday morning to question him about his father's and Harry's death."

"His name is Dimitrius Costas," Selene said. "And Delphi tells me he's single."

Maia continued, "Thenie and Dimitrius are working *very* closely together on the investigation. Lila told me so at yoga."

I gritted my teeth. Sisters! I was already writing my blog for the day in my head.

"How does everyone know this but me?" Mama huffed.

"Stop making it sound like something is going on between us," I snapped at Maia and Selene. "Yes, I'm looking into the two murders because I'm convinced Sonny is involved. I'm sick of how the name Talbot allows them to get away with anything, not just tearing down Little Greece but also possibly murder. And yes, Dimitrius is working with me. Initially it was because he's writing a book based on the murders. But then he got involved in our cause, and he's even uncovered some valuable information, such as that Fatsis is on the verge of bankruptcy."

Mama nodded knowingly. "I had a feeling about Fatsis's business."

I knew that would divert her attention away from Case. "Dimitrius found out that Fatsis arranged with Talbot Senior to pay off his debts in exchange for convincing us not to fight the condo project. When Talbot died, Fatsis and Sonny struck a deal like the one Sonny offered Yiayiá and Pappoús. When Dimitrius confronted him with it, Fatsis stormed out, as you just witnessed."

"How did Dimitrius find all that out?" Mama asked, obviously still skeptical of him.

"He's a writer, Mama. He knows how to research." I turned toward Maia. "Now, Miss Tattletale, answer a question for me. When Harry's body was discovered last Tuesday morning, did Lila show up for yoga class?"

"I can check the schedule," Maia said, getting serious, "but I'm almost certain she did. She rarely misses a class."

"I'd appreciate it if you'd check, just to make sure."

Mama leaned across the table to stare me in the eye. "Is that all that's going on between you and Dimitrius?"

"Yes, I promise. In fact, we might be distantly related through relatives in Tarpon Springs. Somehow. Distantly."

I realized I was twirling a strand of my hair and dropped it.

Mama got up, went to the hostess stand, and came back with a notepad and pen, which she pushed across the table toward me. "Write down his full name."

"Selene already told you his name. It's Dimitrius Costas."

She wrote it down instead, gave me a long, skeptical look, and got up. "We'll see."

"What are you going to do?" I asked.

"Call my aunt in Tarpon Springs. She knows everyone in the Greek community."

Gulp.

After she left, Maia and Selene were all eyes and ears, folding their hands on the table and leaning in to talk in hushed tones. "He's adorable," Selene said. "It'd be too bad if we found out we were cousins."

Maia said, "He's sexy, too. Has Delphi called dibs?"

I gathered my purse and stood up. "I've got to talk to Pappoús and then get back to Spencer's so Dad can take a lunch break."

I headed straight back to the kitchen, where my grandfather was busy cooking. "Pappoús, I need to talk to you about Harry. Can you stop for a minute?"

He wiped his hands on his bib apron, then used a paper towel to dab his perspiring face. "You can see how busy it is here. I'll call you at the office after closing time."

"Of course, Pappoús. I'll talk to you then."

As I walked back to the garden center, my phone beeped. I pulled it out of my purse and saw a text from Case.

Dimitri: *My hunch was almost right. Fatsis didn't run straight to Sonny. Sonny was the client he met at his shop. He even bought a painting, no doubt to make it look like a legitimate reason for being there.*

Athena: *Wish I'd been a fly on the wall. I'm sure they discussed our meeting with him.*

Dimitri: *Speaking of meetings, when is our next strategy session?*

Athena: *My only free time is before I go home to help Nicholas with his homework tomorrow evening.*

Dimitri: *Lunch then?*

I paused. It was risky making trips to the marina during the day, but as I hadn't been there since Saturday, perhaps nobody would notice.

Athena: *I'll make it work. I'll stop and buy sandwiches on the way.*

Dimitri: *I'm looking forward to it.*

I put my phone away with a smile. So was I.

I paused, wondering whether he was looking forward to it for the same reason I was: the thrill of the hunt.

IT'S ALL GREEK TO ME
blog by Goddess Anon

Siblings. They're not all they're cracked up to be.

How can grown-up siblings be so childish in the presence of a parent, like they haven't grown up at all? I'm firmly convinced that when the family gathers, every one of my siblings reverts to his/her childhood traits. Frankly, it makes me want to take my ball and go home. Today, for instance . . . .

Shortly after eight o'clock, after my dad and Delphi had left for the day, I took advantage of the warm evening to sit in the outdoor area at Spencer's to write my blog. A gentle breeze brought the fresh smell of coming rain, and dark clouds were moving in, so I had to hurry before the first drops started to fall.

I had just finished when Pappoús phoned. "What did you want to know about Harry, Athena?" my grandfather asked.

"Pappoús, were you and Harry close when he died?"

"I talked to Harry for the first time in three years the

day before the Talbot auction, and that was because he wanted me to see the statue. He said it would be perfect for the diner. I told him I couldn't afford such a beautiful piece, and he said not to worry about the price because he would arrange a way for me to afford it."

A red flag went up. "Are you saying you didn't actually pay the price on the receipt?"

"*Nai.*" Greek for "yes."

"How much did you pay?"

"Not important."

"Did you pay *something*?" I crossed my fingers, hoping he had so Case couldn't make a claim for it.

"Of course I paid something. Do you think I would take it for free?"

"Did Harry give you anything beside the receipt when you bought the statue?"

"*Nai.* A yellow envelope with papers inside."

"A yellow envelope. Did you look at the papers inside?"

"Why should I look? He gave them to me with the statue, so what would they be about but the statue? I gave the envelope to your father to keep for me. I don't know what he did with it."

"He put it in the filing cabinet for safekeeping, Pappoús."

And no one who'd seen the file marked *Statue* had thought anything of what else might be in there, including me. I'd hurriedly found the receipt, never checking to see what else was in the envelope. Now that I thought about it, I did remember seeing other papers inside. It just hadn't occurred to me that they might be important.

"Did Harry mention anything to you about his boss's decision to cancel his plans to tear down Little Greece?"

His voice suddenly tightening with emotion, he replied, "Harry handed me the envelope and said, '*Paliá fíli, tha eínai oraía me aftá.*'"

"Which means?"

"That you should have attended your Greek lessons," he chided.

"Pappoús!"

"It means, 'Old friend, you'll be fine with this.'"

"Was that all he said?"

"*Nai.* Then he gave me a hug. I wonder now if Harry knew he was in danger."

"Thanks, Pappoús. That's all I wanted to know. Tell Yiayiá good night for me."

"*Kalinýchta,* Thenie."

After ending the call, I pondered Harry's words. He obviously believed that the papers would keep Pappoús safe. But had Harry meant just the diner or could he have meant the rest of Little Greece, too? And if so, why hadn't he said something? Had he been afraid of putting my grandfather in danger?

I put my phone in my pocket and stood. I needed to get that envelope.

A sudden thud outside the fence made me jump. I looked around for Oscar but didn't see him, so I gathered my laptop and slipped inside, locking the door behind me. Then I went straight to the office and opened the filing cabinet.

Thunder rumbled in the distance. I glanced at my watch and saw that it was much later than I'd thought. Nicholas would be waiting. I'd have to hurry.

In the file marked *Statue*, I opened the envelope and pulled out the top piece of paper, which was the receipt showing the sale of the statue. Along with it was a folded document two pages long. When I unfolded it, my heart

jumped to my throat. I was holding the agreement Talbot
Sr. had signed canceling the condominium project. Pappoús *had* been Harry's confidant.

I wanted to call Case to tell him but two more thuds,
these from inside the garden center, set my nerves on
edge. Wishing I had a key to lock the filing cabinet, I
slid the document and receipt back into the envelope,
tucked it inside the folder, shuffled the folders around
so it wouldn't stand out, shut the filing cabinet, and left.

It was dark and starting to sprinkle when I locked the
shop and ran to my SUV, managing to make it just before the skies opened up. With the windshield wipers
going at top speed, the headlights of the oncoming cars
blurred as I made the short trip to my parents' home. I
glanced in the rearview mirror and noticed a big black
SUV close behind me, so close that even in the driving
rain, I could see that the driver had a hood up, but I
couldn't see his face. I turned at the next corner and
the SUV followed. Was I being tailed?

I made an unexpected left turn, then turned right at
the next corner and checked the rearview mirror. The
vehicle was still behind me. My heart started to race,
and my palms felt damp on the steering wheel. Someone was definitely following me.

CHAPTER TWENTY-FOUR

With shaking hands, I reached for my phone, voice dialed 911, and told the dispatch operator what was happening. She instructed me to drive straight to the police station and stay in my car, and meanwhile she'd have a patrol car waiting out front.

I got back onto Greene Street, turned onto Main, the major cross street through town, and the big black SUV was still on my bumper. I had three blocks to go but it felt like three miles. Just before I reached the police station, I glanced in my rearview mirror again and the vehicle was gone. I kept going anyway and when I pulled up in front of the station, an officer was waiting to escort me inside. I gave them a description of the SUV, but without a license plate number or make of SUV, there wasn't anything they could do except follow me home to make sure I arrived safely.

I was trembling when I entered the house. I shut the door and leaned against it to steady myself, then pushed away and headed for Mom's big kitchen to make myself a cup of chamomile tea. My parents were in the living room watching TV and naturally Mama noticed my distress.

"Thenie, what happened?" she asked, both of them following me into the kitchen.

I took a cup from the cabinet, filled it with water, and popped it in the microwave. "Someone in a black SUV was following me. I called the police and they had me drive to the station." I opened another cabinet and found the tea bags. "But the SUV disappeared before I got there."

"Was it a Cadillac?" Dad asked, perching on a stool at the island counter.

"It was raining so hard I couldn't tell. Why?"

"Sonny Talbot has a big black Caddy SUV," he said.

The microwave dinged. I took out the cup and dropped in the tea bag. "A lot of people have black SUVs. And I don't think Sonny would want to chance his Caddy being recognized."

"I don't care who it was," Mama said with a scowl, "that's it for you, Thenie. No more investigating those murders. It's not worth risking your life. From now on you ride to work with your papa."

"Mama, please, I'm not a child. I'll be careful." I took my cup and headed for the back staircase. "I'm going up to see my son and then go to bed."

Mama put her arms around me from behind and hugged me as though it was going to be my last night on earth. "I love you, my precious *moró*. Just remember what I said. This investigation you're so determined to do isn't worth risking your life for."

I went up to Nicholas's room, took a deep breath to steady my nerves, and knocked before entering. "Hey, sweetie."

He got up from his desk and came to give me a hug. "I'm glad you're home."

I put the teacup and my cell phone on the desk next to his bed. "I'm glad I'm home, too, Nick. I missed you."

"It's Niko now, Mom. I keep telling you I like that better."

"Sorry. I haven't gotten used to it. Why do you like it so much?"

"Because it makes me feel like part of the family. They're fun and kinda crazy sometimes, and I like that."

"Then I'll try to remember to call you Niko, I promise. How's your homework going?"

"All done," he said proudly. "Aunt Selene helped me with my math."

"Good. Then how about if we finish *Charlotte's Web*?"

I climbed onto his twin bed beside him, put my arm around his shoulders, and leaned against the head-board to read. Fifteen minutes later, my phone beeped. I checked the screen, saw Case's message, and felt my stomach tense.

Dimitri: *I think someone is outside the boat.*

"Oh, no" slipped out before I realized it.

Nicholas looked over my shoulder at the phone. "What is it, Mama?"

"A message from Dimitri. I need to answer it."

I typed: *Stay clear of the windows.*

No answer came back. I started reading again but kept glancing over at my phone, hoping for an update. Finally, apologizing to my son, I stopped to text: *Do you still hear someone?*

No reply.

"Mom, what's wrong?"

"I think Dimitri is in trouble."

"Can you help him?"

I thought hard but, short of driving down to the marina, didn't know how I could.

My phone rang then, and the name *Dimitri* popped up on the screen. "Are you okay?" I asked immediately.

"I'm off the boat and walking to a coffee shop," came his breathless reply. "If anyone was near the boat, they're gone now."

I wanted to tell him about the SUV but didn't want to frighten Nicholas, so I said, "It could have been one of the ropes hitting the hull."

"That's what I figured." There was a pause and then, "Damn. Now a black SUV is following me."

My heart began to race. That couldn't be a coincidence. "Where are you?"

"On Oak. I'm going to duck down the lane behind Greene Street to see if I can lose it. I might be able to circle around and get a license plate—"

I heard a loud screech of tires and Case's muttered curse, then his line went dead. I started to dial his number but stopped. If he'd had to hide, a ringing phone could put him in jeopardy. I took a deep breath to calm myself and started reading to Nicholas again, but my mind kept conjuring up images of what might've happened to Case.

"Mom, we can finish the book tomorrow. You're distracted."

"I'm sorry, honey. Yes, let's finish it tomorrow." I gave his shoulders a squeeze and kissed him on the forehead. "Do you know how much I love you?"

"I love you, too, Mama. Can I ask you something?"

"Of course."

"Is Dimitri your boyfriend?"

I scoffed playfully. "What a question to ask your mom."

"I heard Aunt Selene and Aunt Maia talking about it. If he is, it's okay. I want you to be happy, too."

"Thank you, sweetheart."

"Can I tell you something else? Promise not to tell anyone."

"I promise."

"I don't like Kevin."

"Can I tell you something, too? And you have to promise not to tell anyone, especially Grandma. I'm not a big fan of Kevin's, either."

We bumped fists. Then I kissed my son good night, went to my room, shut the door, and texted Case: *Where are you? What happened?*

I breathed a sigh of relief when I got an answering ding.

Dimitri: *I'm okay, sitting at a coffee shop.*

Athena: *I heard tires screech and thought you got hit. You scared me!*

Dimitri: *How sweet that you care.*

I ignored his remark and texted: *What happened?*

Dimitri: *The SUV nearly hit another car. At least it gave me a chance to elude him, or them. I couldn't tell how many were in the car, but I did see that it was a Chevrolet.*

Athena: *What are you going to do now? They might still be out there.*

Dimitri: *I've been here a little while and haven't seen any black SUVs driving around. I'm going to head back to the marina in a bit.*

Athena: *Be careful. I was followed home by a black SUV this evening, too. I drove to the police station, but it didn't follow.*

Dimitri: *I'm glad you're ok. But if we're being tailed, it won't be safe to meet at the marina tomorrow. We'll have to arrange another place.*

Athena: *I'll pick up sandwiches at a food truck at the central plaza. Be nearby and watch to see if I'm being followed. If I am, text me and we'll scratch the meeting. If not, I'll continue on to the Páme as planned.*

Dimitri: *Sounds good. See you then, I hope.*

Athena: *Oh, wait! I almost forgot. I found the agreement Talbot Sr. signed. It was in the envelope Harry gave my grandfather when he bought the statue.*

Dimitri: *Wonderful! Do you have it with you?*

Athena: *No. I heard noises and got scared so I left it at the office for safekeeping. I think someone was listening outside the garden center while I was talking to my grandfather about it. And then I was followed, so I'm glad I didn't take it with me.*

Dimitri: *Wise move. We'll have to get it filed tomorrow to stop the project.*

Athena: *I don't know how to get something filed. I'll have to contact Kevin.*

Dimitri: *It's your call. And just a heads-up. Five big bulldozers are parked one block past Little Greece. Talbot's getting ready.*

Tuesday

I had breakfast with Nicholas—Niko—I couldn't get used to calling him that—then watched him get on the school bus before taking off in my SUV. I was angry that I didn't feel safe walking to Spencer's now, especially with the sun out and the temperature in the low seventies, a perfect day for a stroll. But I drove anyway, keeping one eye on the road and the other on my rearview mirror. I parked in a city lot one block behind Greene, cut down the back lane, and went through the gate into the outdoor center. I heard a crunch of gravel in the lane and glanced back but didn't see anyone.

As I made my way through the rows of outdoor shrubs and flowering bushes, and into the patio area, I spotted Oscar sitting in a chair at one of the tables as though he was human, holding an apple in his little paws and eating all around the core. He saw me and kept right on crunching away, not fearful at all.

Suddenly he glanced back toward the lane, dropped the apple, jumped down and was over the side fence in the blink of an eye. I spun around for a look but still didn't see anyone. Now I was spooked. Then I noticed the back door. The glass had been shattered and the door was standing open.

I ran straight to the office where my dad and Delphi were talking with several police officers, Bob Maguire among them. The office was a mess—the desk drawers pulled out, the contents scattered, and more importantly, the filing cabinet had been opened and files were all over the floor.

"Oh, my God!" I cried, and everyone turned to look at me.

"They only targeted the office," Dad said. "Nothing was broken but the back door. They didn't harm anything inside the center. Only in here."

"It appears that someone was looking for a file," one of the officers said. "Do you keep anything of value in the filing cabinet?"

I had to bite my lip to keep from saying yes. My dad replied, "Just client files and purchase orders. Our safe is in a locked closet behind the checkout counter and it wasn't touched."

"Is it okay if I pick up the files?" I asked.

"Go ahead," Maguire said. "We've already photographed everything."

I began to gather the files on the floor, searching for the one that said *Statue*. I spotted it and opened it up. Prickles raised the hair on my arms. The manila envelope was gone.

CHAPTER TWENTY-FIVE

I felt sick. Clearly, when I'd heard that noise while talking with Pappoús, someone had been listening. Why hadn't I taken that envelope with me? Now there was nothing to stop Sonny's project unless we could come up with something fast. The demolition was scheduled to start in six days.

"I told the officers what happened to you last night," Dad said.

"Can you think of any reason why someone would be following you?" Maguire asked.

There was no way I could explain what Case and I had been doing, especially when we didn't know who among the officers was on the Talbot payroll. So I said only, "I've been working hard to stop the demolition of Little Greece. Maybe someone isn't happy about it."

We all knew who that someone would be. I noticed two of the officers glance at each other while Maguire wrote it down.

My hands were shaking so badly I went to the coffee maker to make a cup of coffee, holding it between my palms to ward off the chills that were running up my spine. The statue's sales receipt, the document Talbot Sr. had signed—both gone. My family had been hit on two fronts.

I needed to call Case and let him know what happened.

"Miss Spencer," one of the officers called, "did you notice anything unusual last night after closing? Your dad said you were here alone."

"Yes, I was sitting out in the garden talking on the phone and heard a noise twice that spooked me, so I locked up and went home. That's when I was followed. I think now that someone must have been waiting for me to get home and then returned here."

As Maguire wrote it down, one of the other officers said to my dad, "We'll need a list of everything that's missing."

"It'll take a while to remember what files were in here," Dad said.

"I've been putting client information on the computer," I told him. "I can make a list."

"Drop it off at the station when you're finished," Maguire said.

"I can tell you one thing that's missing," I said. "My grandfather's sales receipt for his statue of Athena. It's a very expensive statue that he bought at the Talbot auction."

Maguire made note of it, then said to us, "I think that should do it. We'll let you know if we find out anything."

As he and the other officers headed to the door, I motioned for Delphi to follow me. I didn't want Dad to hear and tell Mama my plan. "I think Sonny Talbot is behind this."

"Why?"

"Because Talbot Senior's signed agreement stopping the demolition was in that file."

"Tell the cops," she urged.

"That would be as good as accusing Sonny outright of theft. He has a lot of friends on the force. It could even be one of them who broke in." I nodded toward the officers.

"I don't think Bob would do that," she said.

"I agree. We were friends in high school and he was honest to a fault. So what do you think about Bob helping me find out who was following me?"

"I think I can persuade him," she said with a little smile.

"I think you can, too. You know he has a crush on you."

"Of course he has a crush on me," Delphi said. "That's obvious."

"He'd have to be discreet. He couldn't even tell his partner. But you'd have to feel him out before you broached it. If he says he's willing to help, ask him to check the traffic camera video at the intersection of Greene and Main about eight fifteen last night. He should be able to get the license plate number off the black SUV."

"Leave everything to me."

Coming from Delphi, those words usually inspired fear, but today I crossed my fingers that my ditzy sister would be able to carry it off. "Why don't you catch him before he leaves? And try to set up a meeting with him as soon as possible," I called as she hurried off.

I stood at the side of the big picture window at the front of the store, watching as Delphi stopped Maguire before he got into his squad car. Apparently, he had come without his partner today. The other officers had already left.

She said something to him and a big smile spread across his face. He gave her a nod, they chatted a few moments, and she came back looking very pleased with herself.

"We're going to meet at The Parthenon at three when he gets off his shift."

"Delphi, you know Mama will think you're dating him when she sees you together."

Delphi's eyes widened. "Oh my God." And then she made a dash for the door calling, "I've got to catch him."

When she strolled back inside, she was smiling. "Bob's going to meet me in the garden center at three fifteen today."

"Perfect."

Dad stepped out of the office and spotted us. "Hey, girls, I know it's been a trying morning, but we've got a shop to run, so let's take a deep breath and get ready for the day. Thenie, don't forget to check the office to see if anything else is missing. Delphi, we're getting in a big shipment of orchids anytime now. Let's go make a display for them."

"Coming, Pops," Delphi said.

I went into the office and shut the door to text Case: *Are you free to talk?*

My phone rang, and the name *Dimitri* popped up on the screen. I answered it and immediately told him what happened. "Sonny has to be behind the break-in," I said. "Who else would go to those measures to get it?"

"Fatsis. Or Lila. Or anyone else who stood to make money from the project."

"I think we can rule Marie out. She wouldn't have attempted a break-in."

"I'm still going to take her to dinner. After a few drinks, who knows what else I might learn that'll help with our investigation?"

"True. And on a hopeful note, I shouldn't be followed anymore. No reason to now."

The shop was busy until shortly before noon, when tourists started thinking about lunch and looking for restaurants before they filled up. Instead of going down to the diner at noon to eat with my sisters, I told Delphi I was meeting an old friend who'd just bought a new house and wanted landscape advice. As soon as she headed off to the diner, I hurried over to the harbor where a row of food trucks had parked. Picnic tables dotted the green space between the street and the boardwalk and today it was jammed with people.

I scanned the trucks and finally decided on Mexican food, so I stood in line, glancing around as discreetly as I could for Case. I didn't see him—or Sonny for that matter. But, as Case had said, perhaps Sonny wasn't the one who'd tailed me.

I ordered food for two and then stood under a tree to wait. I spotted Dr. Kirkland sitting at a table with a man I didn't recognize. Kirkland was on his phone and when his gaze caught mine, he shifted it away.

My cell phone beeped. I pulled it out of my purse and read the message.

Dimitri: *I haven't seen anyone following you.*

Athena: *That's a relief.*

When my name was called, I picked up the food, paid, and tucked the sack under my arm. I glanced at Kirkland and saw him put away his phone and stand up. Coincidence?

Athena: *Do you see Kirkland? He's standing in front of a picnic table. He got up as soon as I picked up my food. There's another man with him that I don't recognize. Keep your eye on*

*them. I'm going to start toward the marina. If they follow, text
me and I'll go a different direction.*

Dimitri: *Got it.*

I strolled calmly down to the boardwalk and headed
south along it. As I drew near the marina, my phone
beeped.

Dimitri: *Kirkland and his buddy are some distance behind
you. Change directions and I'll let you know what he does. If
he follows you, head back to Spencer's. We'll figure out what to
do from there.*

I stopped at the light at Pine Avenue, crossed Greene
Street, then headed west. Half a block away, I got another text message.

Dimitri: *Coast is clear. They kept walking when you turned.*

Athena: *I'll circle around and meet you at the boat.*

Dimitri: *Not okay with that. Let's meet at the garden center.
I'll use the back lane so I'll know if anyone is tailing me.*

I sent him a thumbs-up emoji and then turned back
toward Greene Street. When I reached Spencer's, Dad
was ringing up a customer at the counter. I gave him a
quick wave and headed toward the back exit. Outside, I
sat at a black wrought-iron patio table as far from the
shop's rear door as possible.

As I was setting out the food, Case entered through
the back gate. "No one followed you here," he said,
pulling out a chair to sit down. "I didn't see anyone behind me, either."

"Good. Then we should be able to work here privately."

Case began eating, wolfing down his taco as though
he were starving. "Delicious. Thanks. Another meal for
which I'm in your debt."

"Don't worry about it."

"I'm not used to accepting charity. I'll make it up to
you."

I'd be satisfied with him not trying to take back the *Treasure of Athena*.

"My sister Delphi has a meeting set up with Bob Maguire this afternoon at three fifteen to see if he can find out who owns the black SUV," I told him, "and my sister Maia said that Lila had indeed shown up for her yoga class on the morning Talbot Senior drowned, just as she had after Harry was murdered."

"The police must have interviewed her quickly and let her go both times."

"That's one of the perks of being a Talbot." I stopped to take a bite of my taco. "We've already spoken with Fatsis. Next up is your dinner with Marie. And I want to talk to Lila, so I thought I'd dash over to the yoga studio and catch her after her class tomorrow morning. I'll have to ask Maia what time to be there."

"Be there at eleven thirty," Case said. "The class starts at ten thirty."

"How do you know that?"

He shrugged. "She invited me to come with her."

At that moment Delphi walked out the door and stopped in surprise. With her hands on her hips she sauntered back to our table. "So this is the old friend who bought a new house. Nice to see you again, Dimitri."

"Afternoon, Delphi."

I said quickly, "I ran into Dimitri by the food trucks and told him my friend had canceled, so he offered to keep me company."

Delphi pulled out a chair at the patio table and sat down. "Right."

"What are you doing back from the diner so early?" I asked.

"Have you checked the time? It's one o'clock, Dad just left, and we're on duty."

"In that case, I'll let you both get to work." Case downed the last of his taco, scrunched the wrapper into a ball, and put it into the sack. Picking up his paper cup filled with iced tea, he rose. "Good to see you again, Delphi."

"Same here," she said, and swiveled to watch him stride along the path through neat rows of shrubs and young trees. As he slipped out the back gate, she said, "Now *he's* the kind of man you should go for, not that wuss Kevin."

I made no comment.

"So," she said, placing her chin in her palm and smiling at me, "are we really related to Dimitri or is that just your cover?"

"Like I told you, Dimitri thinks we're distantly related. He and I are working together to find Harry's murderer and hopefully halt the condo project, and that's as far as it goes."

"Don't forget," she said, rising, "you asked me to talk to Bob Maguire, and that means *I'm* working with you, too. So don't keep secrets from me. I'm not going to tell Mama."

"I'm not keeping a secret from you. We're working together and that's all."

"Okay," she said skeptically, then paused to listen. "That's the front door chime. We'd better get out there."

I watched the clock for the next two hours and when Maguire showed up, I breathed a sigh of relief. Step one of my plan had begun. I made a list of items that appeared to be missing, all fictitious, and after he'd been there for fifteen minutes, I headed out to the garden to give it to him. There I found my sister and Maguire with their heads bent over his coffee cup.

I put my arm across her shoulders. "What're you doing, Sis?"

Maguire glanced up with a smile. "She's doing a reading for me."

"Is she now?" I pulled out a chair and sat down. "And what have you seen?"

"There's definitely a promotion in Bob's future," she said. "It came through very strong. And by the way, Bob would like to help find out who was following you."

"You don't know how much I appreciate it, Bob." I handed him the list. "And here's everything that seems to be missing from the office."

Maguire folded it, stuck it inside his jacket, then took out a notepad and pen. "Tell me the route you took when you were followed, and I'll check the traffic videos."

"You guys don't use iPads?" Delphi asked.

"Sure we do. But then it's online with the PD."

"Got it," I said. Shrewd guy.

I gave him my route information, resisted the urge to hug him, thanked him, and then he stood up to leave. "How about if we grabbed a cup of coffee at Jivin' Java's sometime?" he asked Delphi.

She smiled. "I'd like that."

"What time do you have to be here in the morning?" he asked. "Maybe we can meet before work tomorrow."

I left them arranging their coffee date and headed indoors to rearrange the display of garden tools and gloves. I had just finished when Delphi came scurrying over. "I've got to keep Mama from finding out about our coffee date."

"Don't worry. You're only meeting with him to find out who was following me."

"That's right. And Bob totally gets it about Sonny's influence, by the way. He's going back to the station tonight after the second shift ends to review those traffic tapes when all of Sonny's *friends*"—she used her fingers to put the word in quotes—"will be gone."

"Thanks, Delph," I said, putting my arm around her. "Good job."

I went into the office, shut the door, and phoned Case to update him on Maguire and my plan to see Lila in the morning.

"That's good news on the police front but I keep telling you, Athena, to let me work on Lila. She's not going to . . ."

"To what?"

"Hold on," he said. "A news bulletin just flashed across the TV screen." After another pause, he said, "I think that interview with Lila is going to have to wait. She was just arrested for murder."

CHAPTER TWENTY-SIX

I grabbed the TV remote and hit the power button. "What are they basing the charges on?"

"All it says is that they have DNA evidence that ties her to both deaths. A reporter is going to speak in a minute."

"She *lived* in the house, Case. Her DNA would be all over the place. There has to be something more than that. This doesn't smell right to me."

"On a positive note, at least they won't be looking for me anymore."

I watched the crime reporter move into position in front of the Sequoia courthouse. After he'd recapped the news of Lila's arrest and charges, he said, "Grayson Talbot is going to speak as soon as he and his lawyer arrive."

"And there's a black limo pulling up now." I sat down at the desk, watching as the limo driver opened the back door for Sonny. He emerged dressed in a black suit, white shirt, and black shoes. The driver went around to the other side and opened the door.

I nearly stopped breathing as Kevin stepped out and adjusted his tie.

"Athena? You still there?"

For a moment I was too shocked to answer, and then anger began to set in. Wearing a three-piece gray suit and carrying a black leather briefcase, Kevin marched proudly at Sonny's side across the lawn and up the courthouse steps.

"Looks like Kevin got that new job he told you about," Case said.

"That rat never said a word to me about Sonny hiring him."

"Mr. Talbot," the reporter said, holding the mic up to Sonny's face, "your wife has been arrested for the murder of your father and his assistant. What are your thoughts?"

"I'm shocked," Sonny said, making a bad attempt at playing the part of a distraught husband. "Completely shocked."

"Do you think the detectives made a mistake?" the reporter asked.

"I was told the detectives were seeking the man who broke into my father's office, so naturally this has come as a total surprise. But I put my trust in the detectives right from the start. I know they wouldn't do anything in haste."

"Then you believe the charges against your wife are valid?" the reporter asked.

"Don't put words in my mouth," Sonny chided. "My point is that we have to trust that our system works and let the experts handle things."

"He's talking around the question," Case said. "A born politician."

"I understand you've hired a lawyer for her already," the reporter said.

"As soon as I got the news. In fact, let me introduce him." Sonny put his hand on Kevin's shoulder. "This is Kevin Coreopsis, a local resident who most recently worked for a powerful New York law firm. I know Kevin will do a fine job representing my wife. Now if you'll excuse us, we have business to attend to."

"I can't believe it," I said. "Kevin is supposed to be fighting for *our* cause."

"So was Fatsis, Athena. For some people, money talks. Kevin is obviously one of them."

"He was a bankruptcy attorney. He's never handled a murder case before."

"Probably why Sonny hired him. Sonny's a shrewd man, Athena. He's getting his wife out of the way by hiring an inexperienced lawyer for her and removing your legal advisor at the same time. You can bet Lila won't be cleared or released on bond with Kevin representing her, not in a murder case."

I hit my fist on the desk. "I *knew* he was setting her up. Someone needs to warn her not to use Kevin. She needs a genuine defense attorney."

"Does she have relatives we can contact?"

"I have a better idea. I'll go see her in jail."

"You mean *we'll* go see her."

"You can't, Case. You need a driver's license to get inside."

He muttered something under his breath.

I thought for a moment, then snapped my fingers. "Bob Maguire! I'll contact him and see what he can do to get me in."

I looked up as the office door opened and my dad and mom and Delphi came in.

"Gotta go," I said to Case. "Family is here. Text me after your dinner."

I hung up as Delphi said excitedly, "Did you hear about Lila Talbot's arrest?"

"I've got the report on now," I said, pointing to the TV.

"Can you believe she killed her father-in-law *and* Harry?" Delphi shook her head in amazement.

"What I can't believe is that Kevin is working for Sonny," Mama said. "Shame on him!"

At least she wouldn't be bugging me to date Kevin anymore.

"We're going to have to hire a lawyer to get that injunction," Dad said.

"Lisa Pappas's son is a lawyer in Saugatuck." Mama opened her purse. "He does all kinds of legal work. I'll call Lisa right now and see if she can get him to help us."

While my mom was on the phone, I motioned for Delphi to come with me.

As she pulled the office door shut behind her, she said, "Looks like you're off the hook with Kevin."

"Thank God! Hey, I need a favor. Will you call Bob and ask him to get me into the jail to see Lila tomorrow?"

"Thenie, that's a pretty big favor to ask. We haven't even met for coffee yet."

"Then I'll call Bob myself."

I pulled out my phone and she put her hand over it. "Never mind. I'll do it."

An hour later Delphi sought me out in the garden center, where I was moving tables around to make way for new inventory.

"You've got your interview. Bob listed you as a cousin and no one questioned it. Be at the jail tomorrow at three p.m. when there's a shift change."

"Fantastic. Thank you, Delph."

"Now do me a favor." She turned and started toward

the door. "Figure out how I'm going to pull off skipping breakfast with the family tomorrow morning."

When the shop closed that evening, I already had my blog written in my head, so it didn't take me long to write and post it. Then I sped home to spend the rest of the evening with my son. I helped him with his math, always a tough subject for him; then, while he worked on a reading assignment, I made a list of questions to ask Lila.

I had one eye on my cell phone, waiting for a report on Case's dinner with Marie, but after I'd finished reading to Nicholas, tucked him into bed, and retired to my room, it still hadn't come in.

I'd just about given up when my phone buzzed. "Okay to talk now?" Case asked.

"I thought you forgot."

"Forget you, Athena? I have a mind like a steel trap. I just wanted to make sure you had your time with your son."

I was glad he couldn't see me because I was smiling tenderly. Why did he have to be so thoughtful? "Thank you. How was dinner?"

"Boring for the most part, but I did learn something new. Remember when Marie said she was so distraught over her breakup with Talbot that she saw Dr. Kirkland, and he prescribed depression and sleep meds? What she didn't tell us was that she refused the sleeping pills because she was afraid of what might happen while she was asleep, like driving. He assured her that they were so safe, he'd prescribed them for Lila Talbot."

"Kirkland told Marie that? He's not supposed to reveal patient information."

"But he did and then lied to us about it."

"Kirkland has to know he could lose his medical license for that."

"He took that chance for a reason, Athena. We're going to have to talk to him again."

"He'll never agree to see us."

Case said in a sinister voice, "I know ways to make people talk."

"Yes, you do, but don't get me started on that."

"Subject closed."

"I do have some good news to report. Thanks to Officer Maguire I'm going to see Lila at the jail at three o'clock tomorrow. I've already made a list of questions, so I'll add one about her sleeping pill prescription. Let's meet across the street from the jail ten minutes before so you can look over the questions. There's a Mexican restaurant with a parking lot in back. I'll pull in there and wait for you."

Case yawned. "Sounds like a plan."

"I'll let you go. I'm tired, too."

"*Kalinýchta,* Athena," he said.

"*Kalinýchta* to you, too."

I was still smiling as I hung up the phone

IT'S ALL GREEK TO ME
blog by Goddess Anon

Backstabbers come in all shapes and sizes . . .

. . . but you don't expect it to be someone you trust. Then you see him out with a person you never dreamed he'd associate with, a truly despicable person through and through, and you feel like you've been kicked in the stomach. It happened to me just today . . .

Wednesday

As the school bus stopped at the corner by our house, Nicholas—*damn!*—Niko—gave me a kiss and said, "*Na écheis mia ypérochi méra*, Mamá."

"Niko, I have no idea what you just said."

"Yiayiá's right. You should've gone to your Greek lessons. It means have a great day."

"Okay, Mr. Smarty-Pants, back at ya." As the bus door opened, I gave him a fist bump—he hated to be embarrassed in front of others by a hug—and watched him climb aboard. I arrived at the diner to find Maia, Selene, and Mama gathered around a laptop at the counter as usual. By the way they kept shaking their heads and Mama kept clicking her tongue in disgust, I guessed they were reading my blog about Kevin.

"That poor young woman," Mama said. "She needs to find herself a new boyfriend and make sure the *vlákas* sees her with him."

Curse words I knew. Mama was calling the man she had handpicked for me a jackass. I had to hide my smile.

"Let's leave a comment to that effect," Maia said to Selene.

I smiled inwardly. I'd never flaunt Case in front of Kevin. Goddess Anon would simply thank them for the advice.

Hold the phone. Had I just insinuated that Case was my boyfriend?

"If I knew who she was I would find her a good man," Mama said, shoving back her heavy gold bracelet as if she were preparing to duke it out with someone.

"How do you know she's talking about a boyfriend?" I asked.

"Pah," Mama said. "It's as obvious as the nose on my face." She glanced around. "I haven't seen Delphi this morning. She's usually the first one here."

"She said her stomach wasn't feeling good," I told them, "so she was going to have some tea, then go straight to Spencer's." I stuck my head through the pass-through window to say good morning to my grandparents, then said, "I have to go. I want to finish setting up the outdoor tables so we can hold the GMA meeting outside this evening."

"Good thinking," Mama said. "It's going to be a beautiful night, so maybe that'll soften the bad news about Kevin and Fatsis."

I had parked close to Spencer's and walked to the diner, so as I walked back, I ran over my list of questions for Lila. My phone beeped for an incoming text from Case, and I read: *Look casually over your left shoulder.*

There was a black SUV following me again, and it wasn't a Cadillac.

Where are you? I texted back.

Dimitri: *A block behind you.*

Athena: *Why would someone follow me now? The signed document is gone.*

Dimitri: *I don't have a clue. Could it be because of your jail interview?*

Athena: *Who would know unless someone inside the jail was watching the names on the list? I guess there's one way to find out.*

Dimitri: *Wait, Athena. Don't do anything—*

I came to a dead stop and aimed my phone at the SUV and driver to take a photo, but the vehicle immediately sped away.

"S-Q-A one five three . . ." That was all I'd had time to make out.

I texted Case: *I tried to get a look at the driver, but he sped away. But I did get a partial license plate number. I'll give it to Maguire and let him work on it. I just can't figure out why this joker is following me now.*

Dimitri: *Let's not treat it as a joke. No one should be following you. If you see the SUV again, duck into a shop and text me. If I'm not nearby, I'll be there in a few minutes.*

Okay, I texted back. At least it was reassuring to know Case was close by. But who could be following me and why? Sonny? Fatsis? Marie? I couldn't imagine it being Marie, so it had to be one of the two men.

Delphi was already at Spencer's when I arrived, having her coffee with Dad in the office. We went over plans for the day and then Dad left to get the store ready to open.

Delphi waited until he was gone, then said, "What did you tell Mama?"

"You had a stomachache and were going straight to Spencer's to have tea."

"Good. Unfortunately, I have bad news for you. Bob wasn't able to review those traffic tapes because of Lila's arrest. Too many of Sonny's cohorts were buzzing around. But he's going to try again tonight. He said you need to know that when you see Lila and you're in a room with other visitors, be careful. You never know when a jail snitch might be placed in the next cubicle."

"Got it. Tell Bob thanks for the warning."

The hours seemed to crawl by until two thirty, when I began to prepare for my trip to the jail. I told Dad I had an errand to run that would take about an hour and left. The less he knew, the less he had to let slip to Mom.

Case was waiting in the parking lot, and as soon as I pulled into a slot, he hopped into the passenger seat. He was looking more Greek every day. He had a good tan now, making his deep-set golden eyes stand out. His dark beard was close-cropped against his chin and his hair was thick, dark, and wavy, brushing his collar in the back. His clothing—boat shoes, dark blue jeans, and a blue plaid button-down shirt—fit right in with what the locals wore, nothing like that vogueish stranger I'd first met. He was becoming more of a Sequoian every day.

I told him about Bob's warning and then gave him my list of questions. He read them over and nodded his approval. "Are you ready to do this?"

I took a deep breath. "As ready as I'll ever be. My biggest hurdle will be to gain her trust."

"As you question her, keep in mind that she's still a suspect. She'll want to convince you of her innocence, whether it's true or not."

"Got it."

"I'll wait on the boat. Meet me there when you're done."

He got out of my Toyota and walked away. As soon as he was out of sight, I locked my car and headed across the street. Inside the four-story redbrick building I stopped at the bullet-proof glass window to state my purpose. I had to slide my ID through the opening, put my purse and cell phone in a locker, and then pass through a metal detector. Fortunately, they let me take a pen and notepad with me.

I was escorted into a wide, white-walled room that contained a long gray Formica counter, a glass partition that separated the visitor side from the inmate side, and a row of black plastic chairs with half walls dividing each section. Besides the officer who'd come with me, only one other person was in the room, seated in the last chair. I was given a seat in the middle and told to wait.

"You'll have thirty minutes to talk, Miss Spencer," he said.

In a few minutes, a female officer escorted Lila through the door on her side. Her ankles were cuffed, her usually well-coifed blond hair was straight, and she wore no makeup, just an orange jumpsuit and black flip-flops.

Lila sat down, leaned toward the speaker in the glass, and said arrogantly, "You're the *last* person I expected to see. What are you doing here?"

"Hoping I can help you."

She looked at me with deep suspicion. "Why? You barely know me."

"My sister Maia knows you and she believes you're a good person. And we both believe you've been framed." Maia would kill me if she knew what I'd just said.

Lila looked down at her perfectly manicured nails. "So you're going to help me get out of here, like that sham of a lawyer was supposed to do yesterday?"

"You're exactly right about your lawyer, and that's why I came. Kevin Coreopsis isn't a criminal defense attorney. He was a bankruptcy lawyer in Manhattan. Until your husband hired him, he worked as a legal aide. He doesn't have any criminal defense experience at all."

Scowling, Lila said, "Which is undoubtedly why my husband hired him."

"I think there's another reason, too. Kevin was supposed to help the Greek shop owners stop the condominium project. By hiring him, your husband is trying to kill our chances of doing that."

"It figures. That S.O.B. would do anything to rid himself of me."

"Then let's work together to stop him."

Lila crossed her arms and tried to cross one leg, but the cuffs wouldn't let her. "How do I know you're not working for him, too?"

"I promise you I'm not. What Sonny wants to do to our community makes me sick. My grandparents are going to lose their livelihood and their home, and so are others in Little Greece."

"Hold it. Who's Sonny?"

"Sorry. It's our nickname for your husband."

Lila snickered. "It fits him, the spoiled, selfish little egotist. So how can you help me?"

"Number one is that you need to hire your own defense attorney and fire Kevin. And the rest will depend on the information you give me."

Lila glanced around the stark room, and for the first time, I saw a flash of fear in her eyes. She leaned forward, her face strained and intense. "Look, I don't know who I can trust here. If you really want to help, find me a lawyer from out of town, someone who isn't under the Talbot influence. Can you do that?"

"Yes, I can and will. But I need you to answer some questions first."

"What do you need to know?"

"Let's start from what happened yesterday. The TV news reported that DNA testing confirmed that you killed both your father-in-law and Harry."

"Complete fabrication. And of course, the cops had to announce it in front of everyone at the hair salon when they handcuffed me. I've never been so humiliated." She shook her head. "I can't believe this is happening. I mean, how would they have found my DNA on my father-in-law? I didn't try to pull him out of the tub. I could see that he'd drowned. And I certainly didn't touch Harry when I saw that he was dead."

"Did you touch anything in the room when you checked on them?"

She rubbed her forehead. "I opened my father-in-law's bedroom and bathroom doors . . . and I opened the office door to check on Harry. But the maid would've touched those doors, too, and so would Grayson." Her eyes filled with tears. "I don't understand how they could arrest me based on that."

I didn't want to tell her that they were probably looking for more evidence to indict her, so I stuck to my list. "Is there anything you remember seeing in your father-in-law's bathroom that looked out of place?"

"No."

"Anything that stands out as odd about either man's death?"

She glanced down for a moment, then shrugged. "I don't remember anything odd."

"You're going to have to picture both scenes again and write down everything you remember. The tiniest detail could help your new lawyer."

"Okay."

"Now I want to review the statement your husband made to the newspaper and on TV. He said his father had fallen asleep during his bath, slipped under the water and drowned, and that you found him the next morning."

"Correct, and only because Grayson texted me to check on his father before I came downstairs to breakfast."

I wrote it down. "According to Grayson, because of what you saw, it was an easy call for the coroner to make and that was why no autopsy was performed, which, in case you didn't know it, is against the law. When a person dies alone, an autopsy is required."

"I'm sure Kirkland was following Grayson's orders."

"That's what I figured."

Her arms still crossed, she shook her head, her upper lip curled in disgust. "Nasty man. I never liked him."

"Here's where it gets convoluted. In a later report

your husband was quoted as saying that you gave his father a sleeping pill before he retired for the evening and that caused him to fall asleep in the bath and drown."

Lila banged her fist on the countertop. "That *bastard.* He's lying through his teeth. I don't have any sleeping pills. I've never needed them, and if you don't believe me"—she paused—"I was going to say check with Kirkland's office or the doctor I saw before him, but they can't show you my records. You'll have to take my word for it."

"Does your husband use sleeping pills?"

"Not when we were still in the same room. I can't say whether he does now. Boy, that creep sure is throwing the blame on me, isn't he?"

"Not just him, Lila. Kirkland told Marie Odem that he'd prescribed sleeping pills for you."

"You've got to be kidding me. Why would he tell her that?"

"She said it was to convince her to take them, too."

Lila said through gritted teeth, "I swear I'll sue him for invasion of privacy as soon as I get out of here."

"Go for it."

"I went to Kirkland *once* for a sinus infection, and only because my husband insisted I use him. Otherwise, I'd have gone somewhere else because I can't stand the man."

"Why did your husband want you to see Kirkland?"

"Because his father's medical insurance covered all of us there. I never questioned it before, but now I'm wondering why an insurance policy wouldn't have covered me everywhere."

"Perhaps it was about something more than a simple insurance policy."

"Like putting Kirkland on the payroll? As I said before, my husband wants to get rid of me in the worst way. And this *is* the worst way—accused of murder with a sham lawyer to defend me."

"When you go for your initial hearing, you have to tell the judge you don't like the lawyer your husband hired and ask for one of your own choice." I glanced at the time: I had fifteen more minutes. "Why did your husband ask you to check on his father?"

"Because no one else was available. Our staff consists of two housekeepers and a cook, none of whom were around then. It didn't seem out of the ordinary for him to say, 'Lila, would you check on Dad? He hasn't been down for breakfast and he's usually here before I am,' or words to that effect."

"Describe what happened when you found him." I readied my pen.

"First I knocked on the door to his suite and called his name. When I didn't hear anything, I peered into the bedroom. The bathroom door was closed, and I noticed that his bed hadn't been slept in, so I knew something was up. I knocked on the bathroom door and when he didn't answer I looked in, saw him floating"— she made a face and shuddered—"and ran downstairs to get Grayson."

I wrote it down. "You didn't call 911 first?"

"I was in a panic. I couldn't think what to do."

"Here's something that puzzles me. Grayson gave two statements to the press with different accounts of how he found Harry's body. When I interviewed him, however, he admitted that you'd actually found Harry, and that, because you'd also found his father's body, he didn't want the police to connect you with their deaths."

"Wasn't that gallant of him?" She shook her head in disgust. "I actually thought for once he was trying to protect me."

"He also told me you had given him two different accounts of the position of Harry's body."

With her teeth pressed tightly together she muttered a swear word. "I told him *exactly* what I saw. Harry was sitting in my father-in-law's chair with his face down on the desk, as if he'd just collapsed forward."

"Not lying on the floor on his back with a receipt in his hands?"

"Absolutely not. His arms were limp at his sides. Why in hell would he need to lie about me changing my story?"

Picking up my notepad I said, "I asked him why, and I'll read his exact words. 'Finding both bodies was too much for her mind, which was fragile to start with, even before my father emotionally abused her. I'll forever blame myself for not putting a stop to it. But the truth was, he had us both on tight leashes.' "

Lila stared in openmouthed surprise. "I have a fragile mind?" She squeezed the counter's edge so hard that her knuckles turned white. "I would never have been able to live in that house if I wasn't tough. And as far as Grayson being on a tight leash, what a laugh. He was beyond spoiled. And that's why he was furious when his dad pulled the plug on the condo project. That was going to be his baby, his income, and Daddy changed his mind because something actually caused that ice cold Grinch's heart to melt a little."

After writing down her answer I asked, "Do you know what changed his mind?"

"All I know is that after my father-in-law attended one of your GMA meetings, his last one, actually, he and Harry had a private meeting about it, and Grayson wasn't invited."

"How do you know their meeting was about the condo project?"

"Because Grayson ranted about it all day. I finally said, 'Tell your father how you feel and leave me out of it.'" She huffed louder. "Fragile mind, my ass."

"How soon after that did your father-in-law drown?"

"Two days later."

After noting it, I glanced at my list and then at my watch. My thirty minutes were almost up but I still had a few more questions. "I want to read you one more statement your husband made about you. And I'm quoting him again. 'She was the last one to see my father alive and the first to find him dead, and that does make one wonder at times.'"

Lila hit her fist on the counter again. "See how that S.O.B. is setting me up?"

"Five minutes," the officer announced from behind me.

"What I don't understand is that if you have an iron-clad prenuptial agreement, Sonny—I'm sorry, Grayson—could have simply divorced you."

"Actually, I found out our prenup isn't ironclad after all. A friend of mine told me she got hers broken by a good divorce attorney, so I told Grayson I was going to file for divorce in a different county. He hit the roof, insisting there was no way he was going to split his assets with me."

"When was that?"

"About a month ago." She sat back shaking her head in disbelief. "I *knew* I shouldn't go check on Harry and yet I did because Grayson said he was at the office already, which was another lie."

I wasn't thoroughly convinced Lila hadn't played a

part in at least one of the murders, so I decided to test her. "You're going to have to tell your defense attorney everything you've told me. He'll hire a private investigator to check your facts, so you'll have to be accurate."

She wasn't rattled at all. In fact, for the first time since she came into the room, I saw signs of the old Lila. With a coy smile she said, "Oh, I've got plenty of information for the investigator. I can't wait to see Grayson's face when he gets those divorce papers."

"Time to go," the officer called to me.

"One more minute," I said. Turning back to Lila, I asked, "Do you have anything that would throw suspicion back on him?"

Lila looked up, thinking, then said, "I know Grayson has a lot of pull with the police chief because he and my husband golf together at the country club frequently. I believe Grayson paid the chief's membership dues, too. Same with some of the county councilmen. I'm sure his influence extends further up the ladder than that, but I don't know how far."

"That could be deemed bribery. How about the coroner, Dr. Kirkland? I know he lied about prescribing you sleeping pills."

I stopped talking as the door opened on her side and a female inmate was brought in and seated next to her. A minute later, the officer let in a man on my side who sat across from her. With a whole row of chairs vacant, I knew instantly that they were placed there for a reason.

As they began to talk, I whispered to Lila, "Be careful. That woman could be a jail snitch."

She whispered back, "She's my cellmate."

CHAPTER TWENTY-SEVEN

"Let's go," the officer said sternly to me. "Her attorney is waiting to see her."

So Kevin was waiting outside, was he? I leaned closer to the speaker so our neighbors wouldn't hear me and said softly, "Don't talk to your cellmate about anything connected with the murders, got it?"

She nodded, then whispered, "What about the lawyer Grayson hired?"

"Don't give him any information, either. Tell him you're getting your own attorney and do *not* let Grayson bully you into believing you can't do that."

The two people next to us weren't saying a word. I gave them a sidelong glance and saw that they were both sitting at angles so that they could see as well as hear us. I glanced toward the man, but he didn't look away. "Can I help you?"

He turned and locked eyes with his partner on the other side. I gave Lila a last look—hoping everything we'd discussed had resonated—then rose and went out the door.

Down the hallway Kevin was standing before a metal detector, briefcase in hand, looking sophisticated in a new navy suit, white shirt, and red, blue, and white print tie.

Fuming with anger, I strode straight toward him. "Look who's here. The traitor. I don't know how you face yourself in the mirror, Kevin."

At that moment the female officer brought Lila around the corner, halting Kevin's reply. The officer opened a door to let Lila inside, allowing a view of a small conference room. Closing the door, she said, "Your client is ready, sir."

"I'll be right in." He pointed an index finger at me and said quietly, "We need to talk."

"Yes, we do. I'd love to hear how you were able to turn against your own people."

"Just remember I'm not the only traitor here."

He walked into the room and shut the door firmly behind him, leaving me staring in bewilderment. The officer was watching me, so I turned and walked up the hallway to the exit, retrieved my belongings, and stepped outside. I took a breath of fresh air to clear my head, but it didn't help. My mind was spinning. Why had he called me a traitor?

I got into my car and drove to a parking lot close to the marina, then texted Case: *I'm coming aboard. Make some tea for me.*

I walked briskly along the boardwalk to the last pier, then hopped across to the *Páme* and opened the door to go below. "I'm here," I called.

"Come on down. Your tea is brewing."

I went down the steps, dropped my purse on the small sofa, and pulled out a chair at the table. As I sank into it, Case placed a mug of hot tea in front of me, the bag still in it. "That must have been some interview."

"The interview actually went well. Then I ran into Kevin."

"Ah. Now I understand the need for tea."

I picked up the mug with both hands and took a soothing sip. Case pulled out the chair opposite me and sat down, resting his chin in his hand as he studied me. He was so different than pudgy-faced, self-centered Kevin I wanted to hug him. My thoughts flashed back to what Kevin had called me, and I got angry all over again.

"Tell me about it. Was it a showdown? Did you pull your six-shooter on him?"

"The other way around. After I told him he was a traitor to his people, he said I was a traitor, too, and then he left me hanging. How am *I* a traitor?"

"That's why you're upset? Athena, he's acting like a little kid firing back with the first thing that comes to mind." Case reached across the table and put his hands over mine. "Think of it this way. You're free of Kevin now."

I glanced at his big strong hands and felt a wave of affection flow through me. Instead of recoiling from him in a pure gut reaction, I let his hands stay and placed my other hand on his. He must have felt something, too, because a smile spread across his face and his eyes softened. But a moment later he pulled his hands away and sat back as though nothing had happened.

What *had* just happened? Had Case suddenly realized that there wasn't anyone holding me back now? Did he feel as though he had to move our relationship forward? Was that why he was so quick to take his hand away?

Stretching out his legs and folding his arms, he asked, "What's your assessment of Lila?"

I took another soothing sip of tea, forcing my brain to shift the focus from our relationship onto important

matters. "She was completely forthcoming with the
events that led to both murders."

"I'm glad you two had a frank talk, but if you went
into the meeting with the mindset that Sonny is guilty,
she probably sensed it and played on your sympathies."

"She could have but I don't think she did. It was
clear to me that Lila has been put in a compromising
position. She's never had to take sleeping pills, and she
checked on both men only because Sonny asked her to.
She said that he's been angry ever since she told him
their prenup was breakable and she intended to file for
divorce. She's furious about him hiring Kevin to represent her, too. Which reminds me, I have to find her the
name of a good defense attorney from out of town."

"No matter what you believe about Sonny's role in
the murders, Athena, Lila hasn't been absolved yet."

"Believe me, I kept that in mind. It just seems that
everything is playing out in Sonny's favor, almost as
though he'd scripted it." I glanced at my watch, then
finished my tea and stood up, stuffing my notepad
back in my purse. "I've got to get back to Spencer's. I
said I'd be gone an hour and I'll just make it."

He got up and walked me to the upper deck. "What's
next on our agenda?"

"I'm hoping Bob Maguire will have some information on that black SUV by tomorrow. And I have to be at
the GMA meeting at Spencer's at eight. That means I
need to leave work by six so I have time to spend with
my son before the meeting."

My phone dinged with an incoming text. It was from
my sister Selene.

*Sonny moved up the demolition date. The bulldozers are
going to start the day after tomorrow.*

CHAPTER TWENTY-EIGHT

I stared at the text in horror, then showed it to Case. "What are we going to do?"

"We'll have to find an attorney today."

"Case, it'll take days to get an appointment and I have to find someone who's out of town to be sure there's no Talbot influence."

"Well"—he paused—"you could always gather the GMA members to form a human barricade in front of their shops."

"I'm serious, Case."

"So am I."

I texted Selene back: *Do Yiayiá and Pappoús know?*

Selene: *They got a notice saying to get the diner cleared out tomorrow.*

Athena: *Dad and Mom?*

Selene: *They know, too. Family meeting at the diner tonight after your GMA meeting to discuss plans. Poor Yiayiá and Pappoús are in a panic.*

I could only imagine. I texted her that I'd talk to her

later, put my phone away, and dropped my head in my hands. How were we going to stop Sonny?

"I'll bet that human barricade is looking better and better," Case said.

"There's a meeting tonight. Maybe someone will have another idea."

"I'd like to be there."

I studied him for a moment. He definitely looked Greek enough, but he was still a stranger. "The only way it'll work is if you slip in through the back gate after the meeting starts and stay out of sight."

He gave me a nod, but the little smile that flickered momentarily concerned me.

I left Spencer's at six and made good old hamburgers and French fries for Nicholas and myself, a mouthwatering change from the Greek food at the diner we normally had. We talked about school and a girl who he shyly admitted liked him. Then we cleaned up the kitchen together and started on his homework.

Maia came home at seven and Selene at seven thirty, so I had a chance to freshen up before heading back for the meeting. I took my car because of the threat of a thunderstorm, and as I drove up Pine Avenue toward Greene Street, I saw an army of bulldozers and earthmovers along the curb, ready to turn Little Greece into rubble.

I parked in the lane behind Spencer's and sat for a moment. Through the blowing tree branches and the swaying Chinese lanterns that outlined the patio area, I could see my statue of Athena standing tall and proud among the gathering. This meeting was our last chance to put our heads together to figure out a way to stop the madness. For the first time I felt like the Goddess Athena, strong in my convictions and ready to take on those bulldozers myself. The nerve endings in my muscles twitched at the thought of fighting Sonny—to the bitter end if I had to.

But the energy inside the enclosed garden area was not the same as mine. As I joined my family at the table in front, I could feel a sense of defeat among the members. I was surprised to see Marie Odem there, looking much older than her sixty-five years, her life's work about to be in ruins. Donald Fatsis, on the other hand, was nowhere to be seen. What a surprise.

My father opened the meeting by making sure everyone had received Sonny's notice. My friend Nancy, the owner of Downtown Shabby, stood up and said, "I walked past Don Fatsis's art gallery and it was already empty."

"That's not surprising," Barb said, "considering that he was working with Talbot."

"He left town," someone called. "I saw a moving van in front of his house yesterday."

That started an angry, noisy discussion until my father rapped his gavel on the table.

"We need to work together to get everyone's place of business emptied out. Do I have a volunteer to call truck rental agencies first thing in the morning? We're going to need every truck and all the manpower we can get."

Wait, I wanted to call out, w*e can't give up the fight yet. Surely someone has another idea.* But they were so busy making plans to move that my voice would've been lost in the hubbub. And no one seemed to remember that they were letting Sonny Talbot win. I didn't know what to do to stop them.

"I'll get as many trucks lined up as I can," my mother said.

"Some of us have vans and pickups," one man called.

"My son owns a moving van company in South Bend," a woman said. "I'll ask him to send trucks and men."

Out of the corner of my eye I caught sight of Case by the back gate. Oddly, instead of feeling panic at him being there, I felt a sense of calm. He nodded his head toward the statue of Athena, and as I looked over at her, my warrior spirit began to emerge once again.

"Pops, I want to say something," I said, and climbed onto a bench as he rapped his gavel to get everyone's attention.

"You've been meeting for months to stop the destruction of Little Greece," I began, "and with one paper notice, you're ready to give up? Are you going to let a bully drive you out of the shops you've put every hard-working dime into? You all know that Talbot Senior canceled this project because he saw the good in Little Greece. The only reason his son can go through with it now is because of his father's untimely death and your willingness to give up without a fight."

I let that sink in, watching as people shuffled their feet, looked down in shame, whispered to their neighbors, then finally began to get angry about the situation, and then I said, "Who wins this battle? Will it be us? Or Emperor Talbot?"

"But what else can we do?" Marie called.

"Doesn't anyone here have a son or daughter who's an attorney?" I asked.

"My son moved away," someone replied.

"So did mine," another added.

"Have you called to ask them for advice?" I asked. "We were warned several weeks ago that Talbot Junior was going ahead with the plans. What have you done to stop him?"

There was a general mumbling in the crowd, no one willing to admit that I was the only one who had tried to find help by enlisting Kevin. Finally, one man raised his hand. "My son is an attorney in Detroit, if that will do any good. I can call him."

"Contact him right now," I said. "Tell him what's happening and see if there's any way he can fax over to the court an emergency motion to halt the project."

He pulled out his phone and held it up. "I'll call right now," he said as he headed indoors.

Everyone applauded, so I continued.

"We are not going to be defeated. We cannot and will not let Talbot win. Forget about moving your belongings out. We'll keep your block of Greene Street from being destroyed. At dawn the day after tomorrow, we are going to show up in force to form a human chain from one end of the block to the other. And we'll stay there until we get that court injunction."

"What if Talbot calls the police?" someone called.

"They'd have to arrest everyone in the chain and we'll have another group ready to take their place," I said. "That means all of you have to get on the phone right away and line up family, friends, neighbors, and anyone else you can think of. Are you with me?"

The crowd was silent. Then Nancy called out, "Come on, folks. We can do this. If our ancestors fought against the Roman Empire, we can fight Talbot before he calls Sequoia *his* empire."

"Yes, we can do this," Barb said. "Talbot wouldn't dare mow all of us down with those giant machines. It'd be murder." She turned to me and said, "I'm with you, Athena."

"So am I," Nancy said.

Then many voices called out, "We're with you, too, Athena," and a cheer went up.

"Do we need to discuss this any further?" my dad asked.

"I make a motion that we meet at dawn in front of our shops and make that human chain," David, the owner of the men's clothing store, said.

"I'll second," Barb called.

"All in favor?" Dad asked.

All hands went up and an even louder cheer echoed through the breezy evening air.

As groups formed around the table at the front of the garden area, my dad began taking down names and organizing leaders. I slipped around the crowd and headed to the back gate to talk to Case.

He was smiling from ear to ear. "You did a great job, warrior goddess. I'd give you a hug, but it might attract attention."

"We're going to stop Sonny, Case. I can feel it."

"Athena?"

I glanced at the back lane and saw Kevin standing by my car. I walked up to the gate and asked, "What do you want?"

"A word, please?"

As I opened the gate, Case took my arm. "Are you sure you want to get into it with him now?"

"Oh boy, do I."

"Actually," Kevin said, "I'd like to talk to you both. In private."

I glanced at Case and he nodded. We exited the gate and followed Kevin up the lane away from Spencer's. As we stopped behind a storage garage to talk, headlights came on, blinding us, and then two policemen appeared in the light, walking toward us.

"Damn it," Case ground out. "It's a trap, Athena."

"Kevin, you set us up?" I cried.

"Turn around and put your hands behind your back," one of the officers ordered Case.

"What are the charges?" I asked as he handcuffed Case.

Ignoring me he said, "Case Donnelly, you're under arrest for the murder of Harry Pepper. You have the right to remain silent. Anything you say can and will be used against you in a court of law."

As the officer continued stating the Miranda rights I said, "Listen to me. This is Dimitrius Costas, my cousin. You can't arrest him. We don't even know who Case Donnelly is."

"Athena," Kevin said, "I told them who he is."

"Let's go," the officer said to Case.

I stepped in front of them. "You're making a mistake! He didn't commit a crime."

"Step out of our way or we'll take you in, too," the officer barked. The other officer got into the driver's side as his partner pushed Case's head down to get him into the back seat.

"Find that defense attorney and get him over to the jail," Case said before the door shut.

As the car backed up the alley, I turned on Kevin, so furious I could've scratched his eyes out. "You traitor!"

"*Me*? You want to talk about traitors? I know everything about you two. I was on the dock when you lied to me on the phone and said you weren't on the boat. I even followed you when you left. And I know you didn't meet accidentally at the food truck. You've been lying to me all along."

"And you haven't lied to me? Did you tell me Sonny was going to be your new employer? No, I heard it from

Lila. Did you tell me Sonny's plans to destroy Little Greece were going forward? No. Don Fatsis did."

"I wasn't going to accept Mr. Talbot's offer, not until I saw you with Case. You lied to me about your relationship with this man when I thought we had a future together. Now you're in trouble, too. You've been harboring a fugitive, aiding and abetting a murderer. That carries quite a prison sentence, in case you weren't aware of it."

"Kevin, listen to me carefully. Case didn't kill anyone."

Kevin made a sound of disgust.

"You're a jackass, you know that? If you don't believe me, take me with you to see your client. Remember your client? Lila Talbot? Whom you are supposed to represent as a defense attorney? What a laugh that is. You don't know the first thing about defending someone. In fact, I warned her not to talk to you. So if you want to hear the truth about Harry's and Talbot Senior's death, you need me there because she knows you're working for her husband. And while you're at it, if you're brave enough, question the coroner about why he broke the law and didn't do an autopsy on Talbot. If you *don't*, then let's talk about who's aiding and abetting a criminal."

"I don't want to hear this, Athena."

"Of course you don't, because you belong to Sonny Talbot now. He's been manipulating this whole show, Kevin, and you're going to be the one responsible for letting him get away with murder, not just destroying Little Greece. I hope you're proud of yourself."

I turned and walked away just as the clouds burst open. When Kevin put his hand on my shoulder I pulled away and dashed for my car. Inside, still in shock, I watched the end of the lane as the red and blue police lights faded and Case was taken to jail. Kevin gave me one last disgusted look through the heavy torrents now falling from the sky, and I knew Mama was going to hear about this one.

I glanced over at the garden center and saw that everyone had gone inside. Their plans had been made and the members were finally excited, while I felt at my lowest point ever. If Sonny got his way, I would indeed be charged with the crimes Kevin had listed. What was I going to do?

I looked at my watch. Even though it was past Nicholas's bedtime, I strongly felt the need to hold my son close, afraid of what the next day would bring. I pulled out of the alley and headed home.

Two blocks from my parents' house, I was suddenly jolted forward so hard, my airbags deployed. Momentarily shocked, I realized I'd been hit, so I unfastened my seat belt to get out. But before I could push the airbag out of the way, my car door was opened, and a tight black cloth bag was slipped over my head.

Before I had time to react, I was yanked out of the car and pushed down onto the street on my stomach, where I struggled with my captors as my hands and feet were bound. Then I was pulled to my feet and shoved into the back seat of a car facedown.

I tried to scream, but someone pressed my face into the leather until I was gasping for air. I heard a car door slam nearby and then could tell by the sound of the engine that my SUV was being driven away. The vehicle I was in pulled away, too. Everything happened so fast it took a minute for it to sink in. I'd been kidnapped.

"You won't get away with this," I said, my words muffled by the tight cloth pulling against my lips. "I'm due home. My parents will know something happened."

No one said a word.

I was driven around town, turning corners, as though the driver was trying to confuse me, but I could hear the familiar sounds of the harbor when the vehicle finally stopped. At that moment, my chin was pulled down and a gag was put around my mouth, making it impossible to scream or even talk.

I was dragged out of the door by my feet until they hit the ground, then I was raised up and pushed forward, taking shuffling steps into a building that echoed when the door slammed behind me. I could tell I was on a wood surface, but the room felt empty around me. Another door was opened, and I was shoved forward into another room where my captors forced me to sit on a creaky old desk chair and tied my ankles to the base.

In a panic, I took stock of my situation. My hands were bound behind me, my feet tied down, my mouth gagged, and my face covered. I heard footsteps retreating, then the door slammed, and I knew I was alone. I had no purse, no cell phone, and no way of untying myself. I was stuck and sure I was going to be the next one murdered.

Suddenly something sharp stabbed me in the arm, right through my shirt, and then everything went black.

I was jolted awake at the sound of a door opening, and then I heard heavy shoes walking toward me across the wood floor. I was groggy and hungry but otherwise still alive. I had no idea what time it was nor how long I'd been out, but judging by the gnawing hunger and thirst, it had been a long time.

The cord around my wrists was untied, my hands brought around to my lap, where my wrists were tied together again. My gag was removed, and the black cloth bag was yanked from my head. I blinked at the bright light shining in my face until I could see a lantern held in front of me, as though someone were studying me. The lantern was placed on the floor at my feet, revealing a short, stout man with craggy features, a red-veined nose, and a head full of white hair.

"Have a cup of coffee," Dr. Kirkland said, thrusting a cardboard cup at me.

CHAPTER TWENTY-NINE

"Dr. Kirkland?" I croaked, my throat parched. "You kidnapped me?"

He walked to a window that had been covered with a blanket and pulled back one corner to peer out. It was nighttime, but which night? My belly grumbled loudly, and I was desperate for water. Before I could ask another question, the coroner let the blanket drop, then dragged an old wooden folding chair from the rear of the shop and sat down, the chair groaning under his weight. He set a black medical bag down beside him.

My heart pounded in terror. I tried not to think about what was in the bag and braced myself for an interrogation. Instead he pulled out his cell phone to type a text.

To keep myself calm, I glanced around the room. Redbrick walls, polished cherry floors, shadeless windows, holes in the bricks where picture hangers had been—I was in the back room of Don Fatsis's art shop, near a bright red emergency exit sign over the back door that washed most of the room in a menacing glow.

I checked my watch and saw that it was almost four in the morning. But of which day?

Kirkland hit a button on his phone, then slid it into his white shirt pocket.

"How long have I been here?" I asked.

"Just drink your coffee."

I tried in vain to ignore the steaming liquid in front of me, not wanting to accept his offer, but out of a desperate need for hydration I gripped both hands around the cup and took a sip, then drank greedily, the coffee tasting sweet and pungent and warm. Then a frightening thought occurred to me. What if he'd poisoned the coffee?

As Kirkland glanced at his watch, I took deep breaths, trying to tamp down my fear before it paralyzed me. Putting on a brave front I asked, "You didn't put sleeping pills in my coffee, did you? Like you did with Talbot Senior?"

His lips twitched as he glanced at the empty doorway that opened into the front of the shop, the red sign near his head exaggerating his sunken, weary eyes. Otherwise he gave no indication that I'd struck a nerve.

"You drugged Harry Pepper, too, didn't you?" I gave him a moment as I finished the last sip of coffee. "How did Talbot bribe you into helping him? Offer you new office space or a guaranteed reelection?"

"You should have left it alone, Athena."

"Left what alone? The murders or the destruction of Little Greece? You're a medical professional. How did you get involved in all of this?"

"It doesn't matter. In three hours, this building will be rubble."

I swallowed hard. "You're going to leave me here?"

He glanced down at his clasped hands as though unable to look me in the eye. "That's the plan."

"Because I wanted to save my grandparents' home and diner?"

"No," came a man's voice from the doorway, "because you stuck your nose into my affairs."

I turned to see Sonny Talbot saunter out of the darkness, a smirk on his face. He stopped in the front doorway, half of his body draped in shadow and half bathed in red. He was dressed in a black jacket, pants, and black athletic shoes, which was why I hadn't heard him come in. "Did you really believe you could stop me?" he asked.

"Do you really think you can get away with *three* murders?"

He straightened, his smirk gone. "It's time for the chloroform, Doctor."

Sonny walked over to the window and pulled back a corner of the blanket as Kirkland opened his black bag. My stomach knotted as I watched the coroner take out a small brown glass bottle and a white cloth.

"Is that how you killed Harry?" I asked quietly. "You held the cloth over his face until he blacked out and then suffocated him?" When Kirkland didn't deny it, I asked, "Don't you think it's going to be a little too coincidental that I die the same way?"

"Your body will be buried under so many tons of rubble there probably won't be anything left of it," Sonny turned to say. "And if anyone should happen to find something, who do you think they'll call to test your remains?"

I followed his gaze over to Kirkland.

The coroner, of course.

"So you do all of Talbot's dirty work, *Doctor*?" I asked, trying to keep my teeth from chattering. "I know you prescribed sleeping pills for Lila so your master could murder his elderly father in his own bathtub. Imagine that scene, Doctor, Sonny waiting until his dad fell asleep, then holding his head underwater until he was dead. And then blaming it on his wife. What kind of man does that? A soulless man, that's who."

"That's enough," Sonny snapped, dropping the blanket.

I kept going, hoping to shake up Kirkland. "What was that oath you took when you graduated from medical school? First do no harm? Look at you now. You've become nothing more than one of Talbot's henchmen."

Kirkland's embarrassed shrug sickened me. "Unfortunately, kid, I don't have much more choice in this than you do."

"Doctor, please, why are you risking your life for him?" I began to plead. "Think about your wife. And your practice."

"This quack wouldn't have a practice if it weren't for me," Sonny answered for him.

Ignoring him I said, "Doctor Kirkland, listen to me. You still have time to back out. Cut a deal with the DA and save us both."

Kirkland wouldn't meet my gaze. "I'm sorry, Athena."

"Just shut up and give her the cloth," Sonny demanded.

The coroner glanced toward the rear of the store. "Did you hear that sound?"

"Don't stall, Dan," Sonny said. "Do your job."

"I'm not stalling. I heard something."

"Doctor," I pleaded, trying to regain Kirkland's attention as he stretched a thin pair of rubber gloves over each finger, "Lila knows about the sleeping pill conspiracy. She's going to hire a good defense lawyer and take her husband down. Do you want to go down with him?"

"I'm surprised she was smart enough to figure it

out," Sonny said, keeping his vigil at the window. "But then you were coaching her with your little jail chat, weren't you?" As Kirkland uncapped the bottle, Sonny said, "Lila won't be a problem. Do you know how many inmates are killed in prison each year by their own cell-mates?"

Dear God. Sonny was going to have Lila killed, too. And who would think to blame him for a death that happened in jail?

As Kirkland approached me with cloth in hand, I was trembling all over. I couldn't leave my son without a mother. How could I stop them?

My voice shaking with fear I asked, "How does it feel to be a hired assassin, Doctor?"

Kirkland's craggy face flushed a deep red, but he didn't answer.

I kicked my chair backward against the slick hard-wood floor as Kirkland stepped closer. "How do you sleep at night knowing you helped this power-hungry lunatic murder his own father? And Harry Pepper, too, who never uttered an unkind word to anyone?"

"If you're trying to prod his conscience," Sonny said, "you're wasting your time."

"How would you know? You have no conscience," I shot back. "Your father did, though. That's why he canceled the project. He was a better man than you'll ever be."

"He made a mistake, that's all. Fortunately, he didn't live long enough to regret it." Sonny's phone beeped. He pulled it out, read the text, and muttered, "Damn that stupid kid."

"What is it?" Kirkland asked.

"Kevin wants to talk to me. Hold off on the cloth, Dan. He says he has critical information." Sonny began typing on his phone. "I told him to meet us inside the front door."

"There's that sound again," Kirkland said. "It's coming from the back alley."

"Go check it out then," Sonny said as he sauntered toward me. "I've got a question for you now, Miss Goody Two-Shoes. How does it feel to know that even your boyfriend turned against you?" He bent down at the waist to study me, his eyes sweeping over me as I continued to inch backward. "What did he see in you anyway?"

"Kevin is a good man," I argued. "He took the job with you to get even with me. If he knew what you were really like—"

"A good man," Sonny said, cutting me off. "Who do you think has been following you in the black SUV?"

The news hit me hard, but I wasn't about to let Sonny see it. "I knew it was him," I shot back. "He told me."

"Ah," Sonny said, "he told you. Did he also tell you that he caused your accident and broke into your shop to get the documents? Did he happen to mention who ratted out your new boyfriend?"

I stared at him in shock. If Kevin would do those things for Sonny, he really had turned against me.

"Now Mr. *Donnelly* is going to prison for killing Harry, and guess who his prosecutor will be? My good friend John Glasser."

Cold fear gripped my spine. The DA was on Sonny's payroll, too.

I could hardly hold back my tears. First my husband had let me down, leaving me feeling unlovable and worthless, and now Kevin had gone so far as to hand me over to a killer. The one man who hadn't let me down, who had encouraged me to stand up for myself, who'd shown me that my decisions mattered, would now be caught and tried for murder, and there was nothing I could do to help him. I had let Case down.

"There's the look I was waiting for," Sonny said, his mouth shaping into a crooked grin. "Almost makes this whole damn mess worthwhile." Still watching me, Sonny called to Kirkland, who'd stepped out the back door, "Hurry up, will you? We've got to get to the front before the Boy Scout shows up."

"Too late for that," came a voice from behind him. "Untie her, Mr. Talbot."

Sonny twisted around to see who was talking, and there was Kevin standing in the front doorway pointing a compact handgun at him. Kirkland was nowhere to be seen.

I wanted to shout Hallelujah! "Kevin, thank God!"

"I heard what he told you, Athena," Kevin said, "and everything he told you is a lie. I had no idea what he did to his father and Harry or I would've called the police. And I didn't break into Spencer's or hit your car. That was Kirkland." He aimed the gun at Sonny's chest. "What are you waiting for, *Mister* Talbot?" Kevin asked with a sneer. "I said to untie her."

As Sonny loosened the cords he said, "You're making a big mistake, Kevin. You can make millions if you stick with me. All you have to do is walk away from here. You didn't see a thing."

"He's a psychopath, Kevin," I said, rubbing my sore wrists as Sonny straightened. "Don't listen to him."

"Untie her ankles, too," Kevin said.

I watched as Sonny knelt in front of me and began to work on the knots, all the while thinking, *hurry, hurry*. I knew he was planning something. He fumbled with them for so long, Kevin finally came to see what the problem was.

"Kevin, he's stalling," I said. "Make him stand back and I'll do it."

"You heard her," Kevin said. "Stand back."

But just as I bent down, Kevin collapsed in a heap onto the floor. I straightened with a gasp, and my stomach twisted in fear as I saw Kirkland standing beside Kevin holding a hypodermic needle. "That should keep him out for a while."

"It took you long enough," Sonny said. He picked up the gun and stuck it inside his belt in the back of his pants. "Stupid kid. Tie him up next to her."

"Grayson," Kirkland said, packing up his bag, "I'm washing my hands of this. The police could be on their way right now."

"Tie him up next to her," Sonny shouted, "or so help me I'll make sure you stay here with them."

The implied threat was enough to get the coroner moving. As Sonny returned to my chair to bind my wrists, I put them behind me, then struggled with him to keep my hands free only to have Kirkland grab my arms from behind and pin them down. I fought both men, but I wasn't strong enough to stop them.

I saw something out of the corner of my eye, another man silently approaching, his wavy dark hair and dark beard slowly emerging from under the red glow of the exit sign. Tears of joy and relief welled in my eyes. My Greek hero had come.

Case put his fingers to his lips, warning me to be quiet, then he grabbed the gun from Sonny's belt and backed away as Sonny whirled around. He would have charged Case but then he heard the click of the trigger and it froze him in his tracks.

"Back against the wall," Case ordered. "You, too, Kirkland, stand beside him. Leave your bag where it is. The police are right behind me."

I quickly untied my ankles and knelt down beside Kevin, feeling for a pulse in his neck. "He's alive," I said. "They were going to leave us both here to die."

"That's not going to happen." Case carefully removed his jacket and handed it to me to tuck under Kevin's head. "An ambulance is on its way."

Sonny started to move toward us, but Case aimed the gun straight at his head. "Have I mentioned that I'm an expert marksman?"

Maguire was the first officer to enter, weapon drawn, with at least five officers behind him. He took stock of the situation and started issuing orders.

Case handed over Kevin's handgun to Maguire. "This belongs to him," he said, indicating Kevin's prone figure. Then he came over and wrapped his arms around me, enveloping me in a warm hug. "I'm so glad you're safe."

For a moment all I could do was hold tightly to him, my cheek pressed against his solid shoulder. Then I lifted my head to gaze at him. "How did you get out of jail?"

He looked down at Kevin, sprawled out on the floor, a peaceful expression on his face. "Imagine my shock when this guy showed up at my cell. He said he knew something was wrong when he found your SUV in an abandoned property owned by Sonny Talbot."

"How did he know to look there?"

"He put a tracker on your car."

"Kevin?"

"Yep. He never struck me as the jealous type—or the intelligent type for that matter—but whatever you said to him earlier must have had some impact because he came to me and wanted to hear my side of the story. He was able to get me released and we've been searching for you ever since."

"How did you know to come here?"

"We'd looked everywhere else," Case said. "Your parents even formed a search party that spread out all over town. Then I remembered what someone at the meeting had said about Fatsis's art gallery being cleaned out and I figured it'd be the perfect hideout."

"First to be demolished, too," I said, glaring at Sonny, handcuffed and standing between two officers.

"The ambulance is here," Maguire said to the other officers, putting away his walkie-talkie. "Are you okay, Athena, or do you want them to examine you?"

"I'm fine, just shaken."

He gave me a thumbs-up, then turned to the other officers. "They'll be bringing a stretcher through the front, so take these two out through the back door."

I watched as Kirkland and Sonny were led away, then I said, "Talbot and Kirkland committed the murders together, Maguire. I know how they pulled it off."

"Don't worry about that now," he replied. "We've got enough evidence to arrest them. Come down to the station tomorrow morning and we'll get your statement then. And by the way, Athena, good job." He gave me a high five.

"Thanks, Bob." Turning to Case I said, "I'm about ready to pass out from hunger."

"I know just the place to go," Case said.

CHAPTER THIRTY

We stepped back as the EMTs passed us, and then I leaned on Case. He put his arm around me and walked me out the door. And there gathered along the sidewalk on Greene Street were friends and neighbors who let out a cheer as we appeared. They lined the sidewalk all the way down the block to The Parthenon, greeting us warmly and offering their well-wishes.

Barb and Nancy ran up and threw their arms around us in a big group hug. "We're so glad you're safe," Barb said.

"Thank you," I said. "I'm overwhelmed by all of this."

"Go see your family," Nancy added, dabbing her eyes. "We can talk tomorrow."

All along the sidewalk people applauded Case and me as we passed. I felt my hand tighten around Case's and he pulled me just a little bit closer to him.

When we reached the diner, Delphi was the first in my family to greet me, running out the front doors to throw her arms around me and squeeze me tightly, whispering, "I was so afraid I'd never see you again."

"Stand back and let Mama in," I heard my mother say. And then I was enveloped in her warm arms. She stroked my hair, murmuring, "My *moró*, my precious *moró*." She leaned back to gaze at me as my father moved in to hug me.

"We were so worried about you, Thenie," Dad said. "The whole community has been searching for you for the last day and a half."

I'd been out that long?

Mama took my hand and led me toward the diner. "Come, come. Niko is waiting to see you."

I glanced back at Case and motioned for him to come with us.

The air was redolent with the smells of oregano, basil, garlic, lemon, and mint as I stepped inside, reminding me of how hungry I was and how good Pappoús's food smelled. It hit me then that I'd come a long way, when before, Greek food was the last thing that sounded appetizing. At that moment, however, I couldn't think of anything I wanted more.

Another cheer went up as my big Greek family crowded around, aunts, uncles, and cousins, too, everyone wanting to hug me at once. I was so overwhelmed by their outpouring of love that tears misted my eyes, but I kept them at bay as I was squeezed, hugged, kissed—*smothered*—as I might have called it before.

Now, surrounded by my loving family, uplifted by a community of friends, I felt so incredibly grateful and honored that I didn't mind it at all. I had wanted so badly to escape all the *Greekness,* I hadn't even considered making a permanent home for Nicholas and me in Sequoia. Now I couldn't imagine leaving.

When I saw Nicholas run out of the kitchen, with Yiayiá and Pappoús right behind him carrying enormous platters of food, I couldn't hold back the tears any longer.

"Mama!" he cried, and threw his arms around my neck as I knelt down to hug him. Then he held me at arm's length and wiped the tears from my cheeks. "Mama, it's okay. Come sit by me."

I glanced around for Case and saw him standing alone by the door. "I'll be right there, Niko. Save me a seat."

A big smile spread across his face, filling my heart with joy. "Hey, you remembered!"

I also remembered I was nearly faint with hunger. But I had something to do first.

Still glowing with joy, I said to Case, "Care to join us?"

"Thanks, but you should be with your family. They need you now. And I have to pack."

That stopped me cold. "Why?"

"I'll be leaving first thing in the morning."

"You're leaving town?"

"Our work here is done, Athena. Little Greece is safe, and I have the statue's certificate of authenticity."

I was stunned. "How did you get it?"

"Kevin had it."

"Then he *did* break into the garden center!"

"No," Case explained. "Sonny hired someone to break in, then he turned the file over to Kevin to hold on to. The document canceling the condo project signed by Talbot Senior, the statue's certificate, the sales receipt—it was all there. After Kevin heard my story, he went to his office and got it."

"I can't believe he finally came through."

"He's not such a bad guy after all." Case gazed at my face as though memorizing it. "Athena, you really came through for me. Thank you for trusting me. You're an amazing woman, warrior goddess."

I could feel myself blushing from my neck to the top of my head, and all I could think to say was "Thank you."

"So I'll see you around then. Take care of yourself."

"What are you going to do about the *Treasure of Athena*?"

"She belongs with you. My goal was to make sure the statue was with someone who deserved it in a place where it would be appreciated. I made a promise to my grandfather to find the statue and make sure it had a good home. I can't think of a better home for her than where she is now."

Tears of gratitude filled my eyes as I searched for something to say. "Thank you for entrusting us with your family's valuable treasure. I know my *pappoús* will be amazed and so very grateful when he hears the story behind it."

Case lifted my chin and gazed into my eyes. "*You're* the real treasure, Athena." Then, as though trying to lighten the mood he added, "And hey, thanks for all the help with my novel. I know it'll be a blockbuster."

Despite the heaviness in my heart, I couldn't help but laugh. But it was short-lived. "So you're really going back to Pittsburgh."

"Can you think of a reason why I should stay?"

I could think of a thousand reasons, but I didn't have the words to explain them nor the energy to sort out my feelings for Case, especially not with all the chaos around us.

"I'll lock up the boat before I leave and put the key in its hiding spot." He took my hands in his. "*Antío*, warrior goddess."

He was saying good-bye.

We shared a long look and then my mother came up

to us. "Athena, come eat. Dimitrius, you, too," she called, leading me away.

I glanced back to see Charlie Bolt, the newspaper reporter who'd attended the press conference, step inside to talk to Case. Then the two men left, pulling the door closed behind them.

With a heavy heart, I turned back and saw my family sitting at tables, talking, laughing, and waving me over.

"I'm here," I said, pulling out the chair next to my son.

I spent the next half hour stuffing myself with pastitsio, moussaka, Greek salad, fresh-baked whole-grain bread, and several cups of coffee, and in between mouthfuls, giving everyone a rundown on what had happened to me after the meeting and what I'd learned from Sonny.

Then Dad explained that after my disappearance, Sonny had sent a second notice to all the shop owners warning them that anyone who did not have his store emptied out by this morning would lose everything in it, so that's what they did. Except for my brave, stubborn *pappoús*, of course, who claimed he would go down with his diner.

Mama rose and motioned for me to stand. "My daughter is a hero today. I think we owe her a big round of applause."

As my family clapped and cheered, I knew then I'd made the right decision to stay.

Thursday

My dad handed me the newspaper as I was eating breakfast for the second time that morning. I didn't have much of an appetite, but I forced myself to eat anyway. Dad had stayed home to make Nicholas and me a bowl of oatmeal and then take me to the police station once my son had boarded the bus.

I glanced at the clock. Eight a.m. Would Case be locking up the *Páme* now and heading out or had he already left town? I assumed he'd been cleared by the police, so he'd have no problem getting back to Pittsburgh.

Although he'd told me what his intentions were when we first met, I still couldn't believe Case was leaving. He'd become such a part of my life in the short time he'd been here, I could already feel the hole he'd left in it. And if that wasn't enough to get me down, now I'd be back to Mama fixing me up with another "good Greek boy."

"Thenie," Dad said, when Nicholas went upstairs to brush his teeth, "you look beat. Did you get any sleep?"

"A few hours. I'll be fine once I get to Spencer's."

"Honey, take the day off and go back to bed. You'll be dragging by noon."

"I need to keep busy, Pops. I don't want to think about what happened."

"Then this should perk you up," he said, handing me the newspaper.

The bold banner headlines read:

GRAYSON TALBOT JR. AND COUNTY CORONER ARRESTED FOR MURDER
LITTLE GREECE SAVED FROM DEMOLITION

Grayson Talbot Jr. and County Coroner Daniel Kirkland have been charged in the deaths of Grayson Talbot Sr. and Harry Pepper, as well as for the kidnapping and attempted murder of Athena Spencer and Kevin Coreopsis. Spencer and Pittsburgh resident Case Donnelly managed to hold off Talbot and Kirkland until police arrived.

District Attorney John Glasser reported that Talbot and Kirkland were being held without bond in the county jail. "Had it not been for the determination and persistence of Spencer and Donnelly, Talbot and Kirkland might not have been caught," Glasser said.

Athena Spencer, of Spencer's Garden Center, is now being heralded as the Goddess of Greene Street for halting the demolition of Little Greece, one of Sequoia's popular tourist attractions. Spencer's mother, Hera, said, "There was a reason we named Athena after the goddess of war and wisdom. She's smart and she's not afraid to stand up for her beliefs."

Pittsburgh resident Donnelly, originally a suspect in the murder of Harry Pepper, said, "I credit Athena for her bravery and her fierce resolve to find the true killers. She has more than earned her title, the Goddess of Greene Street."

The article went on, filling in the details of the crimes, with Lila's story in the sidebar, but I didn't need to read more. It just reminded me what a great team Case and I had made.

The house phone was ringing off the hook, but my dad was fielding calls of congratulations for me so I could get ready. My cell phone was ringing, too, but I didn't answer it because none of the caller IDs said *Dimitri*.

After the store closed that evening, I tried to write a lighthearted blog for my followers, but I wasn't in the mood to be funny. I finally gave in to my feelings and wrote:

When Grief Takes the Reins

Sometimes we go through a loss and look back later to realize that it wasn't too difficult to get through. But there are some losses you don't just "get over." You force yourself to go on, pasting on a smile for the benefit of . . .

I heard a crash outside in the garden and stopped typing to go see what Oscar had done now. Sure enough, there was the little critter sitting beside the tipped-over trash can, the black garbage bag inside ripped open. He was nibbling contentedly on a muffin that someone had thrown away after the GMA meeting.

"Oscar!" I said sharply. "Bad boy!"

Oscar saw me coming, scampered onto a table, and leaped over the fence. I went back inside to get a broom and dustpan and began to sweep up the mess.

And then I heard a voice from behind say, "Sometimes even goddesses need help, you know."

Startled, I swung around in surprise, holding my broom like a sword. There stood Case, hands in the air, a big smile on his face, standing in almost the same spot where we'd first met. He was even wearing the same outfit he'd had on that night. He still had his wavy hair, but he'd shaved off his short beard.

"You're not going to call the police, are you?" he teased.

My heart beat faster, and I felt a flush in my cheeks. "I thought you'd left."

"I did leave. I was halfway to Pennsylvania when I thought, what am I doing? Why am I going back to a boring computer job when I could live in this beautiful lakeside town and do something much more interesting? So I turned around and came back. I was even thinking of buying the *Páme* if your *pappoús* wants to sell it"—he took a step closer—"unless you mind me being here."

Mind? A swell of joy raced through me like a tsunami, but I didn't want him to see it. With a shrug I started sweeping again. "I don't mind. And I think my grandfather would be pleased to sell you his boat. You're a hero in Sequoia, you know, especially in our Greek community."

"From suspect to hero, and this coming from the Goddess of Greene Street."

I stopped sweeping to stare at him. "You gave that title to the reporter, didn't you?"

"Yes, I did." He took the broom from my hands and set it aside. "And I meant everything I said in that article."

He was standing so close, his golden-brown eyes so soulful and searching that I was sure he was going to kiss me. And all I could do was wait there like an idiot for it to happen. He put his hand against my cheek, and I closed my eyes.

Oscar chose that moment to jump the fence and land with a loud bang on the garbage can, effectively breaking the spell.

"Oscar!" I called, chasing him away. Awkward moment over, I put a brick on the lid, and said to Case, "Why don't we grab a cup of coffee? I'd really like to know more about this boring computer job."

"Are you actually asking me to share something personal?" he teased.

"Just shut up and let's go."

As we walked down the street together, I realized I had to rewrite my blog. I already had a title for it, too: *Even Goddesses Need a Hero Now and Then.*

Tips for longer-lasting
FLORAL ARRANGEMENTS
from
Athena,
THE GODDESS OF GREENE STREET!

Don't miss the next mystery
coming to you in 2021!

FLORAL TIPS FOR LONGER-LASTING ARRANGEMENTS

Here are some of my top tips for keeping your floral arrangements fresh and beautiful.
—Athena Spencer

1. **Glub-glub. Cut Flower Stems Underwater.**
   Do this especially for flowers of a more delicate nature (i.e., peonies and dahlias) and always on an angle. This helps their ability to absorb water, thus increasing their longevity. If you do not have access to a sink, just fill a large container next to work area. Remember to make sure the container is cleaned.

2. **Big Dippers**
   Submerge the entire flower into water as soon as you've cut it to size. Water enters through all parts of the flower, which results in longer-lasting floral arrangements. Just give it a shake afterward and arrange by the method below.

3. **Make a Grid**
   Many florists make a grid using thin strips of clear tape to create a holder for your flowers, making them look unified and balanced. Just lay the tape horizontally and vertically and, voilà, you have a flower holder to keep your blooms upright and beautiful. This works especially well for short vases and low containers.

4. **Keep Your Foliage Clear of Water**

When arranging flowers in a vase or other water-filled container, be sure to remove all foliage below the waterline. Just one little piece of foliage below the waterline can be detrimental to your floral arrangement by causing mold to grow.

5. **Open Sesame—Er, Flower Buds**

To open up closed flower buds, dip first in warm water and then in cold. This is a great tip for instantly showcasing an open bud arrangement.

6. **A-hum. Try Alum.**

Keep hydrangeas from wilting by using alum powder. After the hydrangea stem is cut, place it into the alum powder and then continue with your floral arrangement. Find alum in the spice aisle of the grocery store.

7. **Ice, Ice, Baby**

Instead of watering your orchids, try using ice cubes. The slow-melting ice cube gives your orchid plant slow, steady hydration and will keep it from drowning. This is also a good way to measure the amount of water to give your orchid plant. One large ice cube per week is all that is needed. If it's a larger orchid plant, use two or three ice cubes.

8. **Remove Lily Stamens**

Stamens are the heavily pollinated center of the lily. As soon as the lily opens, remove the stamen gently and try not to let any touch the blossoms. This allows for longer lasting lilies.

9. **No Fruit, No How**
   Gases emitted by fruit are not friendly to flowers. Remember to avoid keeping your flowers next to fruit.

10. **Spray to Save the Day**
    A product called Crowning Glory is a spray wax that keeps your floral arrangements hydrated. You'll have blooms that last for weeks. *Sh-h!* This is one of the best-kept secrets in floral arranging. Find it at Amazon, Walmart, even Sam's Club.

Connect with Us

Visit us online at
KensingtonBooks.com
to read more from your favorite authors, see books
by series, view reading group guides, and more.

 Join us on social media

for sneak peeks, chances to win books and prize packs,
and to share your thoughts with other readers.

facebook.com/kensingtonpublishing
twitter.com/kensingtonbooks

Tell us what you think!

To share your thoughts, submit a review,
or sign up for our eNewsletters, please visit:
KensingtonBooks.com/TellUs.

Grab These Cozy Mysteries
from
Kensington Books